Oasis

The Last Humans: Book 1

Dima Zales

♠ Mozaika Publications ♠

Copyright © 2016 *Dima Zales*
www.dimazales.com

Published by Mozaika Publications, an imprint of Mozaika LLC.
www.mozaikallc.com

Cover by Najla Qamber Designs
www.najlaqamberdesigns.com

Edited by Elizabeth from
arrowheadediting.wordpress.com and Mella Baxter

e-ISBN: 978-1-63142-131-0
Print ISBN: 978-1-63142-132-7

CHAPTER ONE

*F*ուck. *Vagina. Shit.*

I pointedly think these forbidden words, but my neural scan shows nothing out of the ordinary compared to when I think phonetically similar words, such as *shuck, angina,* or *fit.* I don't see any evidence of my brain being corrupted, though maybe it's already so damaged that things can't get any worse. Maybe I need another test subject—another 'impressionable' twenty-three-year-old Youth such as myself.

After all, I might be mentally ill.

"Oh, Theo. Not this again," says an overly friendly, high-pitched female voice. "Besides, the words do have an effect on your brain. For instance, the part of your brain responsible for disgust lights up at the mention of 'shit,' yet doesn't for 'fit.'"

This is Phoe speaking. This time, she's not a voice inside my head; instead, it's as though she's in the thick bushes behind me, except there's no one there.

I'm the only person on this strip of grass.

Nobody else comes here because the Edge is only a couple of feet away. Few residents of Oasis like looking at the dreary line dividing where our habitable world ends and the deserted wasteland of the Goo begins. I don't mind it, though.

Then again, I may be crazy—and Phoe would be the reason for that. You see, I don't think Phoe is real. She is, as far as my best guess goes, my imaginary friend. And her name, by the way, is pronounced 'Fee,' but is spelled 'P-h-o-e.'

Yes, that's how specific my delusion is.

"So you go from one overused topic straight into another." Phoe snorts. "My so-called realness."

"Right," I say. Though we're alone, I still answer without moving my lips. "Because I *am* imagining you."

She snorts again, and I shake my head. Yes, I just shook my head for the benefit of my delusion. I also feel compelled to respond to her.

"For the record," I say, "I'm sure the taboo word 'shit' affects the parts of my brain that deal with disgust just as much as its more acceptable cousins, such as 'fecal matter,' do. The point I was trying to make is that the word doesn't hurt or corrupt my brain. There's nothing special about these words."

"Yeah, yeah." This time, Phoe is inside my head, and she sounds mocking. "Next you'll tell me how back in the day, some of the forbidden words merely referred to things like female dogs, and how there are words in the dead languages that used to be just as taboo, yet they are not currently forbidden because they have lost their power. Then you're likely to complain that, though the brains of both genders are nearly identical, only males are not allowed to say 'vagina,' et cetera."

I realize I was about to counter with those exact thoughts, which means Phoe and I have talked about

3

this quite a bit. This is what happens between close friends: they repeat conversations. Doubly so with imaginary friends, I figure. Though, of course, I'm probably the only person in Oasis who actually has one.

Come to think of it, wouldn't *every* conversation with your imaginary friend be redundant since you're basically talking to yourself?

"This is my cue to remind you that I'm real, Theo." Phoe purposefully states this out loud.

I can't help but notice that her voice came slightly from my right, as if she's just a friend sitting on the grass next to me—a friend who happens to be invisible.

"Just because I'm invisible doesn't mean I'm not real," Phoe responds to my thought. "At least *I'm* convinced that I'm real. I would be the crazy one if I *didn't* think I was real. Besides, a lot of evidence points to that conclusion, and you know it."

"But wouldn't an imaginary friend *have* to insist she's real?" I can't resist saying the words out loud. "Wouldn't this be part of the delusion?"

"Don't talk to me out loud," she reminds me, her tone worried. "Even when you subvocalize, sometimes you imperceptibly move your neck muscles or even your lips. All those things are too risky. You should just think your thoughts at me. Use your inner voice. It's safer that way, especially when we're around other Youths."

"Sure, but for the record, that makes me feel even nuttier," I reply, but I subvocalize my words, trying my best not to move my lips or neck muscles. Then, as an experiment, I think, "Talking to you inside my head just highlights the impossibility of you and thus makes me feel like I'm missing even more screws."

"Well, it shouldn't." Her voice is inside my head now, yet it still sounds high-pitched. "Back in the day, when it was not forbidden to be mentally ill, I imagine it made people around you uncomfortable if you spoke to your imaginary friends out loud." She chuckles, but there's more worry than humor in her voice. "I have no idea what would happen if someone thought you were crazy, but I have a bad feeling about it, so please don't do it, okay?"

"Fine," I think and pull at my left earlobe. "Though it's overkill to do it here. No one's around."

"Yes, but the nanobots I told you about, the ones that permeate everything from your head to the utility fog, *can* be used to monitor this place, at least in theory."

"Right. Unless all this conveniently invisible technology you keep telling me about is as much of a figment of my imagination as you are," I think at her. "In any case, since no one seems to know about this tech, how can they use it to spy on me?"

"Correction: no Youth knows, but the others might," Phoe counters patiently. "There's too much we still don't know about Adults, not to mention the Elderly."

"But if they can access the nanocytes in my mind, wouldn't they have access to my thoughts too?" I think, suppressing a shudder. If this is true, I'm utterly screwed.

"The fact that you haven't faced any consequences for your frequently wayward thoughts is evidence that no one monitors them in general, or at least, they're not bothering with yours specifically," she responds, her words easing my dread. "Therefore, I think monitoring thoughts is either computationally prohibitive or breaks one of the bazillion taboos on the proper use of technology—rules I have a very hard time keeping track of, by the way."

"Well, what if using tech to listen in on me is also taboo?" I retort, though she's beginning to convince me.

"It may be, but I've seen evidence that can best be explained as the Adults spying." Her voice in my head takes on a hushed tone. "Just think of the time you and Liam made plans to skip your Physics Lecture. How did they know about that?"

I think of the epic Quietude session we were sentenced to and how we both swore we hadn't betrayed each other. We reached the same conclusion: our speech is not secure. That's why Liam, Mason, and I now often speak in code.

"There could be other explanations," I think at Phoe. "That conversation happened during Lectures, and someone could've overheard us. But even if they hadn't, just because they monitor us during class doesn't mean they would bother monitoring this forsaken spot."

"Even if they don't monitor *this* place or anywhere outside of the Institute, I still want you to acquire the right habit."

"What if I speak in code?" I suggest. "You know, the one I use with my non-imaginary friends."

"You already speak too slowly for my liking," she thinks at me with clear exasperation. "When you speak in that code, you sound ridiculous and drastically increase the number of syllables you say. Now if you were willing to learn one of the dead languages . . ."

"Fine. I will 'think' when I have to speak to you," I think. Then I subvocalize, "But I will also subvocalize."

"If you must." She sighs out loud. "Just do it the way you did a second ago, without any voice musculature moving."

Instead of replying, I look at the Edge again, the place where the serene greenery under the Dome meets the repulsive ocean of the desolate Goo—the ever-replicating parasitic technology that converts matter into itself. The Goo is what's left of the world outside the Dome barrier, and if the barrier were to ever come down, the Goo would destroy us in short order. Naturally, this view evokes all sorts of unpleasant feelings, and the fact that I'm voluntarily gazing at it must be yet another sign of my shaky mental state.

"The thing *is* decidedly gross," Phoe reflects, trying to cheer me up, as usual. "It looks like someone tried to make Jell-O out of vomit and human excrement." Then, with a mental snicker, she adds, "Sorry, I should've said 'vomit and shit.'"

"I have no idea what Jell-O is," I subvocalize. "But whatever it is, you're probably spot on regarding the ingredients."

"Jell-O was something the ancients ate in the pre-Food days," Phoe explains. "I'll find something for you to watch or read about it, or if you're lucky, they might serve it at the upcoming Birth Day fair."

"I hope they do. It's hard to learn about food from books or movies," I complain. "I tried."

"In this case, you might," Phoe counters. "Jell-O was more about texture than taste. It had the consistency of jellyfish."

"People actually ate those slimy things back then?" I think in disgust. I can't recall seeing that in any of the movies. Waving toward the Goo, I say, "No wonder the world turned to this."

"They didn't eat it in most parts of the world," Phoe says, her voice taking on a pedantic tone. "And Jell-O was actually made out of partially decomposed proteins extracted from cow and pig hides, hooves, bones, and connective tissue."

"Now you're just trying to gross me out," I think.

"That's rich, coming from you, Mr. Shit." She chuckles. "Anyway, you have to leave this place."

"I do?"

"You have Lectures in half an hour, but more importantly, Mason is looking for you," she says, and her voice gives me the impression she's already gotten up from the grass.

I get up and start walking through the tall shrubbery that hides the Goo from the view of the rest of Oasis Youths.

"By the way"—Phoe's voice comes from the distance; she's simulating walking ahead of me— "once you verify that Mason *is* looking for you, *do* try to explain how an imaginary friend like me could possibly know something like that . . . something you yourself didn't know."

CHAPTER TWO

Campus can look gorgeous when the sun is about to set. It's one of the few times the color red enters the Institute's premises. Green is usually the predominant hue around these parts—green from the grass, green from the trees, and green from the ivy covering all the structures. It would all be green if the ivy had its way, but some of the more resistant parts of the Institute's buildings are still silver and glass.

I pass the triangular prism shape of the Middle-Grade Dormitory and see the children out and about; their Lectures end much earlier than ours.

"Mason is by the northeast side of the campus," Phoe directs me.

"Thanks," I whisper back and turn toward the cuboid shape of the Lectures Building in the distance. "Now can you please shut up and give me ten minutes of feeling like I'm not insane?"

Phoe pointedly doesn't reply. If she thinks that giving me the silent treatment when I ask her to shut up is going to annoy me, then she knows me far too poorly, especially for a figment of my imagination.

As I walk, I attempt to focus on how much I'm enjoying the silence, in part because I am, but mostly because I want to irritate Phoe.

The silence doesn't last long. As I approach the green expanse of the Recreation Field, I hear the excited voices of Youths playing Frisbee. When I get closer, I see that most of them are aged thirty and up, though a few of the Youths are in their twenties, like me.

A little farther, I notice a couple of teenaged Youths deep in meditation. I observe their serene faces with envy. My own meditation practice has recently gone down the drain. Every time I try to do anything soothing, my mind buzzes and I'm unable to find my center.

My stomach grumbles, yanking me out of my thoughts.

I put my palm out, and in an instant, a warm bar of Food appears in my hand. I take a hungry bite, and my taste buds explode with sensations. Every bar of Food has a unique ratio of saltiness, sourness, sweetness, bitterness, and umami, and this specific bar is particularly savory. I enjoy the taste. Eating is one of the few pleasures that insanity hasn't ruined for me—at least not yet.

"Well, Food does have its hedonistic value," Phoe says, grudge apparently forgotten, "if not much else."

I keep eating while trying to make my mind blank. I have a feeling Phoe is itching to say something else. She likes to shock me, like when she explained that Food is assembled by tiny machines at my whim.

"Nano-sized machines," she corrects. "And yes, Food is assembled, just like most tangible objects in Oasis."

"So what isn't assembled?" I ask, though I'm not sure I believe her.

"Well, I don't think the buildings are, though I'm not sure," Phoe says. "Certainly the Augmented Reality stuff, like your Screen and half of the prettier-looking trees on this campus, are not assembled, since they're not tangible in any way. And living things aren't assembled either. Although, if I were a stickler, I'd argue that living things in general are powered by nanomachines, just of a different kind." Her voice is as excited as Liam's gets when he's planning a prank.

Ignoring her prattle, I take another bite and pointedly thank the Forebears for Food.

"Did you do that to annoy me?" Phoe asks. "Did you just thank those technology-fearing simpletons for making this gratuitous choice on your behalf? I told you, your body could be tuned so that your internal nanobots would make eating and waste management completely unnecessary."

"But that would make my already-boring life noticeably more boring." I lick what's left of the Food bar off my fingers.

"We can debate this later," Phoe says, thankfully leaving the topic alone. "Mason is in the rock garden—and you've passed it."

"Thanks," I think at her and retrace my steps.

When I enter the rock garden, I see a guy sitting on the grass at the far end, near the silver dodecahedron statuette. His back is to me, so I can't tell who it is, but he does look like Mason.

I approach quietly, not wanting to startle the Youth in case he's in a meditative trance.

He must not have been, because even though I'm walking softly, the Youth hears me and turns around. His face resembles that of Eeyore, the donkey from an ancient cartoon.

"Hey, dude," I say, trying my best to hide my annoyance at Phoe. This *is* Mason, and he's exactly where she told me he'd be, and I indeed don't have a good explanation for how an imaginary friend would know this.

In fact, I don't have a good explanation for many things Phoe can do, such as make me exempt from Oneness—

"Theo," Mason says, looking slightly surprised. "You're here. I was about to go looking for you or Liam."

"I told you so," Phoe whispers in my mind.

"What did you want?" I say to Mason. To Phoe, I subvocalize, "And you, be quiet. And yes, I'm choosing this way of responding to you because it's easier to show my irritation. I don't know if I can think irritatingly."

"Oh, trust me, you can," Phoe says, not bothering to whisper. "Your thoughts can be *very* irritating."

Mason doesn't hear her, of course, but I notice how hesitant he is to continue speaking. He looks around furtively, and when he's satisfied that we're alone, he whispers, "Eway eednay otay alktay."

"That's, 'We need to talk,'" I think at Phoe.

"I know what that means," Phoe says so loudly that I picture my ears popping. "I was the one who dug up that article about Pig Latin from the ancient archives for you," she adds with less outrage and at a lower decibel level.

"Let's walk as we talk," I reply to Mason in Pig Latin. "We're late for Lectures."

"Whateveray," Mason replies and gets up from the grass. As he stands, I see that his shoulders are noticeably hunched, as though his head is too heavy for his body.

"It's 'ateverwhay,'" I correct him as we begin walking toward the tetrahedron Kindergarten Building.

"Whatever," Mason says without code, shuffling beside me.

I'm about to say something sarcastic, but Mason startles me by saying in code, "I'm too upset to get this stuff right."

I look at him in confusion, but he continues, "No, not just upset." His voice is losing vitality by the second. Stopping, Mason gives me a morose look. "I'm depressed, Theo."

I halt in shock. "You're what?" I say, forgetting Pig Latin.

"Yes. Yes, the *taboo* word." He flexes his fingers, then lets them droop. "I'm fucking depressed."

I look at his face for signs that he's joking, even though this isn't a joke-conducive topic, but I see none. His expression is gloomy, consistent with his revelation.

"Mason . . ." I swallow. "I don't know what to say."

I'm glad he said his revelation in code. Even so, I look around to make sure we're still walking alone.

There are two problems with what he just said. The first one is minor: he said the word 'fucking' out loud. That can lead to a day's worth of Quietude for him and some trouble for me if I don't squeal on him for using profanity (which I never would, of course). Infinitely worse, though, is that he said he was 'depressed'—not to mention, he meant it. That word represents an idea so unthinkable I don't know what the punishment for it would be. It's one of those needless taboos like, 'Don't eat your friends.' The rule probably exists, but since no one's ever eaten someone else in the history of Oasis, you don't know what the Adults would do if you *did*.

"Whatever the consequences are, they would be bad," Phoe thinks. "Both for cannibalism and for not being happy."

"Then we're both screwed," I subvocalize at her, "since I'm not happy."

"You're not depressed," she says. "Now quick, he's still waiting for you to reply with something more supportive than your, 'I dunno what to say.' So please, be a dear and say something along the lines of, 'What can I do to help?'" Then, worriedly, she adds, "His neural scan is unlike anything I've ever seen."

"Atwhay ancay Iway oday otay elphay?" I ask as Phoe suggested.

Mason raises his hands to cover his face, but I glimpse moisture in his eyes. He holds his face as if it might melt if he'd let go, and I just stare at him dumbly, the way I did during a scene of the one and only horror flick I allowed Phoe to show me.

My imagination failing me, I make the small wrist gesture required to bring up a private Screen into the air in front of me. Phoe takes that as a cue to put Mason's neural scan on it.

I examine the image for a second and think at Phoe, "I've never seen anything like it either. He's extremely distraught."

"I think the reason you've never seen this is because you've never met anyone who was genuinely depressed until now," Phoe thinks back.

"So he really *is* depressed?" I subvocalize, barely stopping myself from speaking out loud. "What do I do, Phoe?"

"Ancient texts suggest you might want to put a hand on his shoulder. Do that and don't say anything," Phoe says. "That should comfort him, I think."

I do as she suggests. His shoulder is strangely twitchy under my hand at first, but then, slowly, he lets go of his face. His expression is not completely foreign to me—little kids get it before they learn how to act civilized and look properly happy.

Mason takes a deep breath, lets it out, and in a shaky voice says, "I told Grace how I feel, and she called me a crazy creep."

Stunned, I release his shoulder and step back.

"Crap," Phoe says, echoing my thoughts. "This is bad."

CHAPTER THREE

Like I told Phoe, I'm not as happy as others in Oasis. Coincidentally, my restlessness began with Phoe. Specifically, it began when she first spoke to me a few weeks ago. No, truth be told, it started a bit later, when I learned that certain really cool stuff, like great movies, books, and video games, repeatedly get wiped from Oasis's libraries.

At least I assume it happens repeatedly. On my watch, it happened to *Pulp Fiction*, a movie Phoe had found buried deep in the ancient archives. The movie was awesome, but either because I'd accessed it or because of some horrible coincidence, *Pulp Fiction* got on the radar of either the Elderly or the Adults, and they deleted it. One day it was on my Screen, the next I couldn't bring it up. Phoe said it was no longer in the archives either.

What's worse is this happened before I got a chance to get Liam and Mason to watch it with me. My friends didn't even believe me when I said that the movie used to exist. Phoe was my only witness, and I'm not ready to tell Liam or Mason about her. Actually, being unable to share something with my friends for the first time in my life has also been a source of unpleasantness, but not as much as the questions that now plague me: Why delete such a good movie? Was it because it had all those banned words? Or was it the violence?

If I asked these questions out loud, I'd get a numbingly boring Quietude session instead of answers—and that drives me nuts. So, because of all this, had anyone asked me before today, I would've said that *I'm* the one and only unhappy person in Oasis. Yet even I wouldn't call how I feel 'depressed.'

"I didn't think it was physically possible for anyone to get depressed," Phoe whispers. "The nanocytes in your head regulate serotonin and norepinephrine re-uptake, among a million other variables that synergistically conspire to keep you nice and cheerful. On top of that, the Institute curriculum includes copious amounts of meditation, exercise, and other feel-good propaganda."

"Didn't you hear me?" Mason repeats, his voice quivering. "I told Grace I love her."

He thinks I'm judging him, and it's hard not to. Sexual interest—or romantic love, as it used to be called—is not part of our world. The only reason we even know about it is because of ancient media, which is rife with examples of people our age being 'in love'—a state of being that sounds qualitatively different from love of Food or love for one's friends. People even used to get 'married' back then and start 'families'—two social constructs that are incredibly weird.

Marriage I could sort of understand. It was probably like being friends with a female for a big portion of your life. I can relate to that because we used to be friends with Grace. Family, however, is just bizarre. It would be like being friends with people based on random factors, such as DNA commonalities, and with people of varying ages—including the Adults and the Elderly. Since Youths never meet the elusive Elderly and the only Adults we come across are the Instructors, I find family hard to picture.

As to romantic love, I didn't think anyone has any interest in that stuff. That strange emotion was a form of insanity tied to procreation, and the Elderly take care of that now—though exactly how they do it is the type of question that gets you an hour of Quietude instead of an answer.

I know that from experience.

"Actually, taking procreation out of the game never stopped lust or love for the ancients," Phoe butts in. "They had something called birth control. I think the real reason these desires disappeared is because of the neutering effect of the nanocytes." Before I can ask her about that, she continues, "Of course, given that those nanocytes are also supposed to keep you nice and cheerful, I can only assume that Mason is in this situation because his nanocytes can't cope with whatever is malfunctioning in his brain. If I had to guess, given his prior manic phases, I'd say he's bipolar."

"Theo," Mason says, his chin trembling. "I told Grace—"

"I heard you, dude," I say, shutting out Phoe's rambling explanation to focus on my friend. "I'm just at a loss for words. I told you to keep away from Grace."

"You also told me I was going through a phase and didn't know what I was feeling," Mason retorts. "As did your friend Liam."

Liam is closer to Mason than I've ever been, but now is not the time to be a stickler for definitions. When Mason confided in us, I didn't grasp the extent of his seriousness. I thought he wanted to prove that he could be the biggest misfit in our little band of misfits—and saying shocking things such as, "I like a girl," certainly did it, particularly because he chose the most annoying snitch as the object of his obsession.

"So you told Grace you loved her?" I shake my head in frustration. "Don't you understand? She's going to tell on you, and you're going to be in a world of trouble."

Mason just looks at me. "I don't care. You don't understand, Theo. I've been thinking—" He swallows. "I've been thinking about ending it all."

"Don't say that," I hiss at him, horrified. "Not even in Pig Latin."

"But it's true." He sits down on the ground and stares vacantly into the distance. "Sometimes I—" His throat moves as he swallows again. He raises his head to glance at me, and I see that his eyes are red and watery. "It would be so much better if I'd never been born at all."

I'm overwhelmed by his words. My face must look like one of those ancient Japanese masks Phoe once showed me. Mason has been my close friend for as long as I can remember, yet it's like I don't know him at all. Depression and strange feelings toward Grace are bad enough, but now he's turned the conversation toward even murkier waters.

Death and suicide are beyond taboo. In a way, they're somewhat academic as far as these things go. We all understand their meaning—the concept of death was too ubiquitous in antiquity for us not to come across it—but now that no one ever dies, thinking about death seems pointless. Theoretically, a freak accident could kill someone, but in reality, such an event has never occurred in the history of Oasis. So yeah, unlike cursing, I find it very easy and natural to follow *this* rule and never talk or even think about—

"Stop being so self-absorbed, Theo," Phoe chides me in my mind. "Your friend's in pain."

I look at Mason, who's now hunched over with his head buried in his hands. Taking a deep breath, I step toward him and ask, "What can I do?"

This question is meant for both Mason and Phoe.

"Nothing," Mason says.

"Find a way to get him to relax," Phoe suggests, "and try to fix what he did with that girl."

"Listen, Mason. Let me take you to the Dorms," I say, putting my hand back on his shoulder. "Take a nap instead of going to the History Lecture. I'll tell Instructor Filomena you're sick tonight, and I'll talk to Grace to try to unravel this mess."

"You're wasting your time," Mason says dully. "I don't care if I'm in trouble. I don't care about anything."

"That's cool," I say, feigning enthusiasm. "After you wake up, we'll talk about getting into all kinds of trouble. I'm game to do a prank on Owen if you're still up for that. You know we owe that asshole for leaving dirt in our room. Or tomorrow night we can tell Instructor Filomena to shove her History Lecture up one of her orifices."

The second idea brings a hint of a smile to Mason's face. He hates our History Instructor.

Relieved, I smile back at him. "And remember," I say, trying to capitalize on my success, "Birth Day is in less than three days."

Mason loves the festivities of Birth Day as much as we all do. And why wouldn't he? It combines all of the ancients' holidays of birthdays, Christmas, Hanukkah, Thanksgiving, Election Day, and many others neatly into one celebration. Not to mention that we'll all be a year closer to forty, the age when Youths become Adults and are no longer treated like little kids.

The mention of Birth Day seems to cheer Mason up even more. "You know," he says, "I wouldn't even be lying if I played hooky tonight. I *do* feel sick."

"Exactly." I make my voice extra cheerful. "You have the perfect excuse."

I help him up, and we head toward the Dorms.

As we walk, I steer the conversation onto safer topics, doing my best to distract him from the funk he's in.

"Ask him about his bonsai tree collection," Phoe suggests. "You know how much he likes those things."

Her idea makes sense, so I pretend to have developed a deep caring for Mason's stunted little trees, and he's glad to tell me more than anyone would ever need to know about the subject.

As I pretend to listen, I plan my conversation with Grace. Maybe her silence can be bought with some kind of favor? Or maybe I can convince her we're playing a prank on her? Prank penalties we can deal with.

"This is why you have to use the clippers, not scissors, to prune the tree," Mason says as we enter our room. Stopping, he sighs, and I see his expression darkening as he adds, "Pruning those trees is the only thing that soothes me, but even doing that hasn't been enough."

I point at his corner of the room and say, "Take that nap, dude."

Mason stares at his corner for a moment, and then a bed materializes.

"Actually, it's assembled from scratch by the nanos in the utility fog," Phoe butts in.

"I was just thinking to myself," I subvocalize. "This is the problem with talking to you via thoughts."

Mason walks over, gingerly lies down on the bed, and closes his eyes.

I wait a beat, not knowing if I should stay until he falls asleep and unsure how I'd even tell if he were asleep.

"He's *already* asleep," Phoe says. "He must have requested sleep as a thought command, the way he did with the bed."

"That guy was never a big fan of gestures," I think at her idly and walk out of the room. "Do you know where I can find—"

"Grace will be by the History Hall," Phoe says, her voice echoing off the shiny, arched walls of the dormitory hallway. Clearly catching my thought, she says, "That echo effect is your brain playing tricks." Her voice is in my mind this time.

I start walking faster, and when I think no one is looking, I break into a run. If they catch me running, I can always lie and say I was exercising. That's a trick invented by Liam, the guy who's always in a hurry to get somewhere.

As soon as I'm outside, I move over to the running path. This way no one will question my 'exercise.'

* * *

I see Grace's red hair in the corridor by the entrance to the History Hall, but before I can approach her, a hand grabs my shoulder.

"Dude," Liam says in his excited, screechy voice. "Where have you been all day?"

"Not now, Liam." I give a minute shake of my head. "I have something urgent going on."

"What is it?" He gives me a good-natured shove—an act that can get him as long of a Quietude session as a genuinely violent hit.

"No time to explain." My tone is firm and uncompromising—something that, on very rare occasions, takes Liam out of his hyperactive mode.

"Whatever it is"—Liam bounces from foot to foot—"I'm coming along."

I sigh and hurry toward Grace, grateful that he's at least stopped talking for the moment.

"Ah, if it isn't the Twin Stooges," Grace says, giving Liam a chilly look and me a crooked smile.

"It's the Three Stooges, you ignorant twat," Phoe says, though of course Grace can't hear her.

"I think she calls us twins because she thinks we're very alike," I think at Phoe, trying to shut her up.

"You're tall, blond, and blue-eyed," Phoe says with a slight growl, "while the top of Liam's head reaches your chin, and his hair is brown. More to the point, you're way more handsome and a lot less twitchy than your stocky friend, and she knows it." Her words sound as if they're coming through clenched teeth. "I can see it in the bitch's eyes. You and Liam couldn't be less alike if you tried. And Mason—"

"Mason is the reason I'm here, Phoe. The reason I need to talk to the 'twat'—whatever that means. So please, shut it." Despite my annoyance at her, I can't help mentally chuckling at my imaginary friend calling me handsome. It must be some advanced form of narcissism.

Focusing on the matter at hand, I smile at Grace, and as politely as I can, say, "Hi, Grace. I'd like to discuss something with you."

The bell sounds, signifying the start of the Lecture.

"I think I know what this is about," Grace says as she flutters her big eyelashes at me. "And it will have to wait. I won't be late for the Lecture."

Before I can say anything back, she steps between Liam and me and disappears into the classroom.

"What was that about?" Liam says. "Let's cut History so you can tell me about it."

I look my friend over. When he's excited like this, with his shaggy hair in its usual messy state and his brown eyes twinkling, he reminds me of Taz, the Tasmanian Devil from an ancient cartoon.

"Sorry, I can't skip it," I say. "I can't get Quietude until I speak with her."

Without waiting for Liam to object, I follow Grace into the History Hall.

Everybody's already seated. Instead of gesturing to create myself a seat, I use a thought command and get my Screen up when the desk appears in front of me.

Under the pretext of looking at the syllabus on my Screen, I study Grace.

Like everyone else, she's wearing a boxy, shapeless shirt and a loose pair of pants that conceal most of her body. Still, her tall, slender build is visible, and if I forget about her treacherous personality, I have to admit she's pleasant to look at, as far as physical appearances go.

With her symmetrical facial features, Grace reminds me of a female from ancient times.

"That's because all the ancients you've seen are models and actresses," Phoe intrudes. "The physical attractiveness of the ancients followed a normal distribution curve, but you're only familiar with the outliers left in the media records, and even those, after they were airbrushed . . ."

"And so the history lesson begins before Filomena can open her mouth," I subvocalize at her.

"I had to stop you before you could decide which cartoon character Grace reminded you of," Phoe thinks.

"The Little Mermaid," I reply, mostly to annoy her.

"You're pretty generous." Phoe's tone is strangely tense. "I think she looks more like Ariel's little red crab friend."

"Good evening, students," Instructor Filomena says in her nasally voice as she enters. "Have you prepared yourselves for the wonders of history?"

I cringe. Instructor Filomena has a flare for the dramatic and often exaggerates how interesting her subject matter is.

"In her defense," Phoe whispers, "all Adults are obsessed with the topics they've decided to make their life's work."

I ignore Phoe and hope today's lesson shows more of the ancient world than the usual propaganda.

"I will not be collecting your assignments today," Instructor Filomena says. It's music to my ears, since I just saw the essay on the syllabus. "I'm initiating Virtual Reality right away," she continues, "so don't get startled."

I'd like to know who gets startled by something they've been exposed to most of their lives.

"Well, you do sometimes get—"

"Thinking to myself again, Phoe," I subvocalize at her. "If you want these messages by thought to continue, you need to learn to distinguish which ones are meant for you and which ones are me simply talking to myself—unless, of course, talking to you is the same as talking to myself. In which case, all of this is moot."

Phoe mumbles something, but I miss what, because the VR portion of the lesson begins, and it's one of the few parts of the History Lecture I actually enjoy.

I'm no longer in my seat in the Hall.

I'm no longer even in Oasis.

Instead, I'm standing on a patch of weeds and dirt on top of a majestic green hill. The air is cold and smells of flowers I can't name. To my right is a gigantic wall that extends through the hill I'm standing on, spiraling for miles as far as the eye can see.

"This is the Great Wall of China," I subvocalize. "Right?"

"Yes," Phoe says. "I can't believe she shows you these marvels yet never properly names them."

I don't answer, because before I can savor it all, I'm no longer standing next to the Wall, but next to a giant, half-ruined oval structure I know well: the Coliseum.

"I bet the Taj Mahal is next," Phoe says.

"Shush," I say. "I'm having the only fun to be had in Filomena's Lecture."

"Told you so," Phoe says when the next location materializes around me—or is it more accurate to say I materialize in the next location?

I'm standing next to a white marble structure, trying to take a mental snapshot before the scenery changes again.

The Empire State Building is next, followed by the Grand Canyon, then the majestic waters of Niagara Falls. The scenes of the ancient world come quicker and quicker until they speed by so fast that I can't name them.

Then I see ancient Earth from a tiny round window—a vantage point in space. I love this part because I feel weightless, and because ancient Earth looks so magnificent—a blue world full of life.

Then, suddenly, comes my least favorite part.

It's the same vantage point, only Earth has changed.

The blue oceans of water, the yellow deserts of sand, the green forests, the red canyons—they're all gone, replaced by the orange-brown mess of Goo.

My vantage point zooms in, but I still can't see Oasis, just an ever-increasing, drab-colored layer of Goo. The view zooms in even more, and finally, after a few more zooms, I see a tiny island of green underneath the barrier of the Dome.

"Blah, blah," Phoe says. "The kiddies get it. Oasis is but 0.00000171456 of Earth's surface and the rest is puke-shit. I think this came across after the first thousand times this point was made."

"Much was lost when the technological Armageddon arrived," the Instructor's disembodied voice states. "Oasis survived by mere chance, saved by its isolation and by its people's unwillingness to succumb to the evils of technology run amok. Today, we will study the Amish—the group that inspired our Forebears. Brave souls who shunned the technology of their day, just as we do now."

"Is she really not aware of the concept of irony?" Phoe says. "She gives the 'we denounce technology' spiel, when every one of your brains is currently at the mercy of your nanocytes, every input and output of every neuron carefully controlled to provide a fully immersive fake reality experience—"

"Phoe," I whisper in warning, but it's to no avail; we've hit my imaginary friend's pet peeve.

"Technology, in the form of a force field, protects us from the Goo outside." Phoe's speech gets maniacally urgent. "Technology in the form of nano-machines dresses you, feeds you, creates the air you breathe, and takes care of the waste you excrete."

I don't disagree with a single word Phoe says; I'm just angry that she's speaking, so, out of sheer spitefulness, I subvocalize, "The nano replicators are also what turned the world into Goo."

I hear Phoe take a deep inhale and prepare for an avalanche of objections, but instead, she says, "I know you're just trying to push my buttons."

"What gave me away?" I try to inject as much sarcasm as one can into a thought.

She doesn't reply.

"Two silent treatments in a single day? I'm definitely getting better at dealing with my *imaginary* friend," I think pointedly.

She still doesn't reply, so I return my attention to the lesson at hand.

I'm back in the default empty space, where Instructor Filomena's booming voice is telling us about the virtues of Amish society. I tune it all out, knowing I'll only get angry again. Our curriculum, especially Filomena's History Lecture, is an exercise in cherry picking. For example, she is highlighting our similarities with the Amish but ignoring important differences, like, say, religion. From what I've gathered through my own research, the Amish were defined by their religious beliefs, ideas completely foreign to us.

I expect Phoe to chime in and say something like, "Her parallels are even weaker than the time when she compared Oasis to the visions of the ancient philosopher Plato and his Republic," but Phoe is still holding a grudge.

To provoke Phoe to speak, I subvocalize, "Hmm, I wonder if it's the next stage of my insanity that I can imagine Phoe's words so exactly . . ."

Phoe doesn't take the bait.

Bored, I listen to the lesson. After Filomena further jumbles her message and I feel as if I've just experienced the most boring fifteen minutes of my life, I subvocalize, "Maybe I shouldn't have pissed off Phoe."

Phoe lets me suffer for another ten minutes before she mumbles a hushed, "Serves you right," and makes a point to stay quiet for another torturous half hour—the rest of the Lecture.

"That's all for today," Filomena finally says and the reality of the classroom returns. "Remember," she continues, "as that ancient poet said, those who don't learn from history are doomed to repeat it."

I fight the slight disorientation that always accompanies coming out of VR. In my peripheral vision, I see Grace get up, and I leap to my feet.

Grace exits the Hall and I follow, ignoring Liam's attempt to get my attention.

"Please, Grace," I say, catching up with her.

Grace stops in the middle of the corridor and looks back.

"What?" she says, twirling a red curl around her finger. "Make it quick."

"It's about what Mason might've misled you to believe—"

"Save your lies, Theodore," Grace says. "I already gave my report to the Dean."

CHAPTER FOUR

"F—"

"Don't say anything that will give the snitch more ammunition," Phoe says, her grievances with me instantly forgotten. "Keep your cool."

Focusing on not cursing, I manage to say, "You told?"

I say the words with some strange hope, as if maybe Grace is just taunting me, but her face looks earnest, and I start to feel something older Youths in Oasis almost never experience.

Anxiety.

Some of my turmoil must show on my face, because Grace frowns and says, her voice lowered, "You don't understand, Theo. Mason needs help. I did it for his sake—and to protect myself."

My hands do something unexpected: they turn into fists.

"Theo, what the hell?" Phoe says. "Did you really just think about hitting a girl?"

"No," I subvocalize and take a deep breath. "And what does gender have to do with it?" Before Phoe can respond, I add, "I haven't thought about hitting anyone for years now, with the exception of Owen, but he's such an asshole that wanting to hit him obviously doesn't count."

"Walk away, now," Phoe says, her tone clipped.

"You shouldn't have done that," I say to Grace, ignoring Phoe. "Why are you being like this? We used to be friends—"

"Are you finally building up the courage to call me a snitch to my face?" Grace's usually melodious voice sounds like a hiss. "You think I don't know that's what you and your little band call me? All I'm trying to do is help Mason before he hurts himself or someone else. Just grow up already."

And before I can respond, she storms off.

"That's odd. I think she's running—a breach of the rules," Phoe says, sounding as confused as I feel.

Liam finally catches up to me and stares at Grace's disappearing figure. "What the uckfay was that about?"

"Dude, you can't just say the f-word in Pig Latin," I say in Pig Latin. "It doesn't take a genius cryptologist to figure out what you mean based on the context."

"Owblay emay," Liam says in code, then normally adds, "How's that? That's two words: 'blow,' which is perfectly allowed, and 'me,' which is also allowed." He grins as I shake my head, then says more seriously, "Listen, dude. Something's going on, and you have to tell me what it is."

"Fine," I say. "I'll tell you on the way back to the Dorms."

As we leave the Lectures Building, I begin my tale, speaking Pig Latin throughout and keeping my voice low. Campus is overflowing with Youths, and as we walk, I have to politely refuse an invitation to play hacky sack. A short while after, Liam not-so-politely refuses to join a paired badminton game. It's not until we're halfway to the Dorms that I finish explaining Mason's predicament.

"What did you expect from that *itchbay*?" Liam says as we approach the soccer field. "He shouldn't have told her anything. I mean, what the f—"

Liam doesn't finish his sentence because at that moment, a soccer ball hits him in the crotch.

With a gasp, my friend bends at the waist, clutching the injured area.

Before the ball can roll away, I pick it up and look around.

Several Youths are approaching us.

"Are you okay?" asks Kevin, a Youth we rarely interact with. He looks genuinely concerned.

"Yeah," says the all-too-familiar, hyena-like voice of Owen. "Are you going to cry, Li-Li-Kins?" he says, using Liam's despised childhood nickname. "I'm *so* sorry," he adds, winking at me.

A mix of growls, speech, and Pig Latin escapes Liam's throat.

Owen sneers. "Usually, hitting *sucker* balls is a lot more fun than this."

Liam takes a step in his direction.

Still holding on to the ball, I step between them preemptively. I've seen this routine play out a million times before.

Owen and his band of three other misfits hate our trio. The feud goes back to when we were little, when Owen and co. bullied any kid they could. We weren't such easy prey, though, thanks mainly to Liam. Our crew back then included a few more Youths—Grace among them, if you can believe that. We didn't allow ourselves to be bullied; we fought back.

In those early days, things were both simpler and more savage. The Adults closed their eyes to mild violence, considering it an unavoidable side effect of the developing brain. A push was met with a push, a punch with a punch.

Of course, things changed when we all turned seven and started getting Quietude sessions. The penalties for bullying got so steep that Owen could no longer do it openly, nor could we retaliate without incurring the Instructors' wrath. On top of that, our desire for violence ebbed, situations like this one aside. Instead of outright bullying, Owen plagues us with pranks, trash talk, and nasty surprises—and we make sure to respond in kind.

"No reason to get a Quietude session," I say to Liam with as much calmness as I can muster. "Not over this *unfortunate* accident."

"Yeah, Li-Li-Kins." Owen is watching my right hand, the one with the ball. "You listen to Why-Odor."

Upon hearing my own annoying nickname, I'm tempted to throw the ball at Owen's face. The only reason I don't is because I'm certain he'd catch it and probably thank me for giving it back to him. I also consider allowing Liam to do what he wants, but that's a bad idea, because if Liam really does do anything violent to Owen, he'd be in Quietude for days, if not weeks. Liam getting into trouble is probably part of Owen's plan, or else he wouldn't be goading him. He wants to provoke a response since he knows that out of all the Youths in Oasis, Liam is the only one who seems to get occasional violent urges.

Between my curiosity, Mason's moodiness, and Liam's said urges, we're probably the oddest group of Youths in Oasis—apart from our nemesis in front of me, who is also atypical in his assholeness.

"Peace is a good choice," Phoe whispers. "You're the only one here who's acting his age."

"Shush," I subvocalize. "I have an idea."

"And there goes your maturity." Phoe chuckles mirthlessly. "You do realize that at twenty-three, the ancients were already considered adults? Just because the Adults here treat you like you're still five doesn't mean you should behave like it."

Ignoring her, I feign throwing the ball at Owen's midsection.

His hands go up in a practiced goalie maneuver, but I don't let go of the ball.

Instead, in a rehearsed motion, I gesture with my empty left hand in a way that Liam can see. I'm sticking out my pinky and index fingers—our secret signal from basketball.

Liam grunts approvingly, and I step to my right.

From my new location, I pretend to throw the ball at Owen's head.

Instinctively, his hands go up.

I change direction and throw the ball at Liam so quickly that for a moment I doubt he'll catch it.

But catch it he does.

With lightning speed, Liam throws the ball at Owen's crotch and says, "No hard feelings, dude. Here's your ball back."

With a grunt, Owen clutches his family jewels and falls to the ground.

"Oh no," Liam says in his best parody of Owen's voice. "Do you need us to get the nurse?"

Owen says something in a falsetto. I'm fairly sure they're forbidden words, but he doesn't say them legibly enough to get into trouble. Not that Liam or I would've reported Owen for such a thing, but the others might have.

"It was all a series of accidents, right?" I make eye contact with the other Youths on the field.

Everyone nods, though a few Youths look at us as if we're a bunch of rabid gorillas. I don't blame them. Meditation, yoga, physical exercise, our studies, and other examples of being 'all proper' define most Youths. I envy them their uncomplicated worldview.

With his chin high but his walk a little awkward, Liam leaves the soccer field, and I follow in brooding silence.

As if we didn't already have enough problems with this Mason thing.

After this incident, I'm especially glad that Liam, Mason, and I share a room. Some Youths choose to live in one of the smaller single-person accommodations at the Dorms as they get older, but they don't have my awesome friends. They also don't have to worry about idiots trying to prank them at night.

We discuss Mason's situation some more as we walk. By the time we enter our room, Liam seems completely recovered from Owen's strike, so I guess there wasn't any permanent damage.

Mason is still sleeping, so Liam comes up to Mason's bed and shakes him.

When Mason doesn't respond, Liam turns to me and says, "The dumb dissident is sleeping like a baby."

"Don't rub it in tomorrow," I warn Liam. "He's in enough trouble already."

"But I told him to stay away from her," Liam objects. "*I* told him, and *you* told him."

I sigh, regretting giving Liam the whole story. "I'm sure he'll pay for his stupidity."

"What do you think they'll do?" Liam says, looking worried for a change.

"I have a bad feeling about it," Phoe replies, as though Liam can hear her.

"I have no idea," I say, ignoring her. "I guess all we can do is wait and see."

"Good job thinking up the 'sick' idea," Liam says. "He might milk that a bit before his punishment comes down. Maybe if they think he's sick and has missed too much school, his Quietude sentence will be reduced?"

"Maybe," I say, trying to project a hope I don't feel.

What I do feel is the anxiety from earlier, only intensified. I'm also exhausted.

"It's the aftermath of an adrenaline rush," Phoe says. "You're not used to disturbances in your equilibrium. Sleep should help."

At the mention of sleep, I yawn loudly.

"Oh no, you don't," Liam says, giving me a frustrated look. "It's still early. We can—"

"I'm going to sleep," I say firmly, and to underscore my intent, I make the two-palms-up-and-down gesture to activate my bed's appearance.

"Assembly," Phoe corrects. "It's the nanos that—"

"Pedantic much," I subvocalize back.

"Fine, later," Liam says and creates a chair for himself.

I take my shoes off and get on my bed as they disappear—*get disassembled,* I correct myself for Phoe's benefit.

Out of the corner of my eye, I see Liam plop into his chair. Given his posture, I assume he brought up his private Screen and is thinking of what to do on it.

Feeling generous, I bring up my own Screen and send him a movie recommendation: *The Wizard of Oz.*

With that, I make a gesture for the blanket to 'assemble' and cozy up with it. My eyes close, but sleep doesn't come as quickly as it usually does.

Oh well, I can help nature. I tighten the muscles around my eyes in a gesture that would usually initiate assisted sleep, but oddly, nothing happens. My mind continues buzzing with thoughts of everything that's happened today. I try again, but the result is the same.

Giving up, I attempt to fall asleep naturally again, but several minutes later, I'm still awake, my anxiety worsening by the second. It's so bad that I start worrying about the fact that I'm worrying. Could something be wrong with me, like with Mason?

"You're just really stressed," Phoe whispers. "You need to calm down for the assisted-sleep command to work." She hesitates for a second, then asks softly, "Do you want me to allow them to make you feel Oneness today, just this once?"

"You told me it's psychologically addictive," I say. "I was miserable when I was kicking it weeks ago."

"Yes, I know, and Oneness is complete and utter bullshit." Her voice grows in volume. "It's the Adults' answer to ancient religious experiences, which they hypocritically claim to have transcended." She pauses, as if calming herself down, then adds in a more even tone, "Given that I told you all that, obviously I wouldn't recommend you repeat that experience without good reason."

"And that would be?" I find that injecting sarcasm into a subvocalization is easier than into a thought.

"I can see your neural scan. You're distraught, and I don't know another good way to soothe you," she says. "Not without messing with your brain chemistry in potentially unpredictable ways.

Oneness, for all its faults, has at least been tested on many brains."

"As a form of control," I say, repeating what she told me once.

"Yes, to keep you all pacified and happy, but keep in mind, it's merely a program that expanded on the work of the ancient neurotheologists. It gets your nanocytes to interact with your brain stem, as well as the frontal, parietal, and temporal lobes." Her voice sounds closer, as though she's sitting on the bed next to me.

"Knowing all these things doesn't make it any less weird," I whisper toward where her head would be, if she were really there.

Liam shifts in his chair; he might've heard me whisper.

"You can try meditating instead," Phoe suggests. I'm grateful she didn't use the chance to chastise me for the whisper. "It puts your brain in a nice delta-wave state, lowers your blood pressure, and, in general, gets you some of the same benefits as Oneness."

"Well yeah, doesn't Oneness incorporate a meditative state?"

"It does that too," Phoe says. "And you could use its serenity right about now."

"You know I haven't been able to meditate since you showed up in my life," I think, wondering if she can detect the bitterness in my thoughts. She doesn't respond, so I subvocalize, "It's fine. I'll give Oneness a go. You can help me stop it if I want to, right?"

"I can," she says softly. "And, Theo? I'm sorry I messed up your life."

I begin responding, but at that moment, Oneness begins.

* * *

I feel pleasure.

No, not pleasure. Overwhelming bliss.

With the small part of my brain that retains its ability to think, I recall that the ancients called this intense pleasure 'ecstasy.'

I try to compare it to regular day-to-day pleasant experiences and find them all lacking. This is better than eating Food, more exhilarating than winning at sports, and more exciting than being absorbed in a video game, a movie, or a book, or listening to music.

None of those things come close to this phase of Oneness; the intensity of this pleasure is almost painful.

Then, suddenly, another element of Oneness manifests itself. With some internal vision, I see a bright light and feel a benevolent ethereal presence. If I were an ancient, I would probably think my dead ancestors, or deities, were surrounding me. Without any specific religious backdrop, though, this feeling simply intensifies. At its peak, it morphs into a conviction that the goodness and love of the universe is surrounding me. I feel connected to the distant stars. I recall learning that we are all made of stardust, and I feel like the stars and I are connected by an invisible network of kinship. I feel as though the universe, despite its supreme immensity, actually cares about what happens to me.

Then my breathing evens out, and with each breath, I get the impression that it's not me who's breathing, but that the universe is moving the air into me and then sucking it out, over and over.

I also feel love and wish happiness to the people of Oasis. I feel deep, unshakable love for my best friends, Liam and Mason. I feel love for Phoe. She's a new friend, but in many ways, because of how intimate our communication is, she's become one of my closest. Even if she *is* my imaginary friend, loving her would mean loving myself, and at this moment, I do love myself, wholeheartedly. I want all of us to be happy. I wish for all of us to be well.

I then feel similar love and happiness for people I usually would feel neutrally toward, like the Youths who sit next to me in my Lectures. I even feel magnanimous enough to wish good things to some people I usually don't like. I understand them. They're just human beings. Take Grace, for example. She was doing what she thought was right when she told on Mason. I can forgive her. Or take someone who's wronged me even less, like Instructor Filomena. She's a dedicated Adult who loves teaching. She made teaching her entire life, and I find room in my heart to respect her for it. I wish her happiness and wellbeing.

All this is spoiled, however, by a gnawing fear.

I'm enjoying this too much.

I could get addicted to this again. I could get to the point where I beg Phoe to allow me to experience

Oneness every day, like I used to before she came into my life.

The sense of connectedness with the universe slips as these thoughts surface, and I remember that Oneness is an illusion created to keep us content. A falsehood that some Forebear probably cooked up on a theory that optimum health requires satisfying the need for spiritual fulfillment. Or the Forebears might've created it to prevent us from succumbing to a belief in the pointlessness of existence—an obvious risk for a tiny group on the last patch of Earth not consumed by the deadly Goo.

Yet as these bummer thoughts enter my mind, I'm still feeling love toward everyone and everything. Only the echoes of the pleasure remain, but I still want this pleasure to stop. The possibility of my addiction to it scares me. I can finally verbalize my problem with Oneness. It's the same problem I would've had with the drugs the ancients used to consume.

Oneness, for all its wonder, is the ultimate loss of control. Yet I want—no, I *need*—to be in control of my own mind. I don't want to be a slave to Oneness, or to drugs, or to a spiritual experience. So I shout a thought in my mind as loudly as I can: "Phoe, can you shut this off?"

I have to assume she heard me, because as suddenly as Oneness began, it ends.

* * *

"Well, that was a disastrous idea," Phoe mutters. "I'm sorry I suggested it."

"Don't be so hard on yourself," I subvocalize. "I *am* feeling less anxious."

"Yeah, but that's not what I had in mind. Given how this went, I could've just as effectively given your butt an electric shock," she says. "You're merely feeling better because you got distracted."

"I guess." I rub my forehead.

"Ready to sleep?" she asks. "Or do you want me to come up with some other brilliant idea?"

"No," I say. "I'd like to sleep. I just want to make sure you—"

"I've made it so that Oneness is once again disabled for you," she thinks.

"Phoe," I subvocalize, deciding to ask for something that's been in the back of my mind for a while now. "Can you disable any and all tampering with my mind?" I pull the blanket up to cover more of my body. "Good, bad, I don't care. I don't want it."

She's silent for a while, then says, "I don't think you understand what you're asking me—"

"I know what I'm asking." I say this so convincingly I almost believe it myself. Before she catches me on that thought, I subvocalize, "This is not a spur-of-the-moment request. I've been meaning to ask you this for some time. I don't want the Adults or the Elderly to keep me 'neutered'— whatever that is." My subvocalization devolves into a hushed whisper. "I don't trust them to 'pacify' me either—"

"Calm down," she says. "I'm not saying no. You just caught me off-guard." She pauses for a second. "Truth be told, I've been planning to offer to do exactly that, only in the future when I thought you were ready. There's a favor I want to ask of you, and I don't know if I can trust you with it while your brain is under so much of their influence—"

"When *I* am ready?" The question comes out in a louder whisper than I intended. "*You* trust *me*? Do I need to remind you that you're a voice in my head, and that I have no idea where you came from or what you—"

"Stop, please. Liam just heard you. Luckily, he's ignoring you." Phoe sounds tired. "If it means so much to you, I can expedite my original plans, but I still think it's just your anxiety talking and—"

"Just do it," I think more calmly this time. "Please."

She goes silent again, then whispers, "Are you sure, Theo? At least consider a phased approach. I could start with the serotonin levels—"

"I'm sure," I think at her. "I want it all gone. The ancients lived without all this mind manipulation, so why can't I?"

"Okay," she says. "I will do it, but I have to warn you. This takes time. If you don't like how you feel and decide to go back to your current self, it won't be quick. Your neurotransmitter levels might take a while to normalize—"

"That's fine," I say firmly. "I won't want to go back."

"That's not all," Phoe says. "There will be some things that will still affect you, like fear of the

Barriers, since that works via neural implants that the nanos built into your brain, and I'm sure you don't want me to perform neural surgery on you at this point. More importantly, there are aspects to what the Adults and the Elderly do to you guys that you're not familiar with. I wanted to tell you about that before—"

"I don't care," I say just as firmly. "Please do as I asked. Disable what you can."

"Okay," she says. "Go to sleep and I'll do it as soon as you're under. It might actually be easier, computationally, to undo it all at once. I would just—"

"Thank you," I say, stifling a yawn. "There's something else I want to tell you."

"What is it?" She sounds worried.

"Phoe . . ." I look for the right words to express the conclusion I've been slowly reaching. "I'm beginning to believe you're not my imaginary friend after all."

"You are?" She seems so surprised it's as if she herself thought she was imaginary. "That's good news."

"Don't sound so shocked. I wouldn't ask you to do what I just did if I thought I was talking to myself."

"Well"—she sounds thoughtful—"you've compartmentalized that sort of logic until now. For example, when I spared you from Oneness, you didn't stop to think how you could've done it yourself." She pauses. "I just didn't want to rub your face in it."

I smile in the darkness. "It could be my insanity worsening," I subvocalize, "but I think I'm *not* crazy, which leads me to the big question you've dodged every time I've tried bringing it up—"

"Who am I, if not your imagination?" Her voice is so close that if she had lips, they would be brushing against my ear.

"Right." I take in a slow breath. "That question."

I've halfheartedly asked her this before. It was always a challenge of sorts: If you're not a figment of my imagination, then who are you? She's always responded with something along the lines of, "It's complicated." Her dodgy answers only fed my suspicion that it was *me* talking to myself somehow. I also couldn't see how she could be someone, physically. I mean, she's a disembodied voice. How could someone do what she does? Granted, she gave me some explanations that involved technology, but it's technology no one in Oasis has heard of, so I thought that I, in my delusions, must've made it all up.

Now I have to consider the likelihood that she was telling me the truth, that some form of technology is allowing her to be a voice in my head. But that just makes it harder for me to figure out who she is. Since I don't know how to be a voice in someone's head, I have to assume no other Youth knows how to do that either; we all learn the same things at the Institute.

If she's not a Youth, then she has to be either an Adult or an Elderly. Only she doesn't sound like an Adult at all. She curses and says things that they would find abominable—another reason I thought she was an expression of my own anarchistic tendencies. Though I've never spoken to any of the Elderly or know much about them, I imagine they're worse than Adults when it comes to acting all proper, so she's even less likely to be one of them.

Given all that, I focused on the easiest theory: that she's my imaginary friend. Now, though, I can't ignore all the evidence that suggests she can't be a figment of my imagination.

If Phoe is real, then I have a new friend, a close friend, and I don't really know who she is. Could she be one of those supernatural beings the ancients dwelled on so much? Or—

"I'm not a deity of any kind," Phoe says with amusement. "I know you weren't serious, but still. I'm also not—"

"A banana, nor an ancient proctologist, nor an invisible pink unicorn." I try to make my thoughts sound stern. "There are a countless number of things you're *not*."

"You're right," Phoe says. "But I hope you can forgive me. This is not a conversation I'm ready to have. At least not yet. And especially not before I block the Adults' influence on you. I'll do my best to explain it to you as soon as I can. Like I told you before, it's complicated."

I start to object, but before the words can come out, I yawn again, and with an almost unnatural suddenness, sleep steals my consciousness away.

* * *

I wake up with a start.

I think I had a nightmare that involved falling from a great height. I don't recall the exact details, especially where I managed to find access to 'a great height' in Oasis, but that's just as well.

I'm absolutely, positively terrified of heights, even the not-so-tall ones like the roof of our Dorm building.

Heart still pounding from the dream, I look around my room.

Liam is sleeping in his bed, but Mason's bed is missing, as is Mason.

"Uh oh," I subvocalize. "Where did he go? I hope not to talk to Grace again."

"This is very odd." Phoe's voice is coming from the room's entrance, as if she's sticking her head in to check on me. "After I did what you asked—after I made sure your brain is tamper-free—I was preparing some things related to the 'who am I' question and wasn't paying attention to this room. So I don't know where he is." She sounds worried.

"Don't go anywhere or do anything until I figure this out."

"No, wait," I whisper. She doesn't respond, so I say, louder, "Phoe, come back. What do you mean you don't know where he is? Don't you always know everyone's whereabouts?"

Phoe doesn't answer. Instead, I hear Liam rustling in his bed.

Crap. I have so many questions for Phoe, not the least of which is about the changes to my brain. I certainly don't feel any different.

Pondering that, I sit up and feel the morning teeth cleaning happening in my mouth.

My shoes appear, and I put them on.

"Why are you getting up so early?" Liam says in a sleep-raspy voice.

I bring up a Screen and check the time.

8:45 a.m.

"We're actually late," I say. "We'll have to run if we want to make it to the Calculus Lecture."

"Like I was saying," Liam says, sounding a lot more awake. "Why are you getting up so early?"

I ignore his question and ask him, "When did you head to bed? Was Mason still here at that point?"

Liam sits up and swings his legs off the edge of the bed, giving me a puzzled look. "I went to sleep after I finished watching my movie. And I don't understand your second question."

"I was asking if Mason was still in his bed, but if you went to sleep right after me, then he would have been," I explain. "And if you slept so much, why are you giving me a hard time? I thought you stayed up all night playing with your Screen again."

"I'm still recovering from my last two all-nighters," Liam says. "And what the uckfay is this mason thing you keep rambling about?"

"I'm talking about Mason, who is not here this morning. Mason, who was in bed last night," I say with growing irritation. "And I told you not to say just a single word in code—"

"Dude, I'm too sleepy for some complex historical joke or riddle," Liam says, suppressing a yawn. "Are we talking about a stone builder or a secret society mason?"

"I'm even less in the mood for jokes," I say. "I'm worried about him."

Liam gives me an evaluating look. "Are you okay, dude?" Then in Pig Latin, he asks, "What the fuck are you talking about?"

"Mason, our uckingfay friend," I reply, in my irritation making Liam's favorite cryptographical mistake. "The guy who needs our help today. Ring any bells?"

Liam's face turns uncharacteristically serious. He looks at me intently and says, "This is a dumb joke, whatever this is."

I get up, walk toward the door, and say, "Right back at you."

"Theo," Liam says. "Are you sleepwalking? Like some ancients used to do?"

"Okay." My voice is terse as I continue in code. "Screw this. I'm leaving. I don't have time for your shit."

I head toward the door, and Liam gets an expression I don't recall ever seeing on his face.

He looks concerned.

"Dude," he says. "Wait. If you insist on going to Calculus, let's walk together."

"Not if you're going to continue being a dick," I say in code.

He looks at me with even more worry, and finally, with the most deadpan expression he's ever had, says, "I don't get what's up with you this morning. Are you feeling sick?"

"Me, sick?" My voice rises in volume as I glare at him.

"What else am I supposed to think?" Liam says, frowning. "You sound delirious."

His seriousness makes my skin crawl. "Dude," I say. "Is going insane like one of the ancient viruses?"

Liam blinks at me uncomprehendingly, gets off the bed, and approaches me. Grabbing my shoulder, he looks me in the eye and says, "Theo, buddy, I'm not messing with you."

I look at him like he sprouted horns, but he continues, "I honestly, genuinely don't know what you're talking about." He gives me a pleading look that seems to say, 'Theo, stop this nonsense.'

I grind my teeth. "I'm too worried about Mason to deal with whatever you're playing at." I'm a decibel away from shouting.

"Theo." Liam's expression is one of utter incomprehension. "I don't know what or who this mason is."

"I don't have the patience for this," I grit out, and with a final glare, I storm out of the room.

CHAPTER FIVE

As I hurry toward the Lectures Building, my frustration eases. By the time I'm halfway there, I'm not sure why I even reacted the way I did. Liam was just messing with me, and Mason is probably already in the Math Hall.

As I pass by the pentagonal prism of the Quietude Building—also known as Witch Prison—its unwelcome sight makes me wonder if Mason might be locked up there instead. Could a Guard have gotten him earlier this morning?

I debate walking toward that dreaded place when I see Grace's distinctive red hair between a large oak and a decorative dodecahedron statue. She's meditating, which is a strange thing for her to be doing right now. She should be on her way to Calculus. Could she be trying to calm herself because she had another encounter with Mason?

Once I'm close enough, I don't know what to do, so I just stand there and watch her meditate for a few seconds. Her fine features are serene and placid, like a lake in the morning. I can't believe I'm actually envious of *her* of all people, but I am.

"Grace," I say quietly. Interrupting someone while they're meditating can really startle them. "Grace, you're going to be late for Lectures."

"Theo, what are you doing here?" Grace opens her eyes with a sweep of her long, brown-red eyelashes. Then, looking at her wrist—where I assume she can see her hand Screen—she says, "You're right. I could've been late." With barely suppressed surprise, she adds, "Thank you."

"I was looking for Mason," I blurt out. "Have you seen him?"

"Seen who?" Her forehead creases slightly.

"Mason."

"Who's that?" She blinks. Her blue eyes seem deceptively guileless.

"My friend whom you would never forget, given what he did yesterday."

"Is this a joke?" The crease in her forehead deepens.

"Did Liam put you up to this?" I ask, trying to keep my cool. "If so, it's not funny, especially coming from you."

"Liam put me up to what?" Her confusion seems to increase. "You know how much I dislike that square little friend of yours."

"Mason," I say a bit louder. "The guy who told you how he feels about you." Unable to help myself, louder still, I add, "The person you snitched on."

At the mention of the word 'snitched,' Grace's expression transforms from confusion to anger. Her eyes in slits, she says, "Whatever stupid prank you're trying to pull, stop. Now."

"You should take your own advice," I retort.

"I warned you." She puts her hands on her hips.

"I can't believe your gall," I say, frustrated. "To make light of Mason after—"

"What are you talking about?" Grace's expression abruptly softens with concern. "Are you feeling okay?"

"I'm fine," I say. "But I wish you'd asked Mason that yesterday. He was devastated."

"Theo, I don't understand what's going on."

My frustration boils over. "Of all the nasty shit I expected from you, I never thought you'd fuck with my head like this. I thought you were all about being proper. How did Liam even manage to get you to—"

She jumps to her feet and runs toward the distant cube of the Administrative building.

Realizing the blunder I just made, I chase after her. "Wait." Catching up, I grab her shoulder. "Grace, I didn't mean to use that language. I was just—"

Her gaze flits from my hand to my face, and I see fear in her eyes.

It's like a slap in the face.

I quickly remove my hand from her shoulder. "I'm sorry—"

"I'm sorry too," she says, backing away. "I have to report your language, and whatever else is going on with you."

"You're going to admit you're playing a prank?"

Her expression changes from fear to worry. "Listen, Theo. Why don't you go back to your room? I think you might need help . . ."

The pity on her face scares me.

"I have to go," I say, backing away as well.

"I'm sorry, but I still have to tell them," Grace says, watching me. "I know you'll hate me even more—"

Not waiting for her to finish, I turn on my heels and all but run toward the Lectures Building.

Mason will be in Calculus.

He has to be.

* * *

When I get to the Math Hall, the Lecture is about to start.

I peek in and see other Youths, their faces in varying shades of boredom. Mason isn't among them. Could he be skipping? Math *is* his least favorite subject.

The sound of footsteps coming down the hall interrupts my thoughts, and I turn to see Instructor George, the Calculus teacher, approaching.

He gives me a quizzical look. "Are you *trying* to be late, Theodore?"

"I was just wondering . . . Did Mason give you an excuse for why he's not at the Lecture today?" I ask, hoping I'm not about to get Mason into more trouble.

"Who?" The Instructor's forehead wrinkles in that uniquely Adult way. "I'm not sure I follow."

I realize I'm holding my breath. Exhaling, I say, "Mason, sir. You know . . . my friend. Your student."

"Is this a jest?" The expression on Instructor George's face is the one he gets when someone mixes up an equation. A sort of 'how can you be so wrong?' type of glare. "I don't have a student by that name."

As the meaning of his words registers, a deep terror seeps into me.

Until this moment, I could tell myself that Liam and Grace were playing a prank on me. An Adult, however, would *never* partake in a prank— particularly if that Adult is Instructor George. His sense of humor was permanently replaced by the Pythagorean Theorem.

Which means only one thing: something odd is going on.

Did I jinx my mental wellbeing when I told Phoe I didn't think she was imaginary? Is that what's happening? Did I truly lose my mind? Or did I go crazy because Phoe made my mind tamper-free? Ancients went insane all the time, so this is a real possibility.

Or could I simply be dreaming?

"Phoe," I scream mentally. "Phoe, where are you?"

"Theo, what the fuck is going on?" Phoe's reply is so loud my whole body tenses. I've been jumpy around loud noises ever since Owen startled the crap out of me by suddenly screaming in my ear in the middle of my morning meditation a few months ago.

Instructor George gives me a questioning stare. He must've noticed me jump.

"They don't know who Mason is," I whisper at Phoe. "And don't speak so loudly again."

"Wait." Phoe's tone is pure incredulity. "You asked *him* about Mason?"

"I—"

"Never mind that now," she says sharply. "Get yourself together. I think he just saw you move your lips."

I take a deep breath and make an effort to relax. "It's hard not to panic," I think at her.

"You're doing okay," she says. "Now say, 'I'm sorry, Instructor George. I guess no one told you about the history lesson we're play-acting with Liam. He's supposed to be a Freemason.'"

Robotically, I repeat what Phoe said.

The Instructor looks at me as if I have 'two plus two equals five' tattooed on my forehead. Then he shakes his head and says, "This is one of the most creative ways someone has tried to get themselves excused from my Lecture." Straightening his shoulders, he points at the door. "I'm not falling for it. Get inside."

"Crap," Phoe says. "I guess there's nothing more we can do. Get inside the room and shut up. I have to see how big of a mess you've made."

I march in and notice that Instructor George isn't following me.

Ignoring my growing sense of unease, I plop down in a chair, my mind overloaded with questions.

"He just reported your conversation to the Dean," Phoe says when Instructor George walks in a few beats later. "Let me try to research this further. Don't say a word."

The Instructor begins his lesson. He likes to teach on a giant Screen in the front of the class, not unlike how teaching was done in the ancient world.

I don't hate math as much as Mason does, nor am I as bad at it as Liam is. Mathematics is actually the only subject where I don't feel as if I'm being fed bullshit on a daily basis. For example, when we learned that equilateral triangles are equiangular, I understood both the mathematical proof and the truth of it. Even when we learned that 0.999 with infinitely repeated nines is equal to 1, I understood the truth of it through proofs, even though it felt unintuitive at first. It was even fun to change my mind like that. In contrast, every word that comes out of Filomena's mouth in History feels like a calculated falsehood.

Today, though, I feel as ambivalent about the Lecture as my friends usually do.

To keep myself from panicking, I attempt to focus on the lesson, but every fifteen minutes, I catch myself wondering where Phoe is and what I'd do if she doesn't show up soon.

Eventually, I give up trying to pay attention. At least the Lecture will be over in a few minutes.

To keep a modicum of sanity, I replay the events of this morning in my head. My best guess is that this whole day has been a very strange dream. In that case, how do I wake up?

I pointedly pinch my wrist.

"You're not dreaming." Phoe's sudden words startle me. "Writing usually looks blurry when you're dreaming, but the Screen looks pretty crisp, doesn't it? Believe me, given what I've found out, I wish you *were* dreaming."

"But—"

"I *told* you not to do anything or go anywhere." Phoe's voice grows in intensity. "Which part of that did you not understand?"

"I had to go to Calculus," I object. "Did you want me to cut class?

"Right, of course, because had you skipped your Lecture, you'd have been in trouble, while now, you're all hunky-dory."

"Can you do me a favor and not talk like you're a voice inside my head?" I whisper loudly enough that Owen turns around and gives me a questioning stare. I shrug at him and subvocalize at Phoe, "Just tell me what's going on."

Owen raises his forefinger to his temple and makes a circular motion. Which movie did he learn that 'you're crazy' gesture from? Other Youths usually don't know ancient behaviors that well.

"Ignore that dweeb." Phoe is still, annoyingly, talking inside my head.

"But he might be right," I think at her, pulling my gaze away from Owen to look at the Screen in front of the classroom. I want him to think that I'm bringing my attention back to math. "I think I truly *am* nuts."

"You're not," she says, out loud this time. "But this Mason situation *is* messed up."

"At least *you* know who Mason is," I say, finding surprising relief in that. A little voice—a voice that is not Phoe but my own paranoid self—reminds me that despite what I thought last night, Phoe could still somehow be a product of my imagination.

"So we're back to that nonsense again?" Phoe says. "Now is not a good time for you to be worried about *me*."

"Fine," I think. "Let's get back to the issue of Mason. Did you figure out what happened to him? What's going on? I assume you had a reason for making me wait?"

"Okay." Phoe sounds as though she's sitting next to me. "The bad news is that I *don't* know where Mason is, *or* what happened to him. But I do know this: they truly don't know who Mason is. No one does, as far as I can tell."

Even though I suspected as much, my insides fill with lead. "What does that mean?" I think at Phoe, trying to rein in my growing panic.

"It means when Liam, Grace, and Instructor George acted like they didn't know Mason, they weren't faking it."

"So are you saying *he* was my imaginary friend and not you?"

"Don't be ridiculous," she snaps.

"Then why do they not know who he is?"

"That part is tricky." Her voice acquires a certain distant thoughtfulness. "Do you recall what happened with that movie you liked, *Pulp Fiction*? The one that disappeared?"

"It was deleted from the archives," I say.

"Right. Well, there's something I didn't tell you out of fear of distressing you. *Pulp Fiction* wasn't the first movie that was deleted after I showed it to you."

The mental "Huh?" I reply with sounds like a loud nasal exhale.

"I know how it seems, but it's true. *Pulp Fiction* was merely the first movie I didn't let them make you Forget."

"What?"

"Do you remember *The Silence of the Lambs*?" Phoe asks. "You watched the movie and read the book, but you don't remember either, do you?"

"Lambs?" I fight the urge to whisper out loud again. "Those are baby sheep, right? Those cute white creatures the ancients used to eat?"

"Right. You clearly don't recall. But as I was saying, after the Adults decided to ban *The Silence of the Lambs*, it didn't just disappear from the Archives. You couldn't recall reading or watching it either."

I'm too stunned to reply at first. Then, mentally shaking my head, I think, "No way."

"I'm sorry to spring this on you. I tried bringing it up last night, but—"

"It just can't be," I subvocalize. "If I watched a movie or read a book, I'd remember it. How could I not?"

"Your nanobots were utilized to tamper with the intricate neural pathways required to recall that particular memory. After that was done to you, you confabulated a new reality, one in which you had never read or watched that work of fiction."

"I did?"

"Because you don't remember it now, you can safely assume so, yes. Since then, I've been experimenting with selectively shielding your mind from this sort of influence." Her voice is hushed, almost a whisper in my ear. "It worked with *Pulp Fiction*, which is why you remember *it*. Then, last night, when you asked me to disable all tampering with your mind, I did as you asked. It's my conjecture that the Elderly, or whoever, did the same thing to people's memories of Mason as what happened to your memory of *The Silence of the*

Lambs. It's called 'Forgetting.' You were the only one who didn't fall under its influence."

"Wait—"

"I'm sorry, Theo." She softens her tone. "If I'm right, it's not just those three people you spoke with who don't know a Youth named Mason. If I'm right, you're now the only person in Oasis besides me who remembers your friend."

CHAPTER SIX

"That's impossible," I whisper, but when I see Owen begin to turn his head, I continue subvocally. "How could they make everyone forget?" I look around the classroom as though my classmates' memories might show up on their faces. "Hell, how could they get just one person, Liam, to forget someone he's known all his life? You have to admit it's more unlikely than me having seen a movie and not recalling it."

"As I tried to explain, after Forgetting, your brain goes through a process called confabulation," Phoe

OASIS

says, her tone one of exaggerated patience. "It's a psychological response first noticed by the ancients. Back in those days, they had incidents of something they called amnesia—cases where people forgot things, either due to age-related brain-degenerative diseases, or due to some brain injuries. People with amnesia often told stories that were not factually true, but which felt true to them. For example, they thought the hospital they were in was their workplace. They basically ended up altering their memory and worldview to make it seem as though the things they forgot never existed. Having watched your mind from day to day, I should add that some mild confabulation is a routine part of how your brain operates—"

"Bullshit," I think at her and try pinching myself again, but to no avail.

"Denial is as common of a psychological defense mechanism as confabulation," Phoe says. "Unfortunately, it doesn't change the facts."

"But to erase memories—"

"They didn't erase them. They are blocking recollection, which equates to the same thing but is much easier to do."

"I would never forget a friend." I cover my eyes with the palms of my hands to relieve the tension building behind them. "Nothing would make me forget Liam, or Mason, or you for that matter—even if I do wish I could forget the part of my life after you turned up in my head."

"It's touching, and insulting, and sadly untrue," Phoe says. "Look on your Screen. I just gave you the exact transcript of our conversation about *The Silence of the Lambs*—the conversation you can't recall because it pertains to that movie."

I don't question how she made my Screen appear without my willing it. I'm too overcome with disbelief over the text on the screen.

Phoe is right: I don't recall ever having this conversation with her. Yet the words she tagged as 'Theo's lines' sound like things I'd say.

Exactly like things I'd say.

My pulse accelerates. "You're inside my head," I say, trying to reason it out. "You know me well enough to fabricate that conversation."

"Yes, but why would I want to do that?"

"I don't know." My anxiety intensifies. "I want to wake up and see Mason. I can't accept this."

"I know how you feel." Phoe pauses, then says softly, "I've also been made to Forget."

"You have?" Somehow knowing that Phoe, the ultimate know-it-all, was made to Forget makes me instantly transfer my worry from myself onto her.

"What they did to me was worse than what was done to the rest of Oasis," she explains. "I was basically lobotomized."

"I don't know what that word means." I frown as I shift in my seat.

"You asked me who I am. I told you the answer was complicated, and it is." She sounds as if she's pacing the classroom. "When I asked myself this question some time ago, I realized I actually have no fucking clue. I know bits and pieces, but mostly I only know that I forgot something important." She noisily exhales. "Something huge." She goes silent, as though trying to think of the right words. "The rest of my memory is a series of gaping holes. Not only did they make me Forget this big thing, but in the process, they even made me forget who I am."

"How can that be?" My skin prickles with an icy chill. "How can you forget who you are?"

"It's hard to explain," Phoe says. "I might have guesses, but that's all they are. The favor I mentioned to you has to do with my memory gap. In any case, my situation is very different from yours."

"Obviously," I subvocalize, still trying to process what she told me.

"Listen, Theo." Her voice is hushed and urgent. "The Guard is already waiting for you outside this Hall."

"Crap," I say. "I'm getting a Quietude session *now*, in the middle of all this?"

"I'm not sure whether they're here to take you to Quietude."

I feel as if I've swallowed a tray of ice cubes. "Where else would they take me?"

"I don't know," Phoe says, and I detect a note of fear in her voice. "Wherever they took Mason, I think."

"Which is?"

"I have no idea, but there's a way to figure it out." She's speaking faster now. "A couple of ways, actually. One solution is what I've been itching to have you do—it's that favor. Another thing I could do on my own, though the risk is that they might catch on, but since things can't get any worse, I think we should try both options."

"What options?"

"They're both a form of hacking—"

The bell rings, signifying the end of the Lecture.

"Oh no," Phoe says. "I lost track of time."

All the other Youths jump from their seats and start walking out of the Hall, but I sit still.

"Whether you sit here or walk out there, they will take you." Phoe sounds as if she's about to leave the room.

"I'm just scared," I think at her and wonder whether she can feel my emotions as easily as she knows what I'm thinking.

A helmeted head pops through the doorframe.

"Theodore?" the Guard says.

Why Guards wear that shiny headgear is as mysterious to me as everything else about them. They could be Adults or they could be the Elderly underneath those things. Hell, they could even be Youths like me.

"Please, come with me." The Guard's tone is tense.

I get to my feet. My legs feel shaky and wobbly. Must be from all that sitting.

"Or adrenaline." Phoe's voice sounds as if she's standing right next to the Guard.

I don't chastise her for responding to a thought that was not meant for her; I'm too worried about what's going to happen.

"Hello." I approach the door and look at my googly-eyed reflection in the Guard's helmet. "What do you want?"

"You are to come with me," the Guard says.

I don't move. "Where are you taking me?"

"Please walk with me," the Guard says.

"He won't tell you," Phoe says. "They never do."

"Are you taking me to Quietude?" I ask, ignoring Phoe.

Instead of answering, the Guard extends his hand and moves his palm in the air in a strange, wave-like motion. If it's a gesture command, I don't recall ever seeing it before.

"Theo, he just tried to give your brain a serious calming jolt," Phoe hisses. "Act like you're relaxed. Quick."

The urgency in Phoe's tone forces me to do my best impression of getting calmer.

"Don't ask any more questions," she says. "Just walk."

I do as she says, my anxiety growing.

"He tried to mess with my mind?" I make a point of thinking at her, not daring to whisper or subvocalize with the Guard around.

"Yes. To ease your agitation."

"But I don't feel relaxed."

"Because I made your mind impervious to this sort of influence along with most other manipulations," she explains.

"Oh, right." I try walking straight while looking relaxed—a difficult task given the treacherous shaking of my legs.

"You're doing fine," Phoe says. "Just walk in silence until you exit the building."

I comply. When we're out of the Lectures Building, I wonder whether this is how the ancients who were going to the gallows felt. We walk in silence for a few minutes, and then Phoe says, "I think it will be reasonable for you to try talking to him again. Say, 'Sir, this is a misunderstanding. I was just talking to people about the Freemasons, a group we learned about in Instructor Filomena's class.'"

I say that, plus a bunch of other bullshit Phoe comes up with.

The Guard says nothing for a few steps.

"And the whole thing started with stonemasons—"

Before I can finish Phoe's script, the Guard makes a gesture I don't fully catch.

"What did he try to do to me this time?" I think at Phoe.

"Relaxation again," she says. "Look calm and stop talking."

I try to use external cues to relax for real, as our campus was designed with serenity in mind. Focusing on the rock tower in the distance, I let my eyes glide over the symmetrically arranged rocks.

"That is Augmented Reality," Phoe says. "That tower is not really there."

"Thanks for the useless information." I look at the cherry blossom tree, daring Phoe to tell me it's also not real.

"I'm trying to distract you from gloomy thoughts." She sounds as if she ran ahead of the

Guard. "But if being snippy with me provides relief, then go ahead."

Ignoring her, I try doing a walking meditation. I focus on the light touch of the wind on my face, on the consistent flexing of my leg muscles, on the warmth of the sun's rays on my skin—

"Theo, watch out—"

I don't hear what else Phoe wanted to say, because I run smack into the Guard, who stopped. He's holding his finger to his ear.

He turns his head toward me. Is he giving me a skeptical stare under that mirrored visor?

"I think he just got instructions on what to do with you," Phoe says.

I tense, all traces of my tentative serenity fleeing as I wait to see where he'll take me.

If I'm to get the usual punishment—Quietude— we'll turn right.

The Guard looks hesitant for a moment, as though he's deciding my fate.

I swallow, unable to feign calmness any longer.

The Guard turns to the right, toward the pentagonal prism of the Quietude Building, and begins walking.

CHAPTER SEVEN

"You're going to Witch Prison," Phoe says with relief that the building's nickname doesn't usually generate. "That means Quietude."

"I never thought I'd be so happy to be going *there*." I pick up my pace to catch up with the Guard. "Are you sure that's not where Mason is?"

"I'm sure," she says.

"So where is he then?" I risk a vocalization since the Guard's back is turned to me.

"I don't know. I still didn't get a chance to do the hacking I told you about. Plus, I'm beginning to think the safer route is to get you to do the task I've been talking about—the one only you can do."

"What is it?"

"Something that will make your Quietude session pass faster, I suspect," she says. "Now, if you don't mind, I'm going to prepare what I need."

"Wait," I say. "Tell me what it is I'll have to do."

"Fine." Phoe heaves a sigh. "It's a way for me to remember some of the things I've forgotten. My intuition tells me that if I can recall them, I'll have an easier time finding out what happened to Mason."

"'Intuition' sounds a little wishy-washy."

"I've done many things on intuition, and you've trusted me thus far." Phoe's tone is clipped.

"It just sounds contradictory. You forgot something, yet you know that if you remember it, you'll get specific answers?"

"I know I'll have better tools for hacking at my disposal if you do what I need you to do. In that sense, I'm certain I'll be better positioned to figure out what happened to Mason." It's clear she's doing her best not to sound defensive. "Regarding the memory stuff, I don't know how to best put it into words, but I know something big was erased from my mind—from everyone's minds. I don't know what it is, but I'm sure it's something we'd all want to know, regardless of what happened to Mason."

I consider that for a moment.

I'm about to be punished by boredom—that's what Quietude is, essentially. Whatever Phoe wants me to do might be a welcome relief from that.

"You don't know the half of it," she says, her tone artificially upbeat.

"So what is it that you want me to do, exactly?"

"Merely play a video game," she says. Then, under her breath, she adds, "From the Last Days."

The Last Days is what everyone calls the period of time leading up to the Goo Armageddon, though in some of the texts I've read, it's referred to as the Singularity—a time when technology was invented so fast that human minds couldn't keep up with its rate of development. Everyone knows that any technology from that time should be treated with caution, if not outright fear.

"What about the technology all around us?" Phoe asks.

"Now you're getting into completely private thoughts," I complain. "I thought the technology around us was safer than the abominable things they invented in the Last Days. Weren't we shielded by the barrier of the Dome and separated from everyone else by then?"

For a few seconds, all I hear are the Guard's footsteps and the distant voices of Youths.

"I think that's part of the information I forgot," Phoe says.

"Well, it's a video game," I subvocalize, thinking of what she wants me to do. "How bad can it be?"

"It's a more advanced version of the technology behind the virtual reality they use in your classes—not bad at all, in other words," Phoe says. "I'll try setting some things up. I'll talk to you soon."

"Hold up," I whisper, but she doesn't respond.

For better or worse, we're almost at our destination.

I gaze up at the building.

Even the ivy looks as if it's covering it with great reluctance.

As we get closer, I feel the tightness in my chest that I always get when I'm faced with the Witch Prison. The Quietude Building was nicknamed that because of its unique pentagonal prism shape. It has something to do with ancient witches and how they liked to get naked and draw pentagrams all over the place. I think all of us—those of us who were sent here as little ones, at least—feel uneasy about the place. Due to my record number of 'why' questions and other mischief, I've spent more time in Quietude than most.

We enter the building. With every step down the corridors, I remember why I hate this place so much. Unlike the bright silver of other buildings in Oasis, these walls are a dull gray, and there's an ozone (or is it chlorine?) odor permeating everything.

"This is your room," the Guard says once we've reached the end of the bland corridor.

Knowing from experience how useless pleading with him will be, I walk in without protest.

The room is even duller than the corridor. It's almost as if all the color was sucked out of it. The air lacks any smell, even that unpleasant odor from the corridors.

The layout of the room is the same as it was during my previous visits, with the same uncomfortable chair that's not like the ones we assemble, and the same small bed to the side, near a toilet. In the center is a little table with a pitcher of water and a special bar of Food that, if it's anything like the ones I've had before, is completely tasteless. I'm shocked to see only a single bar. These Food bars are how troublemakers like me gauge the duration of our Quietude sessions. They put out at least a bar for every day of the stay. Since there's only a single bar, I won't be here for as long as I feared.

I walk around the room and, for the umpteenth time, touch everything. These objects are stationary, the way furniture was for the ancients; gestures or thought commands have no effect on them. Gestures and commands don't work in these rooms at all—a fact that I verify as soon as the Guard closes the door behind me.

I can't change the layout, nor can I bring up a Screen.

The lack of a Screen or any kind of entertainment, combined with the blandness of everything here, is what makes Quietude so insidious.

It's torture by boredom.

Sitting down in the chair, I drum my fingers on the table.

"Phoe?" I subvocalize.

She doesn't respond.

"Phoe," I whisper.

Nothing.

"Phoe, I have bad memories about this place. This isn't a good time to be joking around." I say this out loud, knowing she'd never ignore me after such an indiscretion.

Silence is my only reply.

What the hell is going on? What is Phoe up to? Why is she not talking to me when I need her most?

I get up and pace the room.

Five circles later, Phoe still hasn't spoken up.

I pace some more.

No response.

I keep pacing.

* * *

I'm sweating. I swear a couple of hours have passed with me pacing, and Phoe is still silent. I'm ready to do anything at this point, including playing whatever Singularity-technology VR game she needs me to play.

I try lying down but can only do so for a few minutes before I jump up and start making circles around the room again.

My discomfort is increasing exponentially, and I don't understand it. Being locked up in this room has always sucked, but I've never felt this way before.

It's as if the gray walls are closing in on me. It makes me want to bash my head against the door and splatter blood on it.

At least that would bring in some color.

Okay, this is crazy. Am I experiencing some side effect from what I asked Phoe to do to my brain? Is this what it feels like to be anxious without the nano-whatever things messing with my mind? If so, how did the ancients not kill each other?

Then I recall that they *did* kill each other during 'wars' and even on a day-to-day basis. They did a lot of crazy things, including creating artificial intelligence to aid in their wars.

Thinking about the AIs that unleashed the world's end makes me shiver—which is further proof that I'm more sensitive to stress than usual. Sure, those thinking machines were the epitome of all that was unwholesome and evil about the Last Days, but AIs, along with things like nukes and torture, are now a thing of the past.

Maybe I should rethink this no-tampering policy and beg Phoe to change me back to the way I was.

Sitting down on the chair, I fold my legs under me and try to even out my breathing. My mind is racing like that hamster in its wheel at the Zoo.

In. Out. In. Out. I do this for what feels like an hour before I calm down a little.

Then I notice a strange shimmer in the air.

I stare at the apparition for a few moments before I comprehend what I'm seeing.

It's a Screen—a Screen in a room where I've never seen one.

But it's not a normal Screen.

It's faint and distinctly unreal-looking, as though it hasn't *really* formed—as though I'm dreaming this Screen. It's like this Screen is one of those ghosts the ancients were obsessed with, though ghosts were usually shaped like people, not Screens.

A cursor flickers on top of this apparition for a couple of beats and then begins moving, leaving behind an unusual purple text. For a second, all I see are the lines that make up each letter, lines that remind me of digits on an ancient calculator. Then the meaning of the words seeps through my mushy brain.

Theo, this is Phoe.

As it turns out, the Witch Prison is a Faraday cage—or nearly so. It's a place where I can't talk to you. Luckily, I found this one loophole through one of the Guards' communication channels, and I really hope it works.

On the subject of Mason, I tried hacking into their system on my own, but I couldn't—nor could I set up the game interface. But I do have an idea about how we can free up some resources, which might give me a good chance at both tasks.

In any case, none of that matters as much as this: You need to get out as quickly as possible.

"What are you talking about?" I think at her. "I don't understand anything you said, except that you can't talk to me and that I need to escape." I look around, waiting for a reply, and then look at the screen. When no response comes after a few moments, I subvocalize, "How can I get out of this place, Phoe?"

The cursor wakes up again and types:

If you're trying to talk to me, you should know that this is a one-way communication system. I can't even be sure you're reading this, but you better be, because you're in danger.

Someone from the Adult section is on their way to the Prison. That's really bad.

I will try to unlock your door in a moment. I think I tapped into the building's emergency-exit procedures. Once the door is unlocked, exit, make two rights, then a left. Then you'll have to leave through the emergency exit. It will look like a regular door.

I stare at the ghostly Screen in stunned fascination. My daze is broken by the Screen disappearing in the same way it appeared.

Is Phoe serious? She wants me to escape Quietude?

No Youth has ever done this, and I'm sure every single one of them wished they could have.

My pulse racing, I walk up to the door. Unlike regular doors, it doesn't open for me when I gesture at it. Testing out the ancients' method, I push it with my hands.

I could just as easily have been pushing at a wall.

"What now?" I subvocalize by habit.

As though in reply, I hear a sharp noise that makes me jump back.

Then I understand.

It's the door.

Something just happened to it.

I approach the door again and press on it.

Given Phoe's message on the Screen, I shouldn't be surprised, but I am.

The door opens.

Warily, I stick my head out and look around.

The corridor is empty.

I walk out and try not to dwell on what the punishment for doing this will be.

"Two rights and a left," I repeat in my mind as I tiptoe down the corridor.

When I get to the end of the corridor, I crouch and look around the corner—a trick I picked up from playing hide-and-seek with Liam and Mason during our childhood years.

My heart bobs up to my Adam's apple.

There's a Guard walking toward me.

He's half a corridor away.

Is it my imagination, or is he walking faster all of a sudden? Did he see me?

It's impossible to tell with him wearing that shiny visor.

I duck out of sight and swiftly make my way back to the room where I'm supposed to be, staying as quiet as I possibly can.

To my relief, the door closes behind me.

I put my ear to it, but I can't hear any steps coming down the corridor.

This most likely means the door is soundproof, but it could also mean the Guard didn't turn this way.

I count the way I did when I was little—one Theodore, two Theodores—until I reach twenty.

Gingerly, I exit the room again.

When I don't see the Guard in the corridor, a grateful whoosh of air escapes my lungs.

I get back to the corridor on the right and repeat my earlier trick of crouching by the corner.

The Guard is gone.

I get up, turn the corner, and start walking. The corridor is long, and the gray walls blend together to obscure just how far it goes.

I walk for what feels like a couple of minutes, with no end in sight.

I pass a right turn, but ignore it since Phoe told me to make a left.

I walk some more and finally see the end of this monstrous corridor, but it's a good twenty feet away.

"This stupid corridor must curve," I think, unsure whether I'm talking to Phoe or myself.

She doesn't reply and talking to myself has never really appealed to me—unless that is what I do when I talk to *her*, but I've moved beyond that theory.

"Theodore," a voice says from behind me. "Stop."

I think it's coming from where the right turn was.

This voice is male, so I know it's not Phoe. I assume it's a Guard, but I don't look back—that would be a waste of time.

My stealthy walking pace forgotten, I torpedo forward.

He runs after me. Through the beat of blood in my ears, I hear his pounding footsteps. A wall at the end of the corridor looms in front of me. I almost smack into it, but manage to turn left, my shoes sliding on the smooth gray floor.

"Theodore, stop! What are you doing?" The Guard sounds as if he's about to turn my way.

I sprint down the smaller corridor, toward the door at the end. Skidding to a stop in front of it, I make a gesture for the door to open.

It remains shut.

CHAPTER EIGHT

Gasping for air, I gesture at the door again.

Nothing.

I concentrate and think at it, "Open."

No effect.

The definitive sound of running footsteps is growing louder.

My palms cold and clammy, I push at the door with all my strength.

It doesn't budge.

I chance a glance over my shoulder and see the Guard's visor shining from just around the corner.

The door in front of me makes the same sound as the one in my Quietude room. Phoe must've opened it, I realize.

Nearly choking with relief, I push the door open and fly out of the building.

The door whooshes shut behind me.

To my left is waist-high grass, which, according to Phoe, was designed to encourage everyone to stay on the paved pathways. I leap into it and crouch, desperate for cover.

I know I'll be found if the Guard thinks to look here, but I don't see a better option.

"You're fine," a voice says from right next to me. "He's about to run back into the building."

My heart falls back into my ribcage. "Phoe?" My subvocalization is as close to a silent shout as it's possible to get. "You can talk to me again? Where have you been? What's happening?"

An ear-splitting wail fills the air. My head ringing, I realize it's coming from the Witch Prison.

"Since you're here, you clearly got my message," Phoe says hurriedly, her voice somehow audible through the din. "Like I told you, I had a hard time communicating with you once you were in the

Witch Prison." She rattles off the words so quickly that I can barely make them out. "The Guard just headed back. I unlocked more doors. Some of the Youths took it as a chance to take a walk. Someone rang the alarm. I think they'll be busy for the time being."

"But—"

"Get up and run, Theo."

I do as she says.

I didn't think I could run faster than that sprint in the corridor, but I was wrong. I'm surely setting some kind of record; it's too bad no one will give me credit for it.

Youths don't pay attention to me as I fly by. They must think I'm just exercising. Everything around me is a blur. After the grayness of the Prison, my eyes have to adjust to all the different shades of green.

My lungs feel as if they're about to explode, but I manage to gasp, "Can you explain?"

"You just spoke out loud," Phoe chides.

"Yeah, right. Me talking out loud is the problem," I think at her, unable to vocalize too much while out of breath. "I mean, if I keep this up, I might *get into trouble.*"

"If you sprint and talk, you'll run out of breath quicker." Phoe sounds as though she's running alongside me.

I suck in a lungful of air and subvocalize, "What's going on? What's the plan? Why—"

"Theo, you need to do as I say." Her voice gets those commanding overtones I usually associate with Instructors.

"Fine." I need oxygen too much to argue with her even mentally. "Where am I going?"

"Follow the large paved path all the way down, then take the road that leads to the forest in the west."

I can't help but whisper, "But that might lead us to the Adult Border."

"What, are you afraid you might get *into trouble?*" Phoe says, her voice a perfect parody of mine.

"There's trouble, and then there's going toward the Border," I think more calmly. "It just isn't done."

"If it helps, I won't have you officially cross the Border," Phoe says, though it sounds as if she left the word 'yet' unsaid. "I need you to go to the Zoo."

I run in confused silence for a moment. The Zoo is indeed the closest structure we're allowed to visit that's near the Border.

"I can't go there," I think at Phoe. "I haven't been at the Zoo for almost a year." Despite saying that, I head in the direction of the pine trees that are in the far distance.

"Really?" Phoe responds. "I thought it would be your kind of place."

"It is, but I can't enter it. My access is denied. A long-term consequence from when Liam, Mason, and I put Owen's hand in a cup of warm water in the middle of the night."

"I would've thought that would've yielded a Quietude," Phoe says.

"Owen is an asshole, but he's not a snitch. And even if he were, he wouldn't have told anyone that he wet his bed." I mentally chuckle at the memory despite my growing exhaustion. "No. We got into trouble on our way back to our room. They took my access away because we were out after curfew the day after a Quietude session."

"Well, with my help, you'll be able to get into the Zoo," Phoe says.

"How?" I catch the scent of the pines that I'm quickly approaching.

"When you got my frantic communiqué in the Prison, did you notice the part of my message that talked about my failed attempts at hacking into the Adults' and the Elderly's systems? When I mentioned that I couldn't figure out what happened to Mason with the resources I currently possess?"

"Kind of," I lie. "Vaguely."

"What about the part about me not even having the resources to get you into that game that you agreed to stop?"

"Yes. Only I don't recall you ever talking about me stopping anything."

"If you beat the game, you stop the game, but that doesn't matter since I can't even get you in there."

"Why?"

"I just said it a second ago." She sounds annoyed. "I lack the computational resources to either figure out what happened to Mason or get you into that game. That's where the Zoo comes in."

"What resources?" Sweat drips down my back as I continue sprinting. "How can the Zoo help?"

"You'll see," she says. "It's not far now."

Perplexed, I follow the paved path into the pine forest.

Phoe is either busy or giving me space, so I don't talk as I run to the meadow where the signature half-sphere of the Zoo is located.

Unlike most other buildings, the silver metal of the Zoo is exposed. It's as if the pines scared away the ivy that covers everything else.

Slowing down to catch my breath, I walk up to the entrance at a more measured pace.

As I approach, I can't help but recall my futile attempt to get in earlier this year. I tried sneaking in with a large group of Youths, but the doors wouldn't open for anyone until I left.

This time, however, the door slides open for me with no problems.

"Don't be so surprised," Phoe says. "I told you I'd get you in."

"After the stuff you pulled with the Witch Prison, your door-opening capabilities will never surprise me again," I say as I enter the Zoo.

A few steps in, I find myself in the middle of a circular room, the place where one usually stands when the Zoo session is initiated.

As I wait, I amuse myself by looking up at the reflective spherical ceiling.

Nothing happens.

"You're not going *into* the Zoo." Phoe's voice sounds as if it's coming from a few feet away.

"I'm not?" I ask and wonder whether all the adrenaline from my run is intensifying my sense of disappointment.

"We're short on time," she says.

"I see." My shoulders slump a little.

"Fine," Phoe says. "If you *really* want, given what I'm about to ask you to do, I guess we can spare a couple of minutes. Brace yourself."

And just like that, the half-sphere is gone, and I'm standing at the beginning of Zoo Road.

The ground under my feet moves, and I look around.

I almost forgot how magnificent this place is.

To my left is a prairie that stretches to the horizon. There, I note a herd of gazelles running away from a pride of lionesses. To my right, on an equally endless snowy tundra, I spot a penguin escaping a sea lion. Cute animals getting eaten is probably my least favorite part of the Zoo, but it's also fascinating.

"Okay, you saw it. Can we resume our tasks?" Phoe says. "This place breaks all laws of virtual reality aesthetics. Combining Antarctica on one side and Africa on the other? Someone should've told the creator of the Zoo that alphabetization doesn't mean congruency."

"Just a little more," I say as I pass through a couple more luscious environments and observe creatures ranging from komodo dragons to anteaters. "I want to do the petting portion and the safari."

Suddenly, I'm back in the real world.

"I'm sorry, Theo," Phoe says in an apologetic tone. "We really need to get this done."

"What do you want me to do, exactly?" I try not to sound irritated, but it's difficult. I was looking forward to petting a llama again.

"Just step on *that*," she says.

I look about for something to 'step on.' There's a light shimmering right in front of me that looks like a large Screen floating sideways. Then another one shows up right above it, then another. It's like a staircase of sorts. I don't recall ever seeing this before.

"That's because I've put this place into admin mode," Phoe says.

I eye the staircase warily. "Is that thing solid?"

"How else would you step on it?" Phoe sounds teasing.

"Each step looks like a Screen, so it's a fair question."

"It's not an Augmented Reality construct like the Screen," Phoe says. "These steps are made out of the utility fog. But you're right. Whoever designed the admin mode didn't bother to make them look more realistic."

"Oh, great. Fog, the thing I associate with solidity," I think sarcastically as I hesitantly raise my foot and place it on the first step. It feels real, so I put my weight on the step with my right foot and then let my left one join it. The strong feeling that I'm frozen mid-jump makes me uneasy about going higher.

"I forgot about your fear of heights," Phoe says. "But it'll be okay. The platform is just a few steps higher."

I examine the shimmering stairs above the one I'm standing on. They indeed lead to a circular platform made out of the same material.

I take the next step, reminding myself that I'm less than two feet off the ground. Falling from here would be the equivalent of falling from a bed.

I take the next step.

"Now it's as scary as standing on a chair," Phoe suggests. "And the next one will be like standing on a table."

I take the next two steps.

"Keep going." As if to highlight how unreal she is, Phoe's voice is coming from a location in the air that doesn't have a stair.

I take the stairs one after another, but with each one, my stomach fills with ice. When I reach the tenth step, I can't help but look down.

My insides immediately flip-flop.

"Just a little more," Phoe urges. "You can't fall. It's physically impossible. The utility fog that makes up the steps is all around us. If you trip, it will catch you."

Her words reassure me. I take another determined step, then another.

"Two more and you're on the platform," she says.

I inhale a deep breath and go up as quickly as I can.

Standing on the circular platform feels a modicum safer. I let out the breath I was holding. "Now what?"

"Make an exaggerated gesture of pulling down a cord, like ancient train conductors did to toot the train's horn." Phoe sounds like she's right next to me.

I do as she says, making a fist above my head and then bringing my elbow to my chest.

An unusual round Screen shows up in the air in front of me. On it, in a very large font, is written: 'Please confirm the Shut Down.' Under the text are two ginormous buttons that say: 'Confirm' and 'Abort'.

"What does it mean by 'shut down'?" I ask Phoe.

"Shut down the Zoo," she responds matter-of-factly. "Now click the 'Confirm' button."

"Wait a minute. Shut down the Zoo?"

"Yes."

"Permanently?"

"Probably."

"But it's the Zoo." I can't help but say this out loud. "This would deprive everyone of so much . . ."

"I'm sorry for their loss, Theo, but I don't have many other options. The virtual reality simulation that is the Zoo eats up a horde of resources—the computing power we desperately need. I can't think of anything else we can shut down with so little risk to you and such a gain in resources, especially given our time constraints."

"But—"

"Look, Theo," Phoe says. "With this, I should be able to find out what happened to Mason before we deal with the game."

"Can't I just do the video game thing instead?"

"I also need resources for that, remember?" She sighs. "Once you're done with this, I actually hope you can 'do the video game thing' regardless of whether I can puzzle out what happened to Mason." She must sense that I'm about to protest because she adds, "Though I'm fairly sure I will find out what happened to him."

I nod—unconvincingly.

"Please, Theo," she says. "Getting rid of the video game is a way for us to learn that very important secret we were made to forget."

She thinks I have a problem with playing the game, but I don't. I have a problem with denying everyone access to the Zoo.

"It's the only way to figure out what happened to Mason," she says, clearly having read my mind again.

"Fine," I say, growing weary of arguing. "I'll do this for Mason."

I reach out and touch the 'Confirm' button.

"Please say, 'Shut Down,'" the Screen display instructs. "And think, 'Shut Down.'"

"Shut down," I say ceremoniously and follow up the command with the same thought.

"Shutdown commencing," the text on the Screen says.

In the next instant, the Screen goes blank and disappears.

I stand there waiting for some other cue that something has happened, but there's nothing.

Then, a few moments later, I see something on the platform next to me.

I blink a few times.

It appears to be a three-dimensional female silhouette made out of a shimmering fog, like an ancient statue of Aphrodite made of clouds. The ethereal figure doesn't have a defined face or any other distinguishing features other than the slim hourglass shape commonly seen in ancient media.

"It's me," Phoe says, her voice coming from where the mouth of the figure would be—if it had a mouth.

"Phoe." I gape at the figure. "Why do you look like a ghost?" As I say it, an illogical thought flits through my mind. Could she be an actual ghost, like the ancients believed?

"I'm not a freaking ghost," the figure snaps. "I just used the resources you freed up to slightly improve our means of communication. I read in ancient literature that communication is primarily nonverbal."

"I suspect when they talked about nonverbal communication, they meant facial expressions, which you lack," I point out, shaking off the ghost idea.

"Yes, but I can do body language now, which definitely counts as nonverbal communication." She demonstratively puts her hands on her hips.

On a whim, I walk up to the figure and try to touch her.

She doesn't move away from my hand, but when I reach for her slender shoulder, my fingers go through the mirage of flesh the way they would with a Screen.

"I mastered more of the Augmented Reality controls—went visual on top of auditory," Phoe explains. "What you now see works exactly like a Screen."

"Okay, but is that what you really look like?" I step back from Phoe's body. "And where are you now? Who are you?"

The ghostly figure shrugs. "I still don't have a solid answer," she says. "But I do know something far more important."

"You know what happened to Mason?"

"Yes," she says softly. "But I'm not sure if I should share it with you."

"Tell me." I say the words so forcefully that Phoe's illusory figure backs away. I step after her. "Tell me, or you can forget about me lifting another finger to help you."

"Okay." She's all the way at the edge of the platform, and her chest expands as if she's taking a deep breath. "But Theo . . . you should know that what happened to Mason is worse than anything either of us could've imagined."

CHAPTER NINE

The hairs on my arms and nape rise at her words.

"I was hoping I could get you out of the Zoo building before we continued talking about that," Phoe says. "Follow me." Her graceful, shimmering figure approaches the steps and swiftly descends.

"No, tell me now." I run down the first five steps, forgetting about my fear of heights. Then, more carefully, I descend to the bottom.

The Phoe silhouette is waiting for me by the exit. "I got you down without much fuss, didn't I?"

Before I can reply, she hurries out of the building.

I run after her.

When I exit, she's already halfway down the meadow.

I chase after her, my leg muscles burning.

"Theo, I need you to hide in the forest." Her voice is in my head this time.

"Wait," I think at her, but she's already entering the forest line.

I run after Phoe through the pines for at least ten minutes before she stops and waits for me.

"Ideally, you should do the video game first," she says. "They're looking for you."

I plant my feet firmly in the dirt and say, "I'm not moving an inch or doing anything until you show me what happened to Mason."

The shadow-like Phoe looks down. "You'll wish you hadn't insisted."

"It's my decision to make. Stop delaying."

"Okay." She raises her head, as if to meet my gaze. "Bring up your Screen."

I do the gesture, even though I know she could've brought up my Screen for me. She's stalling. This realization sends another chilly tendril into my belly.

My Screen comes up, and I see our dorm room. Mason, Liam, and I are sleeping. The viewpoint focuses in on Mason and gets closer to him, as though whoever is recording just approached his bed. A hand reaches out and touches Mason's shoulder.

"It's a recording from the Guard's visor," Phoe says, answering the question I was about to ask. "I was only able to recover bits and pieces—whatever wasn't deleted from temporary caches and video buffers during the Forgetting procedure."

An explosion of snowy white static interrupts the scene on the Screen, and a new set of images follows right away.

Mason is walking on the wide road that traverses the pine forest I'm in. The viewpoint—one from the Guard's visor, I guess—is staring at the back of Mason's head. In the distance, I see the reflective surface of the Barrier. With its metallic mirror-like wall, it looks like an ancient blimp or a weather balloon—only it stretches through all of Oasis, marking the place where the Adults' domain begins. Mason walks toward it, and the Guard follows.

"They took Mason through the Barrier?" I whisper as I extrapolate what's happening. "But they never let Youths go there."

Phoe doesn't respond, so I watch as Mason approaches the supposedly impenetrable wall that is the Barrier, and it lets him through as though it were some kind of liquid silver bubble. The Guard follows, though, of course, the fact that *he* can pass through the Barrier makes sense.

"How did Mason even approach it?" I ask Phoe. "You can't even walk once you get halfway through this cursed pine forest. I learned this the hard way."

"The fear that the Barrier generates doesn't affect Youths specifically." Phoe's voice lacks its usual vitality; she sounds older and wearier for some reason. "It's merely a matter of the permission profile for the person trying to cross. They gave Mason access before . . ." Her words trail off.

"Before?"

She doesn't respond. The scene on the Screen changes again.

Mason is strapped to a white gurney in a half-lying, half-standing position.

A person wearing white is standing next to him. This person also has white hair, which reminds me of the gray hair on the old people from ancient movies—gray hair even the oldest Adults don't possess.

"I thought we didn't age to the point of gray hair in Oasis," I think both to myself and as a question to Phoe. "Is he an albino?"

Phoe's new shape slowly shakes her head. "He's one of the Elderly."

I look back at the Screen. Everything else in that room is also white, which gives it a medical feel reminiscent of the nurse's office.

In front of the mysterious Elderly man is a big Screen. On the Screen is what I assume is Mason's neural scan.

"His thought patterns have changed since we spoke with him," I tell Phoe. "It looks like he's going through some positive emotions."

"It's Oneness." She turns away from the Screen as if she can't bear to look at what's happening. "They're running Oneness on him nonstop before . . ."

"Before what?" I ask, my chest tightening from an awful premonition.

Phoe doesn't answer.

On the Screen, the Elderly man comes closer to Mason and looms over him. He's holding something. I squint and get so close to the Screen that my nose almost goes through it. It takes me a moment to understand what I'm seeing.

The Elderly man is holding a syringe.

As I watch in shock, he sticks Mason with the needle and presses the plunger.

For a couple of breaths, nothing happens. Then Mason begins to convulse on the table. On the big Screen in front of his head, the brain patterns change.

They get slower.

My eyes feel glued open. I can't blink.

Mason's neural activity slows some more.

I take a raspy breath. "What's happening?" I look at Phoe. "Is Mason falling asleep?"

She doesn't respond. She just stares at the dirt beneath her feet.

Droplets of cold sweat bead on my forehead as I look back at the Screen. Mason's neural activity continues to slow until it, impossibly, ceases completely.

Phoe covers her face with her hands—or, more accurately, she covers the place where her face would be.

"What—" I begin, but the strange activity on the Screen distracts me.

Mason's body disintegrates, as though it was made of sand and a strong wind was blowing on it. It takes less than a second for his body to completely dissipate.

The white bed he was strapped to just a moment ago is empty.

The Elderly man turns to the Guard whose helmet recorded the scene. He says something, but I can't hear him. He then wipes tears from his ancient-looking eyes.

The Screen in front of me goes blank.

On some level, a purely rational part of my brain already knows what happened. The rest of my mind refuses to catch up with that realization.

I feel like screaming, but no words, not even in the form of a subvocalization or a thought, come out.

My muscles tense, and my body begins to tremble.

"Breathe, Theo," Phoe says from what sounds like a distance away. "Breathe, or you'll go into shock."

I take a breath that hurts as it enters my chest and step back. "It can't be."

"I'm sorry I showed this to you." Phoe's voice is even more distant. "I was afraid it would be too much. You've never faced death before."

Death. That's what she just said.

That sinister word snaps something in my mind, allowing it to begin wrapping itself around the fact that this horrid concept is the best explanation for what I saw.

Except it doesn't make sense. Death doesn't happen. It's been eradicated in Oasis. It's an ugly, theoretical construct from yesteryear, like torture and extinction.

Mason can't be dead, can't be gone. The idea is as incomprehensible as the notion of Forgetting him. I can't imagine it. It's like trying to picture the complete absence of matter and space.

I take another step backward and feel the rough bark of a pine tree against my back.

"I'm so sorry, so sorry, so sorry." Phoe's words are like a meditative chant.

I shake my head vigorously, as though to shake meaning into my brain.

"Calm down." Phoe's tone is soothing, but her words feel like acid on my skin.

"Stop trying to handle me," I say out loud. "Why should I calm down? If this isn't the time to freak out, when is?"

"I need you to stay calm because you're also in danger." Phoe's voice still holds a pacifying note. "I need you to help me keep you safe."

"Is he really dead?" I'm still speaking out loud— almost shouting, in fact. "Could those videos be a prank of some kind? A cruel trick? A way to teach me a lesson?"

She steps toward me. "No, Theo. As horrible as it seems, this is how Forgetting people works. The person stops existing. Both in memory and in reality."

Rounding the tree, I back away again, but my foot catches on one of its roots. I fall hard, my confused state not conducive to good landings. My teeth snap together with a loud clink, and a shock of pain reverberates through my back, followed by a wave of nausea.

After a moment, the worst of the pain fades, but I don't attempt to get up. I feel like I want to lie here forever and not think. The crowns of the trees above me sway, and I stare at them without blinking.

Phoe looms over me, blocking my view of the trees and the sky.

"I'm sorry." Her voice is like an echo. "I wish you had time to properly mourn, but I'm afraid you don't. They're searching through these woods as we speak."

"Phoe... If you're making this up, if he isn't really dead and you're just manipulating me into doing this thing you want me to do, please just say so," I think at her in desperation. "I'll do whatever you want. Just please tell me Mason is alive."

"I can't." She sits down on the ground next to me, pulls her knees to her chest, and hugs her legs. "I wish I could."

I shield my eyes with my palms and lie there, trying to even out my breathing.

"That's it," Phoe whispers. "Breathe." Her voice is like a cold drink on a hot afternoon. "We're lucky it's only been a day since I disabled their tampering. All your happy hormone levels are well above those of the ancients. This should help you cope."

Her words make no sense. How could the ancients survive feeling worse than I do at this moment?

"According to what I've read in the archives just now, they went through some of the same things you're going through—denial, anger, bargaining, depression—before eventually reaching acceptance, the last stage of grief."

I lower my palms to glare at her. "I will never accept what I just saw."

"Nor should you." Phoe's hard tone matches mine. "Under the circumstances, of those five stages, anger might be the most productive response."

I replay the image of the white-haired man giving Mason that shot, and my fists clench. If the man were in front of me, I'd hit him and kick him until I saw blood.

"You probably wouldn't," Phoe says. "And I mean that as a compliment."

"You don't know what I would or wouldn't do. The bastard deserves to get punched."

"You're right, and, more importantly, you're on the right track." Her voice takes on Liam's signature conspiratorial quality. "Channel your anger into the next task. Trust me, learning whatever it is that stupid game is preventing me from remembering will be huge. Beating it will help a lot more than hitting an old man."

"Fine." I sit up. "Let's do this thing."

CHAPTER TEN

"First, I need you to calm down some more," Phoe says. "Try eating."

"I don't feel hungry."

"Try to eat anyway."

Almost on autopilot, I make the palm-up gesture that makes Food appear, and the familiar bar turns up in my upturned hand. I take a bite, and for the first time in my life, normal Food is completely tasteless, almost as though it's one of those punitive Food bars they serve during Quietude.

"There you go," Phoe says soothingly. "Food can be comforting, which is good. The calmer you are, the easier the game should be."

Since my mouth is full, I ask mentally, "Why?"

"Because of the nature of this particular game," Phoe responds out loud. "What you're about to experience is a complex neural analysis, adaptation, and response technology. The ancients called it IRES—Immersive Reality Entertainment System."

"I don't understand what that means," I pointedly think at her.

"Immersive Reality is like Virtual Reality, only, well, more immersive. Additionally, the world you'll enter is tailored to everyone who joins the system, which in this case will be you." She points at my chest.

I take another bite of the Food bar and think, "That still doesn't make a whole lot of sense."

"Your teachers have done a number on you guys." Phoe sighs. "How can I dumb this down?" She sits still, apparently thinking, then says, "Think of it like this: the game will analyze your head. It will look at your memories and experiences, and from them, it will create an ultra-realistic world meant to entertain you as much as it can. Does that make more sense?"

"Sort of." On the third bite, the Food starts to taste a little better. "How do I win?"

"Maybe the word 'game' is misleading," Phoe says as I continue chewing. "This thing is meant to be an interactive, fully immersive entertainment extravaganza. Its purpose is to provide a one-of-a-kind experience to each and every player, not to only choose a winner."

"But if more than one person is playing—"

"If multiple people play, the competitive component is enhanced. The game will create a world that's a conglomeration of elements based on the analysis of each player's mind. That's why this thing is so complex; it can support hundreds of interwoven players. Out of that mess, it will create a hodgepodge of a world for them to play in. But you don't need to worry about that, since you'll be by yourself." Phoe pauses as if to catch her breath. "I hope this explains why we have to end its operation. I chose this game as our target because the computational resources it consumes are truly staggering. Plus, since no one uses it, no one will miss it."

"Well," I subvocalize between bites, "what I really want to know is what will happen to me when I enter this game. What can I expect there? How do I do whatever it is you want me to do?"

Phoe's hands fidget in front of her. "What you'll see is very hard to predict, as is what you'll need to do. Suffice it to say, you'll need to play to the end. When you beat the game, you'll get the opportunity to stop it from running. When that happens, make sure to actually select that choice and shut it down."

"Why is this thing even running?" I ask.

"To eat up resources." She puts her arms around her chest as if giving herself a hug. "I think someone tried to find the most resource-intensive piece of software they could get their hands on, and this was it."

I tilt my head. "But why?"

"That's what I'm hoping to find out, *after* you beat this thing." She mirrors my head movement. "I don't want to make unfounded guesses."

"Okay," I say slowly. "But why don't they let anyone play this game? If it's running already, wouldn't it be logical to use it?"

"Since when do Adults go for logical ideas?" She shakes her head dismissively. "If I had to guess, this game is probably on that super-long list of forbidden technology." Phoe's voice lowers, as though she's worried someone might overhear her despite us being alone in the forest and her speaking in my head.

"Great." I catch my hands tightening, squashing the last bit of Food. "Forbidden tech—sign me up." I stuff the tortured piece of Food into my mouth.

"There is nothing to worry about. The Adults are total worrywart-luddites when it comes to technology." Phoe's voice takes on those passionate pet-peeve overtones. "Under the pretext of avoiding the next cataclysm, they label harmless stuff as—"

"Okay. Never mind. Just tell me how to play this thing."

"We'll need to hack you in." Phoe jumps to her feet. "How else?"

"I assume you don't mean hacking a bar of Food into pieces," I subvocalize and clear my throat.

She bobs her head. "Correct. I mean the kind of hacking that lets one do things one isn't supposed to do."

"Right. Can you be a bit more cryptic?" I exhale audibly, the way I would while meditating. "Please just tell me what this 'hacking' will entail this time around?"

"To start, I need to tap into your brain or, more specifically, into the nanocytes that interface with your neurons."

My eyebrows go up, and I squint at her.

"Okay, even more super-specifically, do you remember what you were doing the day we met?"

I nod. How can I ever forget that day? It all started when, on a whim, I gestured for extra Screens after having noticed that if you gesture for one after you already have one in front of you, you get two Screens. On that day, I decided to push that discovery further. I gestured for a third, then a fourth Screen, and kept going (I was very bored while learning about the evils of the Industrial Revolution). Sometime during my three hundredth Screen, the world around me momentarily blurred, and that was when I heard Phoe's voice for the first time.

"Yes, bringing up those Screens created a buffer overrun that I was able to exploit," Phoe says. "So this time, I need you to do the same thing: bring up a ton of Screens. I already created a safe virtual reality space for you to inhabit, a place that will let me pipe you into the game." More quietly, she adds, "In theory, at least."

Not feeling particularly confident, I do as she asked and start bringing up Screens.

"Just a few more," she says when I feel my wrists beginning to ache from the repetitive gesture. "And you could summon these screens mentally, you know."

I decide to play along and mentally summon another boatload of Screens.

When I get to about three hundred Screens again, the world blurs the way it did on that fateful day, and I'm no longer sitting in the forest.

I'm flying.

Or falling.

Whatever motion this is, it's happening incredibly fast.

I'm bodiless, like a ray of light. The world around me is a surreal white tunnel, and I fly/fall through it, heading somewhere.

The experience reminds me of those ancient rollercoaster park commercials, only scarier.

Just as suddenly as the feeling started, it ends.

I have my body back.

I'm standing in a new space.

To call this a room would be the understatement of the decade; it looks more like an ancient cave. It's dark, except for the shadowy light coming from luminescent creatures crawling on top of majestic stalactites and stalagmites. On my left are a couple of big barrels. One has the word 'Gunpowder' written across it, another has 'Gin,' and a third barrel has a skull-and-crossbones sign.

I try the usual illumination-summoning gesture by folding my index finger into a hook and flicking it up, the way the ancients used to turn on light switches.

To my relief, the cave brightens, and I can see details more clearly.

The cave is filled with a medley of forbidden objects, from guns and swords to posters of nude ancient models. Ancient magazines are scattered on the floor, and throughout the cave, Screens are playing violent movies and video games.

"What do you think of your 'man cave'?" Phoe asks from behind me.

"It's something," I say, turning to look at her. "It's like a—"

I don't finish my thought, because I can actually see *her*. I have to force myself to blink a few times as a rush of adrenaline tingles through my body.

She's changed.

She's no longer the ghostly presence she's been since the Zoo.

She looks real now, if 'real' can be applied to a woman who's unlike anyone I've ever seen.

She looks as though she stepped out of an ancient magazine. With her pixie-cut blond hair, overlarge blue eyes, and small, delicate features, she reminds me of Tinkerbell.

"Hey now." She flaps her long eyelashes at me. "That's insulting. I'm five foot nine—hardly as tiny as a fairy."

That's true. She's almost as tall as ancient models were, with the same kind of legs that seem to go on and on. As I stare at her, I also get a better view of her slim hourglass body—more than what was possible when she was ghostly. Her proportions are those of the ancient models too.

Something about her appearance fascinates me, but I can't tell what it is. I look her up and down, my eyes oddly drawn to the cleavage of her dress— something else I've only seen in movies, as Oasis girls don't wear anything that shows that much skin.

"Stop it. You're making me blush." Phoe gives me a mischievous smile. "Your hormones are starting to work the same way as those of an ancient male your age."

She's not really blushing, but I am. She's insinuating all sorts of taboos that I don't even want to think about, so I just say, "Okay, now that we're here, what's next?"

"First, I want to test whether you can come in and out of this virtual space, your man cave, with a gesture I invented for the occasion. I don't want you to have to bring up the three hundred screens every time."

"Okay," I say, ungluing my eyes from the place where her red dress meets her slender shoulders.

"Take your middle fingers and stick them out like this." She flips me off with both hands, the backs of her middle fingers sticking out triumphantly.

"Hey." I narrow my eyes at her. "Did you design this gesture to ensure I get into Quietude every time I use it?"

"Well, if you mentally say, 'Fuck fuck,' it's the equivalent to the physical command." She chuckles. "But we both know you prefer gestures. In any case, you obviously shouldn't escape to this place when you're in front of other people, since in the outside world, you'd be as cognizant of your environment as a rock. So it doesn't matter what the gesture is." She examines the red nail polish on her middle fingers— something I also stare at since I've only ever seen nails painted red (or any color) in ancient media. "I had to invent a gesture and command that isn't already in use, and, well, this was available."

"Right. Usually, like right now, I just want to give you a single-finger gesture," I say and flip her off, even though a part of me instinctively cringes at the accompanying memories of lengthy Quietude sessions.

"That's almost it," Phoe says, her expression deadpan. "You just have to do it with both hands, like this." She double flips me off again.

"Never mind." I make the double-middle-finger gesture just so we can stop conversing about it.

In a whirl of whiteness, I'm bodiless again. I fall through the surreal tunnel and experience the disorienting effect that accompanies the fall.

With startling suddenness, the white tunnel becomes the green of the pine trees around me.

"Now try going back the same way," Phoe's voice says in my head.

I do the gesture, and the trip starts anew.

When I'm back in my virtual man cave again, I say, "Okay, that worked. How do I do the next part?"

"That's easy," Phoe says. "I created a similar gesture." She makes the double flipping sign sideways, and then connects her middle fingers together in front of her chest. "You have to do this, but it will only work from here. You can't get to the game directly from the real world."

I begin connecting my middle fingers together.

"Wait, Theo." She walks over to me, getting so close that I can smell a hint of roses.

Perfume is another thing Youths don't wear, a rational part of my brain thinks. The more irrational part is not thinking at all, particularly when Phoe gets even closer, hugs me—a social interaction from the movies—and pecks me gently on the cheek in another movie-only action.

My breath catches. I feel as though energy is flowing from where her pouty lips are touching my skin. It's moving down through my whole body and into somewhere in my crotch region. I feel a strange urge to grab her and bring her closer to me.

She steps back. "No time for that now. The search party is getting closer."

My heart is beating faster than when I ran through the forest.

Is this what the ancients felt? Again, I wonder how the poor slobs functioned on a day-to-day basis. Then again, whatever I felt from her nearness was not unpleasant.

"Focus, Theo."

I blink at her. "How do I beat this thing? What should I expect?" I say, trying to, literally, get my head back in the game.

"I honestly don't know," Phoe says. "I wouldn't be surprised if there is some kind of a puzzle or quest you'll need to complete, or a phobia you'll need to face. It might be the usual fare of video games, or it could turn weird on you. I simply don't know for sure. Your mind is a key component in this. Colorful, recent, and traumatic past events can play a large role—"

"Sounds lovely." I almost manage to convince myself that my nervousness is related to the upcoming task.

"No matter what happens, it's no more real than this place is." She sighs and gives me a regretful look. "If there was an easier way, I assure you, we'd do *that*."

I suppress the urge to wet my lips. "And if I get killed?"

"Nothing scary would happen in that case." Her tone is gentle. "You'd simply return here and have to start the game over."

"Okay, I'm ready," I say with a confidence I wish I actually felt.

"Once you're in the game, I'll do my best to patch myself through and talk to you," she says.

"Wait, I'm going to be by myself?" I'm unsure why, but this idea scares me more than anything else. "I thought you'd be with me from the start."

"I don't know how to communicate with you once you're in there, but I'll figure it out, I'm sure." She steps toward me and puts her hand on my shoulder.

I feel instant relief. It's as though warmth is spreading from the place where her hand is resting.

"Theo, stop stalling." She pointedly glances at my hands.

I take my middle fingers and connect them in front of my face in some odd parody of the ancients' sobriety test.

As soon as my fingers touch, I become that ray of light again and begin flying through a rollercoaster of whiteness.

CHAPTER ELEVEN

I look around.

I'm back in the pine forest, exactly where I was before I entered my man cave.

"Shit," Phoe's voice says in my head. "It didn't work."

I look around but see neither her ghostly nor her real visage.

"What now?" I think to no one in particular.

"I have to come up with another plan," she says. "I think, given the situation, I have no recourse but to meet with you—physically."

"Wait, what do you mean by that?" I subvocalize.

"No time to explain," she says. "Start heading in the direction of the Barrier, on your left."

I turn.

"No, your other left," she says. This time, her voice comes from behind me.

I turn around and cautiously begin walking.

"You might want to move your feet faster," Phoe says. "The Guards are searching for you."

"I just don't understand." I rub my chin. "What do you mean by 'meet physically'?"

"You wanted to know who I am, right?" Phoe sounds exaggeratingly mysterious. "Due to these unfortunate events, you're getting your wish. We're about to meet in the flesh."

I jerk my head back, in part to dodge a tree branch, but also to respond to Phoe. "But I thought—"

"Theo," a new female voice says loudly.

It's not Phoe's, but it *is* familiar.

"We've searched the whole forest for you," the voice says. "I was so worried."

I locate the speaker; she's standing to my right.

Red hair fills my vision, and I realize it's Grace.

A horrible idea enters my mind: Could Phoe be Grace? She did say she'd meet me in the flesh, and here is a flesh-and-blood girl . . .

"Don't be ridiculous." Phoe sounds as though she's standing next to Grace. "I'm not this pathetic little girl, I assure you."

I take a step toward Grace, raking my hand through my hair.

"Please don't move, Theo." Grace takes a careful step back, her whole body tensing. "Don't move, or I *will* scream."

"She'll probably scream anyway." Phoe's voice wavers. "Fuck."

"Okay." I try to smile at Grace.

"Don't grimace at her like that. You'll make the situation worse," Phoe says.

"Shut up," I think at Phoe. "What now?" I say to Grace.

A *hmm* noise comes from Grace's throat. "You'll come back with me?" She taps her index finger against her chest as if I don't know what she meant by 'me.'

"So that I can follow Mason's fate?" I stare at her incredulously. "So you can get me into even more trouble?"

"Theo, I—" Her lips tremble. "When I told them about your ramblings about this mason thing, I didn't think it would get so bad."

"Mason is not a thing—"

"She doesn't remember him," Phoe cuts in.

"Never mind." I force myself to speak calmly since Grace could decide to scream at any moment. "I don't want to come with you."

"If you don't, things will get worse for you." Grace looks genuinely saddened by this.

"I doubt it could get any worse." Seeing that she's getting nervous, I soften my tone. "Please, Grace. Can you pretend you didn't find me? No one is monitoring this forest, so the Adults will never find out. You wouldn't get into trouble." I inhale, and on the outbreath say, "Please, Grace."

Instead of answering, Grace takes a step in my direction, then another.

Her blue eyes glimmer as she stops in front of me. Lifting her hand, she lays it on my shoulder and gives it a soft squeeze.

Given that Phoe just did the same thing to me, I wonder again whether Phoe is Grace after all.

"I'm not," Phoe whispers. "Now don't spook her or you're screwed."

Fighting the temptation to stare wildly at Grace's hand on my shoulder, I gently cover her hand with mine.

Grace's face contorts with emotions I can't pinpoint. Her lips part slightly, as if she's about to say something, but then she lets go of my shoulder and leans in closer.

"I won't tell them I saw you," she whispers softly, her lips almost brushing against my ear. "But please don't tell on me when they catch you."

I open my mouth to say, "*If* they catch me," but nothing comes out.

"Say, 'Thank you, Grace,' give her a peck on the cheek or whatever, and run." Phoe's voice sounds as though she's talking through gritted teeth.

"Thank you, Grace," I parrot, but I don't kiss her. "Thank you."

I slowly back away, then turn my back on her and start walking.

Grace doesn't say anything.

When I'm about twenty yards away, I look back.

She looks frozen solid, still standing where I left her, her gaze burning holes in my back.

I walk some more and look back again, but Grace is gone.

I begin running. I run as fast as I safely can with the branches hitting my face. I run because I don't know whether Grace will keep her word and not tell on me.

I stop my mad dash when I see a male figure between the trees a few feet away. He's leisurely walking away from me.

I'm glad I spotted him. If I'd continued running, he would've heard me. Maybe if I just wait, he'll move on.

The person stops walking and starts gesticulating. He must've brought up his Screen and is doing something on it.

I flatten myself against a tree and observe the stranger. As I look at him, I realize there's something familiar about this person's slightly stooped, narrow shoulders.

"Walk softly," Phoe suggests. "He shouldn't hear you. Also, before you suggest something as ridiculous as this, that is *not* me."

I decide to do as she suggested and take a soft step.

The forest is so silent and my heart is beating so loudly in my ears that I almost fear he can hear it.

The figure is still playing with his Screen.

I take another step, then another.

The problem with moving this way is that it will take me forever to get beyond his hearing range. The second problem is that it's somehow more nerve-wracking to sneak by than it is to run away, as the deliberate slowness stretches out the unpleasantness.

I continue walking softly, keeping an eye on the guy—which turns out to be a mistake. I should've been looking down. I step on a dry branch, and it makes a cracking sound.

The guy's head perks up, his large ears like those of a canine. That clicks something in my brain. I associate canines with hyenas, and from that, I finally realize whose back I've been staring at.

The Youth turns around, and I confirm my realization.

It's Owen.

I try to hide behind the nearest pine, but it's too late; he's walking my way.

I come out to face him.

Owen gives me a carnivorous smile, then puts his index finger to his lips and makes a *shhh* sound.

"I think he's threatening to scream if you run," Phoe says. "Try to resolve this quietly."

"No shit," I subvocalize at Phoe and stalk toward my nemesis.

"Do I smell Why-Odor?" Owen says when I get near enough that he doesn't have to shout. "Or do I smell trouble?"

I cock my head to the side. "What do you want?"

Instead of answering, Owen closes the distance between us and, before I understand what he's about to do, punches me in the solar plexus.

Air escapes my lungs, and logic goes with it.

I wasn't expecting Owen to do this. Though he's an asshole, he hasn't resorted to violence of this magnitude since we were little. I haven't been in a fight for so long that I've forgotten how unpleasant it is to get punched. I think I was around seven years old the last time I was in a fight, and it wasn't even with Owen; it was with Logan, one of his lackeys. I recall it not being fun, though Logan didn't even hit me in this sensitive spot. I suspect that even if he had, it wouldn't have been as bad, since I was fighting another seven-year-old.

"I have to say, escaping Witch Prison was an impressive feat," Owen says. He's jumping around me, fists raised in the style of an ancient boxer. "I didn't expect anyone to succeed at that, least of all you."

I'm too busy getting air back into my lungs to respond. When I finally straighten my back and take a breath, Owen's fist meets my jaw.

My head snaps back. The pain is exquisite, and the shock is completely dumbfounding.

"I've wanted to fight you for over a decade now." Owen's voice is distant. "Admit it, Theo. Don't you also want to? I know your buddy Liam does."

I'm too dizzy to answer. There's a metallic taste in my mouth.

He punches me in the shoulder—lightly, in comparison to the other hits.

"Oh, come on," he says. "We're in the forest. No one will be the wiser. The Adults keep us from having any fun."

I spit. The spittle is red.

The sight of blood, combined with his taunts, awakens something within me. There's a roar in my ears, angry moisture in my eyes, and a desire to see Owen's blood that overwhelms me.

My hands curl into fists. I raise them, mirroring Owen's stance.

When my opponent notices this, he grunts approvingly and tries punching me in the face again.

Instinctively, I duck. His fist whooshes past my ear.

I see that his miss left him momentarily exposed.

The world goes quiet, and I focus in on my target. I haven't hit another human being in a decade and a half, but I don't hesitate.

With all my strength, I bury my fist in Owen's midsection, cognizant of how hard it was for me to recover from this kind of blow.

A shock of pain travels up my arm, but Owen bends over with a squeal and begins hyperventilating.

Instead of gloating the way he did, I grab his hair and yank his head down at the same time as I jerk my knee up.

His face meets my knee with a satisfying crunch. My knee objects, but I take solace in the fact that his face must feel exponentially worse.

With a grunt, Owen slumps to the ground.

I pull my foot back to kick him, soccer-style, and he whimpers.

"What are you doing?" Phoe says urgently. "Haven't you heard the expression about hitting a man when he's down?"

I stop and stare blankly at the withered mess that is Owen. He's somehow gotten into the fetal position and is cradling his head in his arms.

If Phoe hadn't spoken up, I would've kicked him. What's worse is that I still kind of want to.

With effort, I resist the urge and take a deep breath.

Now I have a practical dilemma. Owen is hurt, and I need to get him help without giving myself up to the Adults.

"Just leave him here and come meet me," Phoe says. "I'll make sure someone finds him in a few minutes, after you're gone. Even if he tells them what happened, I doubt you could get into worse trouble than you're already in."

Feeling an odd thickness in my throat, I turn and walk away.

Owen makes more noises, and I tell myself that means he's relatively okay.

When I can't hear him anymore, I break into a run again, channeling my confusion into physical movement.

"This is scary, Phoe," I think as my feet pound the forest floor. "For a moment there, I lost it."

"You were defending yourself," she says. "You have no reason to feel guilty about that. It's a normal response. The Adults just managed to shelter you from it. Perhaps that is the only positive consequence of their totalitarian meddling."

Too out of it to argue with her, I continue to push my body to its limits. My leg muscles burn, and I feel as if my lungs might explode.

"Hey, cheer up," Phoe's voice cuts in after a minute. "I'm just through this meadow. Get ready for that surprise."

Slowing down to catch my breath, I enter the meadow and see a figure at the edge—a slightly large, round figure that has its back to me. The shape is vaguely feminine, so I assume it's a woman.

I get closer.

Something about this back brings up a memory, but I can't quite place it.

For some reason, I think of the Institute. Specifically, I think of History Lecture.

"Ah, so you do recognize me," Phoe's voice says in my head.

The figure turns around, and in stunned silence, I look at the person in front of me.

It's Instructor Filomena.

CHAPTER TWELVE

I shuffle back a step.

Instructor Filomena smiles.

"So you finally know," she says, her nasally voice *unlike* Phoe's cheerful soprano.

"I couldn't well sound like myself, could I?" Phoe's voice says in my head.

"Not when I wanted to keep my identity a secret," Instructor Filomena continues, picking up exactly where Phoe's mental voice left off. "So, yes, as weird as it might be for you to accept, I'm Phoe."

"You can't be." I rub my temples, staring at her. "You just can't."

"We don't have time for a long debate," Instructor Filomena says. "Follow me."

She walks away.

"Come on," she says as the voice of Phoe inside my head.

Even though I actually want to hide, I follow her.

It still doesn't make sense.

"Stop being so dense," Instructor Filomena says. "Phoe and I both know history really well. We both have access to what only Adults can access. We both like to use Virtual Reality—"

"But I just saw you—I mean, Phoe." I shake my head. "She looked nothing like you."

"What did you think I would do when I could make myself look like anything I wanted?" Instructor Filomena says. "I wanted you to find me attractive, and in my real form, I obviously don't impress someone as handsome as you."

I gawk at her. It's true that Instructor Filomena and Phoe's virtual-reality form couldn't be more different. I might be primed by having just talked to Grace, who looks like the Little Mermaid, but the cartoon character Instructor Filomena reminds me of most is Ursula, the chubby octopus-looking villain.

"That's just plain mean," Instructor Filomena says. "I was right to keep my identity from you."

"Sorry . . . *Phoe*," I subvocalize. "This is just a bit too much for me to handle."

The Instructor sniffs. "We're almost at the Barrier, so I suspect my identity is about to be the least of your worries."

I follow her gingerly, keeping a distance between us.

The fear hits me suddenly, as it did all those years ago when Liam, Mason, and I first got this close to the Barrier.

"The Barrier is a sophisticated bit of technology," Instructor Filomena says. "It emits a signal to everyone's neural implants that tells the brains of unauthorized people that they shouldn't be here."

"I can't walk any farther." I wipe my clammy hands on my clothes.

Instructor Filomena turns around. "Oh, this won't do," she says as the voice of Phoe in my head. "You look practically ashen."

A tingling sensation washes over me.

"That's better," Phoe says. "Those eyes are sparkling again."

I feel lighter. This sudden removal of fear is almost pleasurable.

"I granted you Adult access," she says in her nasally 'Instructor Filomena' voice. "Let's go. They're closing in."

I follow, my gait becoming noticeably less shaky. This is easy, especially considering the magnitude of fear I'd be experiencing had Phoe/Filomena not done her juju.

We walk into a clearing that no Youth has ever reached.

From here, the Barrier is clearly visible in all its shimmering, liquid metal beauty.

"Now we just walk through," she says and confidently walks toward the field, or whatever it is.

I follow carefully. I can't help but compare this spot to the one I saw them lead Mason through.

"We're going to make them pay for what they did to him." Instructor Filomena's tone is sterner than usual. "The Elderly will regret this deeply, as will all of Oasis."

"What do you mean?" I ask mostly to distract myself, as I'm about to cross into the ultimate restricted area. "What is the plan?"

"We're going to shut down something else—something pretty useless anyway," she says as the voice of Phoe in my head. "We're going to shut down this very Barrier and its cousin—the one that separates the Adult section from that of the Elderly."

"We're what?" I ask, but she doesn't answer.

She simply walks into the Barrier and disappears behind it.

The thing ripples like a pond of mercury around a dropped stone—a large stone.

"Hey," Phoe says in a wounded voice. "My metabolism is not as fast as that of Youths."

"Sorry," I mutter. "If you stayed out of my head, you wouldn't have to hear that."

I approach the Barrier, then stop and stare at it.

"Just walk through it," Phoe says. "You won't feel a thing."

I raise my hand and bury it in the silvery surface.

My hand feels as if it's submerged in warm, gentle water, but when it exits the thin obstacle on the other side, it comes out dry.

I guess this is what putting your hand through a bubble feels like.

Emboldened, I take a step.

The warm sensation brushes over my face. Half of my body is on the forbidden side.

I take the next step.

I'm dry, safe, and on the other side.

If I'd made a list of things I expected to see on the Adults' side of Oasis, it would've included many possibilities. Probably a pine forest to match the one I just ran through and an area filled with geometric shapes matching those of the buildings on the Youths' side of the Barrier.

None of these things are present, though.

The scene in front of me is something I never would've expected to see in Oasis. It looks like something out of Instructor Filomena's Lectures or an ancient movie.

A bucolic village sprawls as far as the eye can see, with vineyards, green hills, and clay roofs.

"Inspired by the French countryside," Instructor Filomena says from my right.

I glance at her and note that she managed to change her clothes in the time it took me to cross the

Barrier. She now looks like one of the ancient occupants of said French countryside. She smiles at me, but I quickly return my attention to the landscape.

Something about the warmth of her smile makes me uncomfortable.

As I look around, I realize that the most distinguishing feature in this part of Oasis is a tall tower in the distance—a tower that looks exactly like the Eiffel Tower from the History Lectures.

"Oh, Theodore." Instructor Filomena makes a tsk-tsk sound with her tongue. "Of course that is not the Eiffel Tower." In Phoe's voice, she continues in my mind, "You could just as easily call it the Louvre, because of all the glass."

She's right.

I've seen the Eiffel Tower in those sequences of ancient Earth she shows us before every Lecture, and this tower resembles it only in shape. With the sun reflecting off its glass windows, it's a magnificent sight.

"You like it, don't you?" Instructor Filomena smiles and winks at me. The gesture, combined with her puffy cheeks, makes her look like the cherub the ancients believed shot arrows on Valentine's Day.

"So we're going there?" I let my eyes scan the many miles separating us from the tower.

"Please put these on." She takes a couple of odd objects out of her bag.

After a second, I identify the stuff in her hands as a pair of glasses and an ancient hat.

She steps closer to me. "We have to make you look older."

I try not to back away, figuring it might insult her. She rises on her tiptoes and puts the glasses on my face. Her pudgy fingers brush my temples; then, in a cloud of jasmine fragrance, she takes a couple of steps back. I'm too stunned to react, so I just observe as she looks me over and nods approvingly. Then she steps up to me again and puts the hat on my head.

I exhale in relief when she steps back and studies me. "That should do," she says. "At least if no one scrutinizes you closely. Now follow me."

We walk down to a cluster of houses in silence.

There's feeling overwhelmed, and then there's the state I'm in as I walk on the old-fashioned cobblestone streets. The feeling intensifies as I see long-extinct creatures, including dogs, chickens, and cows. The animals are walking around as if we're at the agricultural part of the Zoo instead of the Adult section of Oasis.

The funny-looking people around us are busy with their farm work. Some are feeding the animals, while others are working in their gardens. I assume they're Adults, but they look more like the Amish we learned about yesterday.

The oddest thing is the ancient technology. Moving vehicles (tractors, I believe they're called) abound, as do some vehicles that I can't name. In the distance, there's an actual windmill.

Suddenly, I spot something that doesn't fit this archaic landscape—something shiny, like the Barrier. A sunbeam reflects off it as it disappears behind a wooden house.

I point in the direction where the strange object disappeared. "I need to go there."

I don't know why I feel the conviction that I must, but I trust the instinct and begin walking that way.

"We don't have much time," Phoe's voice says in my head. "And please don't speak out loud. We don't want to draw attention to ourselves."

As I approach the house, I see that it has large windows through which the backyard of the house is visible. I squint to make out what the shiny object I saw was, but the antique furniture inside the place blocks my view.

All I see is a glimmer of white.

"I'm going to check it out," I think at Phoe. I feel certain of my decision. "You can stay here and wait for me."

Without waiting for her to respond, I jog in the direction of the shiny object. My gait shouldn't look too suspicious since many of these people are rushing about, taking care of their farms.

Three houses later, I think I see the object again, but it disappears behind a parked tractor.

I turn the corner and almost trip on a large tree branch that's been stripped of its bark. On autopilot, I place it in its proper historical context: someone plans to chop it into smaller bits of wood to power a fireplace. Didn't those things predate the tractors? The history question reminds me of my companion, and I look back. She's fallen slightly behind but is still following me.

Seeing no one around, I risk picking up my pace.

When I clear the next house, I finally see my target. The shiny thing and flash of white I saw was the helmet of a Guard and his white uniform. I think I knew this on some level; that's why I felt compelled to follow him.

Seeing the Guard, however, isn't what solidifies my stomach.

There's a person walking next to the Guard—an achingly familiar person.

My friend Liam.

Despite having run the equivalent of a marathon today, I turn around and sprint back to the piece of wood I nearly tripped over. It's still there on the ground, so I quickly grab it. Armed with the wooden stump, I run back even faster, determined to catch up with the Guard.

"This is a very bad idea," Phoe says in my head.

I ignore her, going as far as purposefully whistling one of my favorite melodies: the 'ta ta da dam' beginning of Beethoven's *Symphony No. 5 in C Minor*. I repeat the melody in my head, over and over. It seems to shut Phoe up and gives me a modicum of courage.

When I reach a certain threshold, I run more softly, landing on the balls of my feet to stay quiet.

Liam is walking slowly, which works to my advantage. The Guard isn't rushing him; he's merely following along.

Thinking of what happened to Mason after a similar walk with a Guard strengthens my resolve.

"Seriously, Theo, it's not too late to stop this mad idea," Phoe says to me mentally.

"Ta ta da dam," I subvocalize in reply.

The melody plays in my head as I close the last few feet and raise my makeshift club.

Encouraged by my earlier win against Owen, I smack the Guard on the head with all my force—a classic move from ancient movies.

His helmet makes a hollow, dull sound, and my hand goes numb from the impact of the wood's recoil.

The Guard turns to me. I hear a scary mechanical whir of some kind, but I'm not sure whether it's something the Guard is doing. Though the visor is covering his face, I get the sneaking suspicion that hitting his helmet was a tactical mistake. At the same time, some corner of my mind registers the interesting fact that Liam hasn't even turned around.

The Guard makes the gesture that's supposed to pacify me.

This is my chance to make up for the helmet blunder. I allow my body to relax and pretend his mind control worked on me. Then, as suddenly as I can, I jab the club like a fencer would a sword, aiming it at his midsection.

The Guard catches the club in his iron grip before it connects with his body.

I attempt to pull it back with both hands, but it's as though the stick became part of the Guard. My shoulders scream in pain. Before I can even think of something else to try, the Guard rips the weapon from my hands, leaving my palms torn and stinging.

Without saying a word, the Guard breaks the thick piece of wood over his knee and throws the pieces into the nearby bushes.

My heart jumps into my throat, and I back up a few steps.

He follows.

I back away some more, hoping to at least lure him away from Liam.

"Run, Liam," I yell at my friend—who would have a good head start if he were to run.

Except he doesn't run. He doesn't react at all.

I hear that mechanical noise again, and it distracts me for a moment.

When I focus back on the Guard, I see the white-gloved hand flying toward my face—and my world explodes.

CHAPTER THIRTEEN

Owen's punches were like the brush of a bird's wing compared to this. This is mind-crushingly painful.

I spit out the tooth that Owen loosened when he hit me. The metallic taste in my mouth is overpowering, and I have difficulty breathing.

My ears are ringing—or is it that noise again?

For some reason, the rage that came over me during my fight with Owen hasn't returned. All I want to do is double over and fall to the ground, but I know if I do, the Guard will lead Liam away, and that just isn't happening.

The thought of Liam getting hurt brings colder, more rational anger to the surface.

I straighten, gritting my remaining teeth. Audibly inhaling, I focus on the Guard.

He's reaching for me with both hands.

I only understand his intent once his hands are locked around my neck, and then I'm suffocating, his fingers cruelly cutting into my windpipe.

I grab at his wrists, trying to pry them away, but they're as unmovable as oak tree branches.

An unintelligible croak tries to escape my throat but doesn't make it past the barrier of the fingers choking me. Desperate, I kick at the Guard, but all I get is a burst of pain in my toes.

My vision starts going black, and my struggles grow more frantic.

Suddenly, I hear that mechanical noise again. It's getting louder—and then, over the Guard's shoulder, I see a giant lumbering machine.

A mechanical tractor is heading for us, its insect-like headlights seemingly ready to swallow us whole.

Given that I'm about to suffocate to death, getting killed in this novel way shouldn't matter. It should even seem preferable since it's a more interesting way to die that will have the added bonus of killing my attacker. But my fight-or-flight response violently disagrees with this logic. My guess is it has something to do with our fear of giant, loud, fast-moving things—a fear that might be programmed into our DNA.

Hearing the same sound, the Guard turns.

White flecks dot my vision as my brain grows increasingly oxygen-deprived. This is my last chance. If I'm right that this fear is universal, the tractor should serve as a sizable distraction.

Gathering every bit of my remaining strength, I kick the Guard in the groin.

I'm not sure if it's because of my kick or his fear of the oncoming tractor, but he lets go of my neck and jumps aside.

Wheezing, I leap in the opposite direction, toward Liam's immobile figure.

The tractor swerves toward the Guard and rams into him. I hear a dull thud, followed by a short-lived yelp.

Horrified, I watch as the machine drags him toward the wall of the nearest house. My heart slams against my ribcage as I gulp down frantic breaths to re-oxygenate my brain.

The tractor crashes into the wall with an eardrum-shattering bang.

Dazed, I stare at the site of the collision. It's hard to tell the extent of the damage. The tractor backs out, and I see the Guard's legs sticking out from under the rubble.

Is he dead? Bile rises in my throat.

"No, he's fine." Phoe's speaking in my head. "Come on. Get on."

I turn to look at the tractor and see its rotund driver—Instructor Filomena.

"Who else did you think it was?" Phoe's tone is snarky.

"I don't know, Phoe," I think, unable to bring myself to call her Instructor Filomena. "Thinking was at the bottom of my agenda."

The tractor door opens, and Instructor Filomena climbs down with surprising agility. "I told you this was a bad idea," she says in her own voice.

"What, attacking a Guard was a bad idea?" I say out loud. "You don't say."

"It's over now," she says, glancing at the Guard's still-pinned legs. "And we really have to hurry."

Nodding, I take a few steps toward Liam.

Throughout all the commotion, my friend never even turned around.

"Liam," I say when I reach him. "Liam, what's wrong with you?"

Instructor Filomena approaches us and waves her hand in front of Liam's eyes.

"He's on cloud nine," she says to me, then turns her attention to him. "Liam, follow me." She makes a strange gesture, and Liam looks at her with glazed-over eyes.

Apparently satisfied, Instructor Filomena heads toward the tractor.

In a stupor, I watch her get in and help Liam into the cabin.

"What are you waiting for?" she says as Phoe's voice in my head. "Let's go."

"You want me to get into that?" I think.

The tractor door opens again, and Instructor Filomena pokes her head out. "No. I want you to slowly walk to the tower, even after all this," she says, her nasally voice making Phoe's usually friendly sarcasm sound kind of mean.

As if to help the Instructor make her point, I see a group of people heading toward us. They must be wondering what all the noise was about.

Self-preservation kicks in, and I hurry toward the tractor, deciding we can always continue our conversation en route.

"Genius," Phoe says mentally.

Unsure whether she's being sarcastic, I simply climb into the tractor. Knowing she might read my mind, I try my best to suppress my relief about having Liam between us.

She starts the contraption, and we slowly pull away. She isn't even trying to stay on a road of any kind. We drive through farmland, destroying fences and gardens, and we gain a funny tail of ropes with dry clothes attached to them.

The people who were walking our way are chasing after us, shouting as they run. I feel anxious just looking at them, so I turn my attention to my friend.

"Liam, dude, snap out of it," I say, waving my hand in front of his face.

He looks as responsive as a drunk-on-brains zombie.

"I've undone what the Guard did to him." Instructor Filomena briefly looks away from the windshield to glance at me. "Still, Liam needs a few minutes to get back to normal."

We drive in silence until I see something that makes my pulse jump.

"What are we going to do about that?" I point at a large group of Adults/farmers in our way.

Instructor Filomena doesn't answer, but her face gets very focused, and she floors the gas pedal like a racecar driver in an ancient movie.

The tractor engine complains loudly, but we begin moving noticeably faster.

To distract myself from my anxiety, I examine Liam. Maybe it's my adrenaline-infused imagination, but I think there's more recognition in his gaze than there was even a minute ago.

We get closer to the crowd.

Instructor Filomena presses the middle of her wheel, and the most annoying sound escapes the tractor's maw.

The crowd ignores the honk.

Instructor Filomena grips the wheel.

"Phoe, err, Instructor Filomena? You're going to run them over."

She doesn't respond, but her knuckles turn white on the steering wheel.

The crowd probably realizes she means business, because they disperse, and not a moment too soon. I swear she would've run them over if they hadn't moved. What was she thinking?

She doesn't respond to my thought, and I decide against asking the question out loud. My hands are still shaking from the near miss.

We're halfway to the tower when I see telltale shiny objects in the distance.

I squint, and as we get closer, I know for sure that my eyes aren't deceiving me. There are at least fifty Guards waiting for us. I didn't realize we even had that many in Oasis. Until this moment, the most I'd seen in one place was three.

Will Instructor Filomena try to go through them the same way she did with the farmers?

She doesn't.

She turns the wheel all the way left.

I expect us to violently spin out, but we simply lumber to the left. Perhaps swerving out of control isn't something tractors can do.

The Guards must've registered our change of course, because a couple of them jump into a vehicle that looks like a metallic cube. As they close the distance, I get the eerie impression that a miniature version of the Administrative Building is chasing after us.

On the bright side, we're getting progressively closer to the tower. On the not-so-bright side, so is the Guards' cube-shaped car.

Something whizzes past us with a high-pitched whine. A second later, the mirror on my side shatters, peppering the tractor's window with shards of glass.

"Are they shooting at us?" I'm glad Phoe can't see me as I ask this, because I'm certain my lips are trembling.

"Liam," she says, ignoring my question. "Liam, can you hear me?"

Liam gives a half-hearted shrug.

"Liam, sweetie, I need you to run when I say 'run,' okay?" Instructor Filomena's body tenses as she says this.

"Okay," Liam says in a robotic voice, but he looks as if he isn't done talking. After an eternity of a pause, he adds, "I'll run when you say so."

Another projectile whizzes by.

"It would be such a shame to get shot so close to the tower." Instructor Filomena bites her puffy lower lip.

She's right. The tower is close enough that we could sprint for it.

As though she read my mind, Instructor Filomena stops the tractor.

"Nothing 'as though' about it," Phoe's voice says. "Go," she adds in Instructor Filomena's voice.

I blink at her. "Wait a minute—"

"Run," she shouts at us. "Run now."

CHAPTER FOURTEEN

My pulse spiking, I swing the door open and jump out, dragging Liam out with me.

Something whooshes by my head.

On instinct, I look back.

The tractor's engine is roaring once again, and the car with the Guards is approaching fast.

I start running, pulling Liam behind me. Another projectile whines by my ear, and I duck, accidentally letting go of Liam's arm.

He stumbles but keeps running.

Relieved, I pick up my pace, and after another moment, I sneak another look back.

My heart rate threatens to reach superluminal speeds.

The Guards' car is no longer heading for us. It turned. They're following the tractor, which means Phoe's plan of us separating worked—assuming she actually had a plan. Maybe her plan was to distract the Guards by using us as bait?

"You think so poorly of me." Phoe's voice is mock-hurt. "My plan has always been to get you to this tower to disable the Barriers."

"Why can't you disable them yourself?" I reach the first metallic staircase of the tower and look back. Liam is a few steps behind me. Though he's technically running, his gait is so leisurely that it can barely be labeled as a jog.

We're lucky the Guards aren't on our heels.

"Disabling the Barriers requires a two-person confirmation sequence," Phoe says in my mind, "and there isn't another Adult I can trust with this."

"Theo?" Liam says, sounding slightly less dazed as he catches up to me.

"Yeah, dude, it's me," I say. To Phoe, I say mentally, "Where to now?"

"Go to the first floor and take the elevator," Phoe says. "Make sure Liam goes with you."

"Right," I say as I usher my friend up the stairs to the first floor.

Once we reach the platform, I press the elevator button.

Liam observes me dully and then, with the flattest tone, asks, "So what are we up to?"

"Doing something that could get us into a boatload of trouble," I say and watch his expression.

His gaze wanders. Had I told him that today is Monday, I would've gotten a similar level of excitement. Then again, he's getting more engaged by the minute.

Closing his eyes, he mumbles, "Oh, okay."

Okay, relatively more engaged. At least he's talking.

A *ding* announces the elevator's arrival. My eyes widen as the door opens. I've only read about these contraptions.

We walk into the elevator. The back of the thing is made of glass. The door slides closed, and I press the only available button.

The elevator begins to rise.

With each foot we ascend, my heart climbs higher in my chest. Through the glass wall, I get an extremely unwelcome view of Oasis shrinking below me.

I hadn't realized this, but when you don't like heights, an elevator is a very creative form of torture.

Beginning to feel sick, I tear my gaze away from the glass wall and look at my friend.

Liam is staring at me emotionlessly. I think there's a spark of something resembling interest again, but maybe it's my adrenaline making me see what I want to see.

The elevator stops with a loud *ding*. I scurry out of it, my stomach churning, but find no relief.

If anything, my situation's worse.

I have a bird's eye view of the Adult section.

Far below is a small tractor carrying Instructor Filomena. The Guards' car is much closer to her than it was minutes ago.

"Quick, you two need to begin your task," Phoe says. "Bring Liam through that corridor."

Her words snap me out of my height-induced nausea. Glancing at Liam, I say as calmly as I can, "Hey, dude, walk with me."

"Okay," he says. He's noticeably more animated as he follows me. "Where are we?"

As we head down the corridor, I do my best to explain to him what happened, though I leave out the stuff about Phoe. I talk quickly, hitting the most pertinent points. He's not nearly as shocked by my tale as I would've been had our roles been reversed. Clearly, he's still under the effects of the pacifying crap. And speaking of calm, talking to him has been distracting *me* from looking through the windows.

"Okay," he says, his voice almost as chipper as it was earlier this morning. "So what do we have to do?"

"Getting to that part," I tell him. "I have to learn that myself."

The corridor ends in a staircase that's next to a huge window with a stomach-knotting view.

"Open the window," Phoe says urgently. "I'm running out of time."

I make an 'open' gesture at the window, but nothing happens.

"It's manual," Phoe explains. "There should be latches, like they had in ancient times."

Trying to steady my hands, I flick the latches into the 'up' position and pull the window open.

If I hadn't glimpsed the ground below, the breeze coming from this window would've actually felt pleasant. But since I did look down, all I can think about is not embarrassing myself in front of Liam by throwing up or worse; he might be cognizant enough to remember and never let me live it down.

"Do you see that large ledge in front of the window?" Phoe sounds out of breath for some reason.

"Yes."

"Walk onto it."

I back away from the window, whispering, "What?"

Phoe lets out an exasperated breath. "It's a large freaking platform. You'd have to go out of your way to fall."

I look at the platform and decide to just go for it. Face my fear and all that. Pressing my elbows to my sides as though I'm trying to make myself smaller, I attempt to climb out.

I say 'attempt' because, in reality, I take another step back.

Suddenly, I hear a loud bang come from below. I look down and see that the tractor and the Guards' car have stopped. There's smoke coming from the tractor.

"I don't have much time." Phoe sounds desperate.

"Tell me what to do once I get up there," I subvocalize urgently. *If* I get up there, I think for my own benefit.

"It's exactly like what you did in the Zoo." Phoe's ragged voice sounds like it's coming from behind Liam. "Do this and they will all see the errors of their ways—" A bang is followed by a hiss, followed by silence.

"Phoe?" I think in panic.

Nothing.

"Phoe, are you okay?" I subvocalize.

Still no response.

"Phoe, what happened?" I whisper desperately.

Another loud bang comes from below. My heart hammering, I glance down.

Darker, more sinister-looking smoke is coming from the tractor, which looks tiny from this distance.

What happened? Did the Guards just blow Phoe up? I can't think about that right now, not when her last concern was about this task that I have yet to do. I take a step toward the window, take in a breath . . . and freeze as I see the gaping emptiness below.

"Dude, are you planning to jump?" Liam's voice startles me. I glance back and see that he's looking me up and down. "'Cause, please, don't."

"Thanks, Liam. You saved my life. I was totally going to jump." I turn away from him and focus on the platform, staring at it as though I'm trying to hypnotize it.

"No need to be snide," Liam says, my sarcasm seemingly helping him clear his head. "If you're not jumping, then what are you doing?"

"I need to get onto this ledge and do a couple of gestures," I say, turning my attention from the ledge to him.

He bobs his head. "Okay. If that's all you need to do, then why are you standing there all intense like that?"

"Because it's outside." I know an avalanche of teasing might be coming my way, but I still say, "I'm afraid of heights."

"Oh." He scratches his cheek. "I didn't know that."

"Not a lot of heights around," I say, edging closer to the window. "So how would you?"

"True." He looks very contemplative, especially for Liam. "You know, *I* am not afraid of heights."

"Good for you." I take a step back. All this talk isn't soothing my nerves.

"No, you nimrod." Liam's eyes twinkle with the glow of his usual mischief. "I can do whatever it is you need done on that ledge."

"Oh." I feel pretty dumb. Then, after a moment's consideration, I say with a sigh, "No. I can't accept you taking such a risk for me."

"Dude," he says pointedly.

The fact that he's not already on the ledge proves he's not completely recovered, but I can tell he's getting there and that this debate might be pointless soon.

"You can't exactly stop me from going," he says, echoing my thoughts.

"Okay," I say. "But you have to promise to do it carefully."

"I pinky-swear and shit." Liam resolutely approaches the window. "What do I do?"

"Once you're there—"

Before I can finish my instructions, Liam leaps onto the ledge with the same enthusiasm as when he jumps onto his bed—which, despite being a year older than Mason and me, Liam still does regularly.

"As I was trying to tell you," I say once he's sitting in a lotus pose on the ledge. "Make a choo-choo train gesture."

Liam grimaces. "I'm trying to help you. Is this really the best time to show off that you're a smartass?"

I take a deep breath, feeling a major case of vicarious fear. Trying to steady my nerves, I explain the fist-up-and-down gesture I used in the Zoo.

Liam executes the move.

An enormous Screen shows up in the hallway next to me.

"I think it worked," I tell Liam. "Come back— carefully."

Like in the Zoo, the screen has text on it. "Initiate the double confirmation?" it says in red letters.

As before, two giant buttons are also there: 'Confirm' and 'Abort'. What's different this time is the huge, detailed image of Oasis, seen as though from a helicopter hovering just below the clouds. It reminds me of the History Lecture images meant to show how little of the Earth's surface was spared from the Goo.

"Wow," Liam says.

"Yeah," I reply.

The image has details I've never seen before. Usually, the view in the History Lecture is too brief and from too far up to make out the Adult section. Here, however, I can easily see it in all its countryside glory. The Elderly section is also clearer, but it has such a dense forest that it might as well be hidden for all that it's telling me about the Elderly's way of life. What really stands out are the clearly defined Barriers that separate the sections. Their silvery, shining edges cut Oasis into three pieces that run parallel to one another.

I reach for the 'Confirm' button but hesitate.

"What's that going to do?" Liam says.

"Bring down the Barriers," I say softly.

"Wow," he says.

"Yeah," I return in kind.

To myself, I wonder: What is the point of doing this? With Phoe dead, whatever she wanted to accomplish, whatever resources she wanted to free up would—

"I'm not dead. I jumped out in time, and the Guards are running after me," Phoe's mental voice says. "Do it. Now. Once it starts, they'll have bigger problems than me."

"Phoe!" I mentally scream. "You're—"

"Yes, yes, I'm alive—for now," she says. "Now do it."

Knowing my friend needs me erases any remnants of hesitation from my mind. Without further ado, I press the 'Confirm' button.

The Screen has me triple-confirm my choice the way the one at the Zoo did.

"Two people have to confirm the shutdown procedure," the text after the triple check says. "Please exercise extreme caution."

A new set of buttons shows up, one marked 'Primary' and the other 'Secondary.'

"Press the 'Secondary' confirmation," I tell Liam.

"Why am I the Secondary?" he asks.

I roll my eyes and press the 'Secondary' button, nodding him toward the 'Primary' button. He looks pleased as he goes for that choice and presses his button. Right away, more follow-up buttons prompt us, and we wade through all of them.

The messages get more threatening. I think I get a dozen 'Are you sure?' prompts. If you think about it, it makes sense. The Barriers between the sections are a big deal.

"This action will not be reversible," the Screen warns in big letters. "Please triple-confirm for the last time."

Liam and I touch the 'Confirm' buttons and say, "Shut Down," when the Screen display commands us to. When it comes to the mental command, I think 'Shut Down.' I assume Liam also thinks the last 'Shut Down' instruction, because the Screen picture changes. It blinks red and says, "Barrier shutdown commencing."

"So it's done," Phoe's voice sounds tense in my head. "It's finally over."

I stare at the image of Oasis, waiting for the Barriers to come down.

Except they don't.

Something else happens, something so terrible it chills my blood.

I look over at Liam. His ashen face confirms that I'm not hallucinating, even though insanity would be preferable to this situation.

A Barrier is disappearing, only it's not one of the ones separating the sections of Oasis.

The shimmering, dome-like barrier that protects all of Oasis from the Goo flickers and goes out.

We both watch, frozen in place, as the Goo begins eating Oasis. It consumes it with such hunger it's as though it's been waiting for this moment for centuries.

CHAPTER FIFTEEN

"What did you make me do?" I think at Phoe in horror. "What did you make me do?" I repeat out loud, my words coming out in a whimper.

Liam blinks at me. "*I* made you do?"

"I'm not talking to you," I tell him, fully cognizant of how mad this makes me seem. "I did this because Phoe—I mean, Instructor Filomena—asked me to."

He gapes at me. "Instructor Filomena?" A bead of sweat drips from his eyebrow, and he mutters, "Weren't we *just* in the car with her? Why do I have trouble remembering that?" He looks the most scared I've seen him. The idea of forgetting something seems to frighten him more than the Armageddon we just unleashed. "How did I get here?" He looks around in confusion. "Am I dreaming?"

I don't reply. My eyes are glued to the Screen.

The Goo has moved through the bushes that surround the Institute and is approaching the Campus.

"I'm sorry, Theo." Phoe sounds genuinely sad. "This was the only way to stop this mockery . . . this excuse of a society."

Her words snap me out of my dazed horror. "What the hell are you talking about?" I scream. "You just used me to kill everyone."

Liam looks at me, his face contorted in confusion.

"Not you, Liam," I say in a calmer tone. "This isn't your fault, not at all."

Liam backs away from me.

"You wouldn't understand, even if I tried explaining it to you," Phoe says. "They had it coming, the Elderly. This was our only way to freedom . . ."

I don't listen to the rest of her monologue; she's making as much sense as a movie villain. Coming out of my shock, I frantically prod at the Screen. "There has to be a way to stop this," I mutter. "Come on, there has to be a way."

Liam backs up some more, does a one-eighty, and leaps up the stairs.

I don't call out to him. I continue pressing at the Screen, my desperation growing.

After about a minute, I realize my actions are futile. There's no way to undo this.

"I suggest you run up the way Liam did," Phoe says at the end of her crazy 'explanation.' "You might buy yourself a few precious minutes."

I take one last look at the Screen.

The Goo seems to be moving faster, the green that was Oasis quickly becoming the same revolting orange-brown mess as the outside world.

I run for the metal stairs, my leg muscles burning as I take the steps two at a time. I'm trying to catch up with Liam, but to a larger degree, I'm attempting to outrun my inevitable doom.

As I climb, all kinds of thoughts race through my head. Regrets. Ideas. I wish I had watched more movies, read more books, spent more time with my friends.

Ancient books often talk about seeing your life flash before your eyes in near-death situations. In my case, I'm just remembering certain scenes, starting with my earliest memory. None of them are from my time at the Nursery; intellectually, I know there was a period when I was a baby and the Elderly took care of me, but I can't recall it. My first memory is of being embarrassed on my first day of Lectures. I asked a 'why' question for what I assume was the millionth time, and that, in combination with my full name of Theodore, got me the nickname of 'Why-Odor.' After this, I remember more positive moments from childhood, like the first time I met Liam, even though we actually got into a fight that day. Also, my first—

Spotting the real-life Liam brings me out of my recollections. He's standing with his back to me, seemingly mesmerized by the view beyond the window.

I cover the remaining three steps in one jump and stop next to him to look out the same window.

Instantly, I wish I hadn't looked. I can now see the Goo with my naked eye.

It's midway through the village below.

Until now, a part of my mind thought that perhaps the Goo attack on the Screen was some kind of cruel joke, a lesson designed to teach us not to disobey—anything other than this horrible reality.

When I tear my eyes away from the nightmare below, I see that Liam is staring at me gravely, as if he's about to say something.

"Liam," I begin, but he takes off and starts running up the stairs again.

My lungs straining, I run after him. I have no idea what we're going to do once we reach the top—which, judging by the continually narrowing staircase, will be soon.

Instead of obsessing about it, I keep running. When I run, the world kind of disappears. Thoughts of the past visit me again. I wonder if on some level these memories are a defense mechanism my mind made up to cope with the panic and horror that will accompany my last moments. The fact that the rest of the human race will die alongside me makes the idea of death even more incomprehensible. It's like trying to understand what might have existed before there was a universe.

This time I'm brought out of my dark reverie by a terrible mental shriek that I barely recognize as Phoe's voice.

"It burns," she screams. "Oh, Theo, it burns . . ." She makes a gurgling noise that sounds like, "I'm sorry."

Then there's silence.

Sick to my stomach, I stop in front of one of the staircase windows and look down.

The place where I last saw Phoe and the Guards is now covered with Goo.

She's finally dead. Really dead.

Despite her horrible treachery, I can't help but feel a sense of loss. Pushing it away, I focus on the physical pain of the muscle fibers in my legs tearing from the strain of my rapid climb.

The ascent lasts for ages before I get a whiff of Liam's body odor. It's such a little thing, but the knowledge that my always-brave friend is sweating enough to stink makes my chest constrict and my eyes prickle. I recall this feeling; it usually precedes crying—something I haven't done since I was little. Youths have no reason to cry as they grow older.

Instead of giving in to this weakness, I follow Liam's rapidly climbing figure.

On the next landing, he stops and turns to face me.

I'm about to say something—anything—to him, but the words never leave my throat because suddenly, the tower shudders and tilts with a metallic groan.

My foot misses the last step, and then my arms are windmilling as I fall in speechless terror.

The tower seems to be rotating around me.

There's a moment of weightlessness, followed by an explosion of nauseating pain as my left shoulder smacks into something hard.

Gasping, I grab at it with my uninjured arm, and my fingers close around a handrail as the rest of my body meets the staircase with a bone-jarring slam. I continue to slide down for a few seconds before I jerk to a stop, my wrist screaming in agony.

With some still-functional portion of my mind, I realize the tower must be leaning sideways. The wall is now a sharply angled floor, while the stairs have become the new wall, like something out of an M.C. Escher painting.

The tower emits another groan, tilting even lower. I can now crawl up the wall, and I attempt to do so, despite the agonizing pain in my shoulder and a sickening sense of vertigo. My left shoulder must be dislocated, and the entire left side of my body hurts like nothing I've ever experienced.

My stomach heaves, and sweat dampens my clothes as I desperately crawl upward, imitating soldiers from ancient war films. I try not to dwell on the fact that the steps of the staircase make up the right wall. That surreal image strikes at the heart of my panic, and panic is something I'm trying to stave off.

Somewhere above me, I hear a moan and crawl toward the sound.

"Liam?" I yell as I reach the downward-angled platform. "Are you okay?"

"Careful," Liam hisses back. "Or you'll join me."

His voice is so warped by terror it's almost unrecognizable. I always thought Liam might've been born with a genetic defect in his amygdala, making him unable to feel normal fear, but now I see that's not at all the case.

My heart thudding in my ears, I crawl up to the edge of the topsy-turvy staircase platform.

Liam's voice is coming from what used to be a window, but is now a hole in the sloped floor.

On the window's edge, I spot fingers, their knuckles white from exertion.

"Liam!" I slither on my belly toward the hand and look down.

My friend is hanging out of the window, his legs dangling in the air. Blood is running down his arm. Below him is an enormous drop that ends in a putrid orange-brown mess. The Goo is consuming the base of the tower.

Fighting lightheadedness at the sight of the far drop, I grab Liam's forearm with my uninjured right hand.

"Liam, I've got you. Now climb up." I note a tiny spark of relief in his fear-glazed eyes, so I add, "Seriously, get back in. Stop messing around."

The strain and horror on his face eases slightly. "Nah, I'm just hanging, you know."

I grimace at his joke. "Grab onto my arm with your left hand and climb up. It should be easier than grabbing the window's edge." I style my stern tone after that of an Adult.

Liam reaches up, but his flailing hand misses my arm by an inch.

The tower shudders again.

"Come on, Liam!"

He reaches up, his face scrunching from the effort, and this time, his fingers connect with my arm.

"That's it." I tighten my grip on his forearm, my fingers slippery from sweat. "Come on!"

He tries to lift himself up, but his grip on the window doesn't give him much leverage.

"Pull me up, Theo," he gasps. He lets go of the window to latch on to my arm with his right hand. The strain on my right shoulder is enormous as his full weight dangles off my arm.

Forgetting about my injury, I reach down with my left hand to assist him.

The resulting agony makes me stop and hiss in pain. The dislocated shoulder doesn't allow for that range of motion.

Seeing this, Liam grabs higher up my arm, using it as a rope. I inch backward to drag him in.

The strategy looks like it's working—for a heartbeat, at least.

Then Liam's fingers slip on my sweaty skin, his palms sliding down my arm uncontrollably.

"Liam!"

I make a desperate grabbing motion and catch his right hand just as his grip slips off completely.

He's now hanging by the tips of his fingers off my right hand, and I feel his grip slipping with every second.

As if realizing the futility of his efforts, Liam looks up, his gaze growing oddly distant as he stares up at something. "You have to reach the top, Theo. You must."

"You're not making any sense," I say urgently. "Come on, climb back up."

With my bad left arm, I make a monumental effort to reach down, ignoring the crippling pain. Liam's fingers slip out of my grasp, but he twists his body and grabs my left wrist just as I reach for him. There's a loud crack in my left shoulder, followed by a white-hot flash of excruciating pain.

An unbidden scream escapes my mouth.

I think I'm about to black out from the pain when I hear Liam say, "I'm going to let go."

At least that's what I think he said.

Through the pulsating haze of agony, I hear him say, "You have to get to the top of this thing."

The darkness at the edges of my vision closes in, dimming all my senses. Fighting it, I clench my teeth and try pulling Liam up with all my remaining strength, but he's not even trying to help me. His eyes are wide as he keeps staring up past me.

I try to follow his gaze. Something important is up there, and I want to know what it is.

Just as I start turning my head, Liam lets go.

"Liam!" I scream, but it's too late.

He plummets to the ground, and I stare in horror as his body disappears into the writhing mass of Goo.

A pained roar escapes my throat. As though in answer to my anguished cry, the tower creaks again and rotates in violent, jerky movements.

My arms shaking, I grab onto the windowsill with both hands and watch with dazed vertigo as the window faces first the horizon and then the sky.

Now I'm the one who's hanging out of the window, only my feet are not dangling over a long drop. After the tower did its spinning maneuver, the window that was on 'the floor' ended up on 'the ceiling.'

Dimly, I register that my left side hurts a little less. Did Liam pop my shoulder back into place when he grabbed it? If so, it saved my life.

Glancing down, I see that the other wall of the tower is under my feet. If I let go of the windowsill, I probably wouldn't hurt myself too badly. I consider doing exactly that but see that a streak of Goo is running up the wooden handrail. I'll be running the chance of touching it if I jump down. The fact that the Goo is already here, right below me, sucks what little hope I had left.

How is it on the handrail? I wonder with strangely academic interest. I guess the Goo must find it easier to eat away softer substances, such as wood, than the heavy-duty steel that the rest of the tower is made out of. I don't have any illusions, though: the Goo can eat through anything.

We have a desolate ocean of the stuff to prove it.

Still, I can't hang like this for long. My left shoulder, though somewhat better, is still in agony. Gritting my teeth, I use the last remaining bit of my strength to pull myself up. Once my head is sticking out the window, I lever the rest of my body up and try to stand on what used to be the outside wall of the tower.

My head spins. The wall of the tower is tilted at about a forty-five-degree angle, sloping toward the sea of Goo that is the ground. It's probably a matter of moments before the Goo eats through the tower's base, toppling the entire structure into its abyss.

The knowledge of impending death sharpens my senses. The tiniest details of my environment jump out at me. I notice how the sky looks a bit bluer without the Dome, and how strange it is that the tower looks weather-beaten, given that in Oasis, there's no erosive weather to cause this sort of damage. Then another detail catches my attention: a light where the tower's peak would be.

I recall Liam staring that way in his last moments.

What is that light, if that's indeed what I'm seeing?

I carefully run on what used to be the tower's wall. It's not a solid surface, but a patchwork of metal beams and some surviving glass windows.

It's hard to focus on running after everything that's happened, but I force myself to. I will the pain of losing Liam out of my head. It seems more manageable than trying to suppress the pain of losing everyone else I've ever known.

My thoughts narrow on one goal: figuring out what that light is. That much I can do, and it enables me to pretend that I still have some modicum of control over the events around me.

As I get closer to the top, the light becomes clearer.

It's the biggest Screen I've ever seen, yet it also looks like an ancient neon sign, all pink and bright. In some way, it reminds me of a Times Square billboard from ancient times—if the billboard were merged with a gate-looking Barrier, that is.

I run faster, ignoring the pitfalls of broken windows and protruding metal rails.

I must reach that billboard-like Screen.

As I get closer, I realize there's a message on it—a very simple one.

'Goal,' it says in garish, flashing font.

Goal? Why would the top of the tower have such an odd decoration?

My lungs scream for air, but I push my muscles to move even faster.

The tower shakes.

I wave my arms to catch my balance and inadvertently look down.

Instantly, my legs give out and I stop.

I'm rooted to this spot. This paralysis feels like a culmination of everything that has just happened to me and the rest of Oasis.

Everyone is dead. The world is over. These thoughts hit me hard, overwhelming me, and I double over from the pain of it all. Maybe I don't need to wait for the Goo to get me. Maybe I'll just die from the horror and the guilt.

An oddly familiar shimmer next to me catches my eye, bringing me back to reality.

When the Screen appears, I'm actually not as shocked as I should be, because I've seen a Screen like this once before, when I was in Quietude.

It's ghostly, and like last time, there's a cursor flickering on it.

Theo, the Screen writes slowly, one letter at a time. *Theo, I'm not sure if you can see this.* The Screen continues typing each letter at a pace that matches my heartbeat. *I'm worried,* the Screen informs me. *Your neural scan is out of control—*

Before I can even blink at it, the Screen dissipates into thin air, but the hairs on my arms stand up.

An idea forms in my mind. It's a faint one, yet it's enough to motivate me to move again.

I must reach the top and the word 'Goal.'

I focus on that one task, leaving all other concerns behind.

The tower quakes again. Trying not to fall, I balance on the metal beams like an ancient surfer. As soon as the bout of shaking subsides, I resume running and jump over the gaps between the steel struts.

I run like a berserker, the concept of time erased from my mind, and stop only when I reach the biggest gap I've encountered so far.

This gap is an unfortunate part of the tower design and is about seven terrifying feet wide.

Though I've been successfully suppressing my phobia, looking at the gap brings it all back.

The Goal sign is still beckoning me. It's just beyond this last obstacle, and I'm almost there.

I decide to break down the impossible into manageable steps.

Step one: calm my frantic breathing. This step is semi-successful.

Step two: jump. My leg muscles tighten, ready for the action of jumping, running, or whatever else might burn some of this adrenaline off.

I back up, figuring the jump might be easier to execute with a head start.

When I'm a good ten feet away from the gap, I start running toward it.

This is it.

This is when I face my fear of heights and become victorious.

Only when I reach the gap, I don't jump.

I stop, my whole body trembling uncontrollably.

Can't give up, I think and back up again.

I run.

I jump.

Time slows.

I see the Goo swooshing menacingly far beneath my feet.

I'm almost on the other end of the gap when the tower shakes again with a deafening screech of metal scraping against metal. The other edge of the horrible gap moves away from my feet just as they're about to touch it, and the top of my chest hits the unyielding metal edge.

Air escapes my lungs, and I flail my arms, trying to grab on to something. Only my index and middle fingers manage to connect with cold metal.

Right away, I realize this hold is tenuous at best. The weight of my body is too much for those two fingers to handle.

My fingers go numb and begin shaking. Worse, they start to slide down the sleek steel surface.

I hold on to the edge by my index finger for a breath before I completely slip.

I'm not holding on to the edge at all, I think dimly.

Either time slows down, or like a cartoon character, I first have to look down before my descent begins. So, masochistically, I look down. I see how far above the ground I am, and then my plummet begins.

Air lashes at my face.

My body feels weightless—a feeling that would be pleasant if it weren't for the fact that I'm about to die.

This fall reminds me of my most awful recurring nightmare, the one where I'm falling toward something. Turns out this nightmare was a dark prophecy.

I look down again.

The Goo is approaching.

Futilely, I try to enter the Goo head first, like the insane ancient sport of high diving.

I hit it hard and submerge deep into the Goo.

All I can see is the orange shit vomit of it, which feels surprisingly smooth on my skin. I squeeze my eyes shut and hold my breath, wondering why it hasn't eaten me yet. Even through my closed mouth and nose I can taste and smell it, and it's worse than I ever imagined. I'm on the verge of throwing up, but I don't dare open my mouth.

I realize I've been holding on to the same breath since the drop. My lungs are burning, but so is the rest of my body. The burning of my body must mean that, despite my secret hope, the Goo is about to take me apart molecule by molecule.

The burning increases in earnest. My whole body feels like lava for a fraction of a second, and then the sensation multiplies a hundredfold.

I gasp in pain, knowing I'm about to inhale the Goo into my lungs.

CHAPTER SIXTEEN

I inhale the Goo, but the pain doesn't worsen.

In fact, the burning stops.

I feel insubstantial. I feel like a sunray that's beaming through a bright corridor of white light.

An ancient would probably think they're entering the afterlife, since it matches their description of what that experience might be like. Given the circumstances, I might consider that theory plausible, except I have a better one.

I've gone through this already, earlier today, though it feels like it happened ages ago.

I feel the sensation of my body returning, but I close my eyes. When I open them, I'll know for sure if I'm right.

"Theo?" Phoe says.

I open my eyes.

I'm standing in a cave. Stalactites hang overhead, and on the floor, there are stalagmites and an inventory of various dangerous objects.

Phoe's beautiful pixie face is contorted with deep worry.

There's a large Screen next to her. On it is what I assume is my neural activity. My brain looks like a beehive going to war against an anthill, at ten-speed. The sight of it causes me to relive the terrors in a strange biofeedback.

The Screen disappears. Phoe must've realized I'd recover better without it in my face.

"Calm down, please," Phoe says. Her voice is the epitome of soothing. "You're back."

Deep down, I know the answers, but I still can't help but voice the questions. "You didn't destroy everyone?" I take a step forward and do a jerky sweeping gesture with my hands, as though the people of Oasis are hiding at the edges of the cave. "You're not Instructor Filomena?"

Phoe looks at me, incomprehension taking over the worry in her eyes.

"Was all of that the fucking game?" I say louder and step back. "Was none of that real?"

Phoe approaches me and wraps her arms around me. I don't fight this hug, the second one I've received in my life, even though this time, it feels different. This time, the ancient social gesture is meant to soothe me, and it's pretty effective at that. As the fragrance and warmth of Phoe's body envelops me, my heart rate slows from hypersonic to merely three hundred miles per hour.

She rubs my back in random circular motions that are also soothing.

"Shh," she whispers in my ear. "You're here. You're safe."

"But it was so real. I died." I take in a shuddering breath. "Liam died too. Everyone did." I try to pull away, halfheartedly, but she tightens her arms around me. Lowering my voice to almost a subvocalization, I say, "You betrayed me."

"It's over." She gently strokes my hair. "I would never betray you. How could you ever think that?"

I take another breath, and as I exhale, I say, "It all happened so fast."

She lets me go, backs up a step, and regards me solemnly. "Can you talk about what happened? Judging by the fact that the memory gap is still here"—she points at her head—"not to mention the lack of new computing power, I have to assume you didn't shut down the game."

"You couldn't see what happened? You don't have access to that place?"

"As I told you, not to see, no. I did try to get a message *in*. It seems it didn't work." Phoe looks dejected.

"It did," I say. "I saw the Screen you sent. It looked like the one I got in the Witch Prison. It gave me hope, but . . ." I shake my head.

"That's great." Her eyes brighten. "That means next time I should be able to—"

"Next time?" I feel my cheeks heat up. "There will never, ever be a next time."

She frowns for a moment, then asks, "Can you tell me what happened?"

I begin my story, starting with how the game tricked me into thinking I wasn't in the game. Phoe listens quietly. She clearly has questions but is saving them for later. I finish with, "And after I inhaled the Goo, I came back here."

"That is so peculiar," she says. "I don't even know where to begin."

"At the beginning," I tell her. "I can tell you're upset."

"Well"—she makes a chair appear out of thin air and sits on it—"there are things in your story that should've been clues about how fake everything was."

I decide I also want to sit, and as soon as I do, another chair shows up. "Such as?"

"Well, for example, Grace just let you go? And she actually touched you?"

"I know, odd," I admit. "But I was in a rush and didn't question it. It seems like she had some kind of . . ." I feel my face flush. "I don't know, secret feelings for me or something."

"Fine." Phoe crosses her arms over her chest. "I can always chalk that one up to your inexperience with hormones. Same goes for the part where

Instructor Filomena showed interest in you." She makes a disgusted face. "But, Theo, the Adult section of Oasis was the French countryside? With Amish-looking people? You don't think it's rather convenient that you learned about them just yesterday? And you actually believed I was Instructor Filomena?" Her lips press into a thin line.

"I just—"

"And Owen attacking you physically... You know he's too pacified by the Adults and too cowardly for something like that."

"He kicked a ball at Liam yesterday," I remind her. "Nothing stopped him from doing that."

"Fine. Maybe that could've happened, though I have my doubts. But a tractor chase? I made you do something that brought on the end of the world?" She shakes her head. "Out of all the problems with that scenario, don't you realize that if there *was* a way to shut down any of the Barriers, the control room for that would be managed by the Elderly. It wouldn't be in an incongruent, anachronistic tower, which, from what you told me, fell in a very odd and physically improbable manner."

I feel a warm, tingly sensation in my face. I know Phoe's biggest gripe is with the fact that I thought she was capable of killing everyone. Truth be told, now that I'm out of the game, I find that idea extremely hollow.

"It was like a dream," I tell her and attempt to reduce the warmth in my cheeks by rubbing at them. "You know when you're dreaming and the dream makes sense, but then you wake up and wonder why Liam was Santa Claus and why you didn't question it? I mean he's not *that* fat."

Phoe nods, as if she's urging me to explain further.

"Look." I mirror her arms-folded posture. "The world was ending. I didn't exactly have a moment to reflect on anything."

"But Instructor Filomena with her bullshit history?" Phoe's slender face is pinched. "You know she represents everything I loathe."

I force myself to speak calmly. "Well, if you'd told me who you really are, I wouldn't have concocted a theory, misguided as it might've been."

She bites her lip, a gesture that fascinates me for some reason. "Let's not throw blame around."

"So all I have to do to shut you up is ask you who you are?" I narrow my eyes. "Why don't you just tell me? Maybe if you did, I—"

"It's not that simple." She gets up from her chair. Her ears perk up as though she's listening to some distant noise. With worry on her face, she says, "Shit."

"Let me guess." I give her my best effort at a condescending smile. "Some emergency came up, and I need to run, right? The last thing we have time for is to continue talking about your least favorite topic."

Her long eyelashes flutter as she sighs and says, "That *is* pretty much what I was about to say, yes."

"How convenient."

"Without you beating the game, I don't have much to tell you anyway," she says. "I wish I was just dodging your question, but look." She extends her palm.

Out of her palm streams an image. It's not exactly a Screen, but it might as well be as far as its function goes. Only, unlike a Screen, the image in her hand is three-dimensional, like a hologram. It's showing us a small section of the forest.

There I am, lying on the forest floor, surrounded by greenery and looking fairly bored. My eyes are unfocused.

"You're jacked into this place," Phoe says. "Your neurons are only receiving inputs from your nanocytes instead of real sensory inputs. Only things like your parasympathetic nervous system are active in the real world, allowing you to breathe and digest Food, among other things. If someone were to approach you out there, you wouldn't even blink an eye at them."

I nod. Though this isn't something I'd thought about, it makes sense as she says it.

Content that I'm following her so far, she tilts her palm. The image moves deeper into the woods, away from my comatose self. I watch as the camera, or whatever it is that's behind the point of view, reaches a small clearing.

There's the shiny visor of a Guard's helmet.

I get up from my chair and fight the urge to run. With my system still overflowing with adrenaline, the fright that comes over me is stupefying.

This Guard is walking through the clearing. What's worse is his direction: he's heading straight for where I'm lying, and my unconscious self is as aware of him as the trees are.

"Crap." I begin pacing and nearly trip over Phoe's chair.

"Yeah. You can say that again." Phoe follows my frantic movements calmly, as if I pace like an insane person all the time and she's gotten used to it.

"What do I do?" I circle her a third time.

"Use the gesture and run." With fanfare, she flips me off with both fingers. "I'll be with you."

I mimic her gesture, too preoccupied to feel any hesitation at doing something the Adults would consider obscene.

Instantly, through that same white tunnel, I'm returned to my body in the forest.

The pine fragrance is in my nostrils, and Phoe is next to me, only she's ghostly again.

She turns her back to me, starts jogging, and says over her shoulder, "Run."

I jump up and run. Dry pine needles crunch under my shoes. My legs are tired, but not as much as they were toward the end of the game—which makes sense since all that stair climbing wasn't real.

"I think I prefer you the way you were in that cave," I tell Phoe mentally. Speaking out loud might cause me to run out of breath faster, or worse, the Guard might overhear me.

"Funny you should say that," she says over her shoulder before her insubstantial figure disappears into thin air. "The only reason I took on this guise at all was to point you in the right direction," she explains as a voice in my head. "You're running toward the Barrier. I'll need all my resources for what I need to do next."

"Barrier?" My pulse skips a beat. "Why?"

"Either you or, more likely, the game came up with a decent idea by using your knowledge."

My feet feel cold despite the exertion. "What idea, exactly?" I ask, though given the mention of the Barrier, I think I already know.

"I can use what little resources I have to temporarily authorize you as an Adult, at least as far as the Barrier is concerned," Phoe says. "You can then enter their section. Just don't expect to see the French countryside."

"I don't think—"

"I'm going to disconnect for a bit as I do this," Phoe says. "Just keep running straight ahead. It looks safe all the way to the Barrier."

"Wait, Phoe," I whisper. "I don't want to cross the Barrier."

Phoe doesn't respond.

I'm running alone.

"Are you ignoring me on purpose?" I subvocalize.

No reply.

So I run.

And keep running.

After a time, my pace becomes completely steady, and I feel like an automaton—dodging branches, moving my feet, and breathing, all without any conscious thought. This lack of awareness allows my thoughts to wander. At first, I go over everything that happened. After I tire of doing that, I start asking myself questions: How long is this forest? Were we at the farthest point from the Barrier before, or did Phoe set me on a diagonal path?

My foot catches on a root, and I trip, barely managing to avoid slamming into a big stump to my left. I hit the ground awkwardly, my palms sliding on the pine needles and dirt.

My ankle objects violently. I see white specks, as though I've been staring at the sun. Blinking the whiteness away, I turn my head as I start to get up—and freeze in place.

There's a person staring at me from behind the stump.

A very familiar person.

His mouth is open so wide I can't help but say, "Dude, you realize something might fly into your maw, right?"

Liam gets up and comes toward me.

"You okay?" His voice is rough. "Where the hell did you come from? Why did you run away?" His tone gets progressively more incredulous. "Why the uckfay are you grinning at me like that? Don't you understand the uckingfay trouble you're in?"

Only when he points it out do I realize that I am indeed smiling. I can't help it. Seeing him, hearing him misuse Pig Latin, solidifies a single thought in my mind.

Liam is okay.

Rationally, I already knew it was a game-inspired figment of my imagination who fell from the tower. Fear is rarely rational, however, especially when it comes to that kind of loss. Given how realistic the cursed game was, on some level, I felt like Liam was gone.

"Help me up," I say, fighting the urge to say something sappy. "What are you doing here?"

Liam forgets his questions and helps me get to my feet, muttering, "I wasn't going to help those uckersfay find you. I'd sooner sniff Owen's feet."

Leaning on Liam's arm for support, I test stepping on my right foot.

He's watching me intently, so I try not to cringe too much.

He narrows his eyes, so I let go of his arm and take a tentative step on my own. Right away, I have to swallow a yelp. I don't want Liam to know I'm fighting nausea and the desire to sit back down.

"Come with me, dude." Liam's eyebrows draw together into what Mason and I nicknamed 'the forehead caterpillar.' "I'll take you straight to the nurse's office."

"No, you won't," I say. "I'm not going anywhere near the Adults."

"Dude? Have you gone completely insane?" His forehead caterpillar gets all wrinkly. "The longer you stay out here, the worse it'll be for you."

"Trust me. There's no way things can get worse for me, no matter what I do."

As I say the words, the hopelessness of my situation fully dawns on me.

Unlike ancient fugitives, I have very limited options when it comes to escape. Even if Phoe manages to get me into the Adults' side of Oasis, we're still talking about a very small surface of habitable land that they would have to search before they find me.

"Seriously," Liam says, and I realize I missed something he said. "I ought to knock you out and take you back for your own good."

"Liam, trust me, I can't go back." My voice cracks, and I pause to clear my throat before continuing. "Please, promise you won't tell them where I am."

"But you're not well." He chews his cheek. "You can't expect me to ignore—"

A rustling sound comes from the trees behind the stump.

Without fully realizing what I'm doing, I dive for the place where Liam was sitting earlier and crouch, ducking my head. The pain in my ankle is so sharp I'm surprised I haven't fainted.

The sound of someone moving through the forest gets louder.

Liam steps toward me but doesn't look at me. His eyes are glued to a point far above my head, behind the stump.

He stops right next to the stump, so close I could reach out and tickle his leg were I in a more jovial mood.

"Liam," a horrifyingly familiar nasally voice says. "Were you just talking to someone?"

I recognize this voice. After the game, I don't think I'll ever not shudder at hearing it.

"Hi, Instructor Filomena," Liam says. "There's something you need to know." He makes his hands into fists, relaxes them, turns them into fists again, and then sticks his hands in his pockets. "It's about Theo."

CHAPTER SEVENTEEN

Forgetting about the pain in my ankle, I coil up, ready to pounce, but Liam is standing in my way. It would be impossible for me to spring without knocking him over.

"Theodore?" Instructor Filomena's voice rises with each syllable. "What about him?"

"I saw him," Liam says. "I was speaking of my discovery into my Screen."

"You saw him?" she repeats. "Why are we standing here then? Where is he?"

Liam takes his hand out of his pocket. Raising it, he points southeast. "He was running that way. I yelled for him to stop. He looked at me but kept running." He shifts his weight from one foot to the other. "Do you know what happened? Why he ran?"

"Don't you worry about that." Instructor Filomena tries but, in my opinion, fails to sound soothing. "Come with me. We can cover a wider area if we work together."

"Okay." Liam takes a step to the left and stops next to the stump—I'm guessing to block Instructor Filomena's view of me. I hear shuffling footsteps and realize she's probably heading in the direction Liam pointed in. After a few moments, Liam follows her.

I sit quietly, not daring to even sneak a glance at them. I massage my ankle as I wait and wonder what I'm going to do next.

A shadowy figure suddenly looms over me. I jump, nearly smacking my head against the stump.

"Sorry," Phoe says. "I didn't mean to startle you."

"You didn't," I say and attempt to swallow my heart back down my throat. "I thrive on sudden movements and menacing shadows."

She chuckles, raising her transparent hands to her head with no face. Now that I know what she would look like had this been my man cave, or had she possessed enough resources, I can picture that sly, crooked smile.

It's an oddly pleasant visual.

Phoe clears her throat. "Anyway, you're now authorized to enter the Adult section."

"Great." I rub the back of my head, where it touched the stump. "One thing you never told me is why I would go there. Won't I be like the proverbial lamb going to the slaughter?"

"Not necessarily. They won't think to look for you there. At least not for a while."

I use the tree stump to help myself to my feet. My ankle hurts when I put my weight on it.

"Shit," Phoe says. "You can't run like that."

"Yeah," I say. "I'll be lucky if I can limp my way there."

"This development just strengthens the need for you to cross the Barrier." Her ghostly form makes a motion of running a jerky hand through her hair. "I can get you transport once we're on the Adults' side."

I take a step and wince. "Damn. This really hurts."

"I'm sorry I can't ease your pain with my current resources." Her voice is full of regret. "Not without undoing the anti-tampering protection I put in place per your request."

I carefully balance my weight when I take the next step. I'd rather be in pain than have my mind messed with.

Suddenly, Phoe's spine straightens, and she runs ahead. "Come here," she exclaims. "There!" She points to the ground.

I limp over and look at where she's pointing.

"That's a dry stick," I say, not even trying to hide my disappointment. She was so excited I was expecting to see an invisibility cloak or something.

"An invisibility cloak would require extremely complex manipulations of the Augmented Reality interface—and for tons of people. With my meager resources, I have trouble dealing with just yours. This—" She makes a showy two-palm gesture at the dry branch. "This here is a *walking stick*." She's using the overexcited style of speech common in ancient advertisements. "Like all the famous explorers used."

"More like a cane," I mutter but pick up the stick.

I take a tentative step with the assistance of the stick.

Then another.

"Much better," I reluctantly admit.

"Good," Phoe says. "The Barrier isn't far now."

* * *

"We just passed the threshold, the place where fear would've stopped you had my authorization not worked," Phoe says as I see the shimmer of the Barrier in the distance. She looks at me worriedly. "You don't feel fear, do you?"

I shrug. "Nothing outside what's normal. And by that, I mean normal for someone who has the whole population of Oasis chasing after him and who fell to his death the last time he went this way."

"I'll take that as a sign that my manipulations worked," Phoe says. "You clearly have the Adult privileges required to cross this spot."

Mumbling about why I'm justified in being afraid, I move forward with the help of my stick/cane.

After a couple of minutes, a long stretch of cut grass with no trees that ends in the Barrier comes into view.

"I know," Phoe says. "I also dislike the lack of cover, but it can't be helped. We can't afford to walk toward the section where the Barrier crosses the forest." She glances down at my ankle.

We walk in tense silence until we get to the clearing. "Theo, wait—" Phoe starts saying as I step out from behind the last tree, but it's too late.

I see the Guard, who must've just stepped out from the tree line to the left of me, some sixty feet away.

"Maybe he didn't see us," Phoe says urgently. "Back away slowly."

I begin complying when she hisses, "Never mind. Get to the Barrier."

I glance at the Guard and see that he's running toward me.

He must've seen me after all.

I grit my teeth and limp toward the Barrier as fast as my ankle and cane will allow.

The distance I have to cover is about fifteen feet. A quarter of the distance between the Guard and me, I reassure myself.

"Except if you take into account his current velocity, he *will* catch you," Phoe says. "You have to run."

I attempt to increase my speed, but my ankle pulses in waves of aching complaints, and the wooden stick feels as if it's about to break. I steal a glance at the Guard.

He's closer than I expected.

Desperation coils in my chest. Stopping, I raise the stick and hurl it like a spear at my pursuer.

He ducks to the side to avoid it, and his foot catches on a protruding piece of rock. I watch in amazement as he sprawls across the ground, sliding forward.

I bought myself a few precious seconds.

I resume my rapid limping. Without the stick, the pulsing in my ankle morphs into a violent throbbing.

It pays off, though. I get so close that if I were to reach my hand out, I'd touch the Barrier. Out of the corner of my eye, I notice the Guard is struggling to his feet.

Without testing the Barrier as I did in the game, I rush through it.

Nothing happens.

I don't feel as if I walked through a bubble, or wetness, or anything else.

One moment I was on the Youth's side of the Barrier, and the next I'm on the Adults'.

"That's because the Barrier is not real," Phoe says next to me. "It's Augmented Reality that works on the same principles as Screens and my current image." She sweeps her hands down her body.

I don't respond. I'm looking at a stretch of grass that leads into a pine forest, and it hits me how unlike the game everything is. Aside from the Barrier working differently, this side of Oasis looks like a mirror image of the one I came from.

"Well, yeah. Did you expect the French countryside to make an appearance?" Phoe says. "Now, quickly, get on that." She points to a metal disk lying on the ground. "Remember that Guard? Just because you can't see him through the Barrier doesn't mean he's not about to come through it."

Her reminder jolts me back into action, and I limp to the disk she pointed at.

"It's just a shiny circle of metal," I whisper after examining it cautiously. "How do I 'get on it'?"

"Given your injury," she says, "you should sit in the center of it, probably in the lotus pose."

My mind is full of questions, but I step on the disk. A shimmering bubble forms around its edges.

"That's to make sure you stay safely inside," Phoe says, answering the question I was about to ask. "Now sit."

I get into the lotus pose, which allows me to massage my injured ankle.

A shimmering ghostly copy of a disk appears on the ground. Phoe steps on it and sits down in the same pose.

"Go like this," she says and raises her hand, palm down, keeping her fingers tightly together.

I do as she showed me.

My disk twitches under me.

"Don't move," she says as I'm about to jump up. "The field around you won't let you get off anyway."

The disk moves smoothly and slowly, as though I'm on an ice slope instead of grass.

Then I realize I'm not sliding on the grass; I'm actually hovering above it.

Phoe begins to hover as well.

At first she's just an inch above the top of the tallest grass stalk; then she's almost a foot off the ground.

Before I get a chance to voice any objections, the same thing happens to me.

I'm about a foot off the ground, which is low enough not to activate my panic, but high enough to prove a frightening point.

I'm sitting on some sort of flying device. It must be the transport Phoe mentioned earlier.

"Don't dwell on that," Phoe says. "Turn your hand to the right like this"—she tilts her palm rightward—"to turn right."

I carefully tilt my hand, and the disk rotates in the same direction.

"Same with the left," Phoe explains and tilts her hand the other way.

I turn my palm to the left and the disk straightens at first, but then tilts to the left.

"Shit," Phoe says suddenly and points at the Barrier.

The Guard steps out of it and heads straight for us.

"Do this." Phoe points her palm upward, at about a seventy-five-degree angle. In response to her gesture, Phoe's disk whooshes upward at the exact same angle as her palm.

I look at where the Guard was.

He's no longer there.

He's a foot in front of me, his hand extended.

If I don't do what Phoe said, he'll grab me.

I point my palm upward, though at a narrower angle than Phoe's.

The disk whooshes over the Guard's head, leaving his outstretched hand empty. He leaps after me, but I'm already too high for him to reach.

"You're moving smoothly," Phoe says. Somehow she's flying next to me, even though a moment ago she was far away. "Do this to add speed." She thrusts her palm forward in a jerky motion, looking like an ancient martial artist.

Her disk speeds up. Given how fast it's going, its flight is surprisingly smooth, reminding me of a stingray swimming after its prey.

I hesitantly repeat her gesture.

My flying device moves faster too—much faster.

What's worse is that due to the slight slope of my palm, I also gain altitude.

"There wasn't a choice," Phoe says soothingly. "Not unless you wanted to fly into the trees."

She's right. I clear the nearby trees, flying a couple of feet above their tops.

"What now?" I think, mostly to distract myself from my overly rapid breathing.

"I have no idea." Phoe's voice is inside my head. I guess she didn't want to pretend to scream over the wind in our ears. "My plan of hiding you here is shot to shit, though."

I nod, wondering how I can feel the wind in my ears if I'm enclosed in a protective bubble. This thought is interrupted by the enormous city I spy in the distance.

I stare at it openmouthed.

This is no French countryside, obviously. I didn't truly think it would be. But I didn't expect this . . . conformity. Why keep the Youths away when everything here is so similar to our section, with the same geometrically perfect metal structures and bucolic greenery, only scaled differently?

"Scale is pretty important," Phoe says. "You can figure out the ratio of Adults to Youths from the scale, and that ratio can reveal other things, such as birth rates."

I unpeel my eyes from the distant buildings and look at Phoe's disk.

"How is it that this thing can fly?" I ask. "I didn't think that was possible."

"I already told you: I'm not here in the real sense of the word," Phoe says. "This form you see is an Augmented Reality construct."

"I meant *me*," I say. "How am I flying on a disk? I'm not Augmented."

"Oh," Phoe says innocently, as though she didn't realize what I meant. "Similar to those stairs at the Zoo, this probably has to do with magnetic fields and room-temperature superconductors."

"Ah, why didn't you tell me that before?" I say sarcastically. "Now I totally get it."

"And I wouldn't go so far as to say you're *not* Augmented." She snickers. "Though you're not an AR avatar, with your nanocytes, you're pretty augmented all right."

"I get that too," I say without sarcasm.

"Then I assume you also get that we can't fly any farther," Phoe says, her tone turning more serious. "They could spot us."

"So where do we go?" I ask.

"I'm thinking we should turn back and return to the Youths' side, even if it means we can't fly." She raises her hands and massages her temples. "The Guard we fled from has undoubtedly reported our encounter and—"

She stops talking and stands up on her flying disk. Her whole body locks as if she's frozen. With the way she's standing, it looks as if she's staring into the distance to her right.

I follow her gaze.

"Crap," I say at the same time as she says, "Shit."

Like a flock of migratory birds, a group of Guards is approaching us, their disks reflecting the sun's rays.

Phoe comes out of her reverie, swerves her disk sharply to the left, and shouts, "Follow me."

I tilt my palm so sharply left I nearly pull my forearm muscle in the process. The result is worth it, though.

I follow Phoe's trajectory perfectly.

We torpedo forward, the tops of the trees becoming a solid green blur below us.

"Stop, Theo," Phoe yells at me. "Make your hand into a fist to do that, like this."

She follows her words with a gesture that I mimic right away. My nails dig into my palm as I make a fist, and we both come to a sudden stop.

There are Guards in the direction we were flying in.

They're still in the distance, but it doesn't make them any less of a problem.

"Left?" I say urgently. "Or right?"

"They have us surrounded. I think we should go up."

"Up? But—"

"Your fear of heights is a phobia," Phoe says. "In this case, a pretty irrational one."

"But—"

"Just think how ironic it would be if the fear that's meant to help with your survival causes you to get killed," she says, then tilts her hand up.

"Fine," I say and raise my palm with my fingers upward, the way she just did.

I meant to raise it at a sharp ninety-degree angle but ended up with only half of that. Still, I climb higher, and the trees below get farther and smaller.

"Now you need to go forward." Phoe's voice is in my head. "As fast as you can."

I motion to go forward.

"Now swerve around unpredictably—it's our only chance." She starts dashing around violently to illustrate her point.

I do as she instructed. It's actually not hard. My hands are shaking, my fear giving me a swerving advantage. I maneuver so unpredictably that even *I* don't know where my disk will go next.

It doesn't help, though.

The Guards don't need to know where I'm going when they have numbers on their side.

"There are at least sixty of them," Phoe whispers.

I suspect she's lowballing it to make me less scared. I would've guessed there are closer to a hundred Guards in my path.

I turn back but see Guards about forty feet behind me.

I look left—Guards.

I turn right—even more Guards.

I look down—a ton of Guards are flying up.

It hits me then: the Guards have formed a sphere, with me at the center of it, and they're executing their plan by flanking me from every direction.

"Stop and raise your hands." Phoe's voice is a frantic whisper in my ear. "If they're going to take you anyway, let's at least make sure they don't harm you in the process."

I scan my surroundings. My stomach twists with hollow terror.

"Screw that," I say and raise my palm at a perfect ninety-degree angle.

At the same time, I make an almost-punching motion with my hand.

My disk dashes upward.

Though I know I've been flying up to this point, this is when I see what flying *really* means.

"Theo, what the hell?" Phoe's voice says in my head.

I don't answer, but my plan is simple, and I'm sure she'll figure it out.

Since I have the shield bubble surrounding me, I plan to ram into the Guards above me. They won't be expecting this, since even I wouldn't have expected me to fly upward.

"Stop, Theo. Your plan won't work."

I ignore Phoe, focusing on the Guards.

"It won't work because I lied," she says urgently. "There isn't a protective bubble surrounding you."

In time with her words, the bubble around my disk shimmers and disappears.

"It was Augmented Reality," Phoe says, "like the Barrier." She sounds on the verge of crying. "I wanted to ease your fear of heights, so I—"

I don't listen to her.

I stare at the approaching Guard.

He, like the others, is standing on his disk.

He has no bubble either.

None of them do.

Because, like Phoe said, mine wasn't real. This device doesn't come with one.

All these thoughts race through my mind as my disk rockets toward the Guard.

I'm not sure why, but instead of making my hand into a fist to stop the device, I jab my hand forward to increase the speed and stand up on my zooming disk. The ancient movies had a concept of 'playing chicken,' and in my desperation, it's the only thing I can think of to try.

The guard will either move, or we'll collide.

Unfortunately, the Guard has a third option.

He spreads his arms as though he's planning to give me a hug.

At breakneck speed, I ram my body into his, my shoulder colliding with his helmet like a bullet hitting Kevlar armor.

Through the ringing blast of pain, I feel a strong hand grab me and see a disk fly away.

Clearly, the Guard wasn't fazed by the impact of our collision. As I flail in the air, he tightens his grip on me, dragging me up onto his disk.

Out of the corner of my eye, I see another Guard flying toward us.

I struggle to free myself, but I might as well be trying to jump out of my skin.

The approaching Guard is holding a shiny stick-like object in his hand. Stopping in front of my captor's disk, he jabs my exposed forearm with it.

I feel a painful jolt, and my vision blurs. I open my mouth to protest, but it's too late.

My consciousness turns off.

CHAPTER EIGHTEEN

The world comes back in a haze of sensations. Dimly, I hear voices.

"What's the point of healing him if he's to be Forgotten?" a man asks.

"It's protocol," another man replies. "Until they hold a formal Council vote, he's a citizen of Oasis, with all that it entails, and he's hurt."

"We both know that vote is a formality," the first voice says. "You heard what Jeremiah said. But if you insist . . ."

I feel a pinprick and warmth spreads through my body, easing the pain in my ankle and shoulder—the shoulder that hit the Guard in what seems like a bad dream.

I attempt to open my eyes and say something, but there's another cold jolt and all sensations fade.

* * *

I struggle into wakefulness again.

There are no voices around me this time.

I peer through a sliver between my eyelashes.

There's a white floor and a white chair nearby. I also detect a medicinal scent in the air. If I didn't know the horror of the true situation, I could tell myself that I'm in a nurse's—

"I know you're awake," says an unfamiliar raspy voice. "Your brain frequencies were alpha and theta just a few minutes ago, but they're different now."

I open my eyes and take in my surroundings.

This is where Mason was strapped to a table. I'm sure of it.

Worse than that realization is the next one. The man in front of me is the white-haired monster who gave Mason that fatal shot.

I blink away the remnants of my grogginess.

Close up, I can't help but marvel at this man's leathery, wrinkled skin and his frail muscle tone, which is noticeable even under his robes.

These are signs of aging, something that shouldn't exist in Oasis.

I try to speak, but only a hoarse noise comes out of my throat.

The man's eyes are piercing blue and bottomless. He catches my gaze, and I feel like if I stare him down, I might get lost in those eyes.

I swallow, try again to speak, and manage to say in a hushed whisper, "Who are you?" Saying something feels good, so more confidently, I add, "What do you want?"

"I'm Jeremiah, Head Councilor and Keeper of Information," he says, his gaze turning more intense. "You may call me Keeper."

The man's imperious tone snaps something inside me, and I remember that this is the very man who killed my friend.

"What the fuck do you want from me, Jeremiah?" I use the F-word on purpose. To break his hypnotic gaze, I give him a harsh squint. "How come you look like an old man from the movies?"

Taken aback by my vehemence and outright disrespect, the Keeper glances to his right.

I use his momentary discomposure to scan the room and realize he looked at the Guard, as if saying, "What are they teaching these Youths?"

The Guard's mirrored visor conceals whatever emotion he may be feeling, so I quickly survey the rest of the room.

There's a second Guard here, unlike on that recording of Mason. Thinking of what happened to my friend threatens to send me into full-on panic mode, so I focus on something else, like on this double Guard business. Do they consider me more dangerous than Mason and thus added a second Guard? Of course, even a single Guard is overkill since I'm tied down the way Mason was.

"Your fingers have free range," Phoe whispers in my head.

Happy for the distraction from the iceberg growing in my belly, I wiggle my fingers. They are indeed free. And I know what Phoe's getting at. I could, if I wanted to, do the obscene gesture required to get back into the cave and from there be a gesture away from the game. Thinking of playing the game again doesn't frighten me as much as it ordinarily would have. Compared to my current situation, my adventure inside the game doesn't seem so bad.

"But don't do it. Don't go back to the game," Phoe whispers. "At least not yet. They can't know anything about me or that game. With your brain scan on display like that, it would be risky, since we don't know what—"

"I look like an old man because I am one. I'm two hundred and nine years old," Jeremiah finally says, responding to my old man comment from what feels like an hour ago. "I'm one of the Elderly and should be treated with respect."

The implications of what he says whoosh through my consciousness. He's been alive nearly ten times longer than I have. I must seem like an infant to him.

Then my mind goes into scarier waters. If this guy ages, that means the rest of the Elderly probably do too. And if *they* age, that means the rest of Oasis does as well—including me. Youths have been taught that once you reach Adulthood, the developing process stops. We all believe we stop changing at the peak of health and maturity, which is around forty years old. No one ever calls the process of a Youth becoming an Adult 'aging.' Similarly, we were told that an Adult becomes an Elderly when he or she acquires enough wisdom to join the leaders of our society— nothing to do with aging, per se. Aging is one of those ancient words, like famine. Horrible in theory, but poorly understood in practice.

"When Adults reach their ninetieth birthday, they join us, the Elderly," Jeremiah says as though he deduced my train of thought. "Before they show any signs of degeneration." He holds out his spotted hands in front of him. "It allows everyone but the Elderly a rather carefree existence for a very long time, don't you think?"

The implications are too horrible to bear. If this is all true, that means we're no different from the ancients. It means we grow old and eventually die.

Unable to deal with that right now, I put that thought aside, locking it in a box. Gathering as much bravado as I can muster, I say, "Are you asking me if I agree that ignorance is bliss?"

"I don't like this, not one bit," Phoe whispers, her voice quivering. "He wouldn't tell you so much if he was intending to let you go."

"I don't understand, Theodore." Jeremiah stares at me, and I see a flash of something almost like hurt in his pale gaze. "Where is this hostility stemming from?"

"Don't say a word about Mason." Phoe's voice turns shrill. "In general, don't tell him about anything to do with me." I hear her exhale a burst of air in my head. "Please."

I glare at Jeremiah. "You give me Quietude." I fold my thumb with as much emphasis as possible while tied up. "You have the Guards hunt me down." I fold my index finger. "You tie me up." I chance pushing my body against my restraints, testing them. They, of course, don't budge, so I add bitterly, "And you have the balls to say I'm acting hostile?"

He gestures and a chair shows up next to him. "Since you bring that up, why *don't* we discuss your act of running away from the Guards?" He sits down on the chair. "I would not have expected you, or anyone, to run from them."

"You don't know what happened to Mason," Phoe reminds me.

"I'm not stupid." My mental retort is harsh, so I add, "Sorry, Phoe. I'm channeling some of my frustration with this asshole the wrong way."

"I deserve your anger," she replies softly. "I couldn't protect you."

"Why did you run away?" Jeremiah repeats patiently. "And how did you manage to cross the Barrier and get a disk?"

I look at him stoically and say nothing.

"What about Quietude? How did you get away from that building?" Jeremiah asks, his voice tenser. "How did you open the doors?"

I shrug as much as my restraints allow and stare at the wall behind Jeremiah as if its white blandness is more interesting than his bullshit.

He sighs heavily. "What about Mason?"

I flinch.

The Keeper squints, his features tightening. I curse myself for my instinctive reaction. He got a confirmation that I know that name—not that it should've been big news to him, since in my ignorance, I spoke of nothing else this morning.

"Let that go," Phoe whispers. "You didn't know about Forgetting. You still don't, as far as Jeremiah is concerned."

I don't argue with Phoe. I simply make my face impassive and resist confronting Jeremiah about Mason, as hard as that is.

"Who is Mason?" Jeremiah runs a frustrated hand through his hair, bringing my attention to the fact that his hair is thinning throughout, especially around his forehead. "Why did you ask Grace about Mason this morning?"

"We were merely discussing the Freemasons," I say. "They were one of the ancients' largest and best-known secret societies." As nonchalantly as possible, I stretch my neck by turning my head from side to side. "Kind of like the Elderly here in Oasis. You're the first one I've met."

Jeremiah starts to get up, but then sits back down again. "It's just a matter of time before you stop insulting my intelligence," he says through gritted teeth.

"Well, why don't *you* tell *me*"—my voice rises in volume—"what the word 'mason' means to you?"

"My role here is to ask the questions. Yours is to answer them." Jeremiah's pale cheeks redden. "How is it that you know who Mason was?"

I purse my lips in response. Subvocally, for Phoe's benefit, I say, "Did you notice he said 'was'?"

"Don't subvocalize," Phoe whispers. "What if Jeremiah notices you muttering?"

"Let him think I'm cursing him under my breath," I subvocalize and shift against my restraints, feeling the strain and soreness of my muscles.

Jeremiah lets out a sigh at my non-response, and I clench my teeth to avoid screaming obscenities at him. If I give in to the anger, I might blurt out something I'll regret. Besides, my silence seems to be pissing him off more than any yelling would.

As I continue to stare him down, Jeremiah sighs again, his expression unexpectedly softening. "Please, Theodore." He looks almost regretful. "I don't want to coerce you to speak, but . . ."

"Shit," Phoe says. "Tell him *something*. I don't like where this is going."

"You want me to speak?" I think at Phoe. "Fine."

Loudly, relishing every syllable, I say, "Fuck you, Jeremiah."

The left side of his upper lip twitches slightly. "You don't leave me with any choice." Jeremiah glances at the Guards as though he said this more for their benefit than mine. Turning his attention back to me, he says, "Last chance, Theodore. Will you tell me what I want to know?"

I do half of the gesture that would send me to my man cave.

Seeing my middle finger, Jeremiah does a strange gesture of his own. With his outstretched hand, he makes a tight fist, as if he's trying to squash something.

His face looks menacing, and I flinch, expecting something bad to happen.

"He just tried to hurt you." Phoe sounds horrified. "Had it worked, it would've been terrible. It was supposed to stimulate the pain center of your brain."

I examine myself.

I feel absolutely nothing.

"That's because of the shielding I created for you," Phoe says. "The shielding he's about to learn about, given your lack of a reaction."

"I'll make him think it worked," I think at her and let out an animalistic roar.

In case the sound didn't convince Jeremiah, I also thrash side to side, figuring if I'm going to pretend to be in pain, I might as well test my bonds some more. The bonds are, sadly, unyielding.

Jeremiah watches all this with a darkening expression. His eyes are locked on the Screen above me.

"How is it that you're not in pain?" The twitch in his upper lip becomes more pronounced as his voice grows louder. "How did you just resist the Punish gesture? Did you know what I did? How did you know to pretend like you're in pain?"

I mentally curse my neural scan, stop my thrashing, and give him an uncaring shrug.

"I'm so sorry." Phoe's voice gets smaller. "I should've tried faking your neural scans. I was a coward. I was just afraid that—"

"Don't worry about it," I say out loud, figuring the reply suits both conversations.

Jeremiah reaches out as though he's about to repeat the gesture, but then stops, no doubt realizing it would be futile.

Getting up, he looks at the Guard to my left, then to the one to my right. As if in answer to his look, the

Guard to my left says, "He also resisted the Pacify command, back at the Quietude Building."

He must be the same Guard who chased me down that corridor.

"How did he do that?" Jeremiah's tone is hard. "How *could* he do that?"

The Guard who spoke up shrugs.

"Why didn't you tell me this earlier?" Jeremiah's voice rises. "This is important information."

"I'm sorry." The Guard takes a step backward, but his back hits the white wall. "I wasn't sure what happened. I didn't think it was possible to resist—"

"It's not." Jeremiah jerks his head from one Guard to the other. "I swear by the Forebears, it's supposed to be impossible."

The Guard on my left flinches, as though he's expecting Jeremiah to use the Punish gesture on him next. In contrast, the other Guard meets the old man's gaze calmly—or so I assume, since it's hard to tell with the reflective visor.

"Do you see why I have to find this out?" Jeremiah says to the Guards. "We must know."

The Guard on my left shrugs.

The Guard on my right speaks up for the first time. "Perhaps someone on the Council will know?"

Planting his feet farther apart, Jeremiah gives the Guard an evaluating stare. "You're Albert, right?"

"Yes." The Guard reaches for his shiny helmet and takes it off.

He's a man, something I could've guessed by his voice. What's interesting about him is his age. He isn't as old as Jeremiah. He looks closer in age to the Adults at the Institute.

"Except for the gray hair and wrinkles," Phoe says, "if you look closely."

She's right. Albert's temples are gray—something that happened to ancients with age. And he does indeed have slight crinkles in the corners of his gleaming eyes.

"That is my name," Albert says, meeting Jeremiah's gaze. "Yes."

"Well, you're fairly new here, *Albert,* so I understand your confusion." There's menace under Jeremiah's even tone. "I'm the oldest on the Council. The oldest in Oasis, for that matter. As such, I'm the Keeper of Information. Do you know what that means?"

Albert looks at him noncommittally.

"It means *I* tell the Council these types of things. It means I'm the only member of the Council who carries these burdens. I don't get to have the 'bliss of ignorance,' as this child called it." Jeremiah takes in a breath. "I do not get the peace of mind that comes with not knowing the terrible secrets of statecraft." His voice is quieter when he adds, "I do not even get the luxury of Forgetting. Can you imagine what that's like? Remembering your friends who have passed on?"

Albert's confident mask slips slightly. "I didn't mean any disrespect," he says. "I was only giving you a suggestion."

"Jeremiah openly admitted Forgetting," Phoe whispers. "And the Guards seem to know about it too, though it sounds like they, as well as the rest of the Elderly, Forget with everyone else—"

Jeremiah sits down in his chair and turns his attention back to me. "Theo, please. Tell me what I want to know, and I'll take you to see Mason. He's been asking about you."

His lie and chummy use of my shortened name infuriate me, but lashing out would only give away my knowledge of Mason's fate. I take a deep breath and exhale before asking, "Are you now talking about the stonemasons?"

Jeremiah jackknifes from the chair. "I'm sick of this charade." A little bit of Jeremiah's spittle lands on my cheek and the restraints prevent me from wiping it away. It's disgusting.

Jeremiah begins pacing back and forth in front of me. He looks deeply troubled. Stopping next to Albert, he extends his hand and says, "Give me your Stun Stick."

Albert reaches for a metal object on his belt, then stops. He looks at his colleague with desperation but sees what we all see: his own reflection in his partner's visor. He then gives Jeremiah an uncertain look and takes a few steps back.

"You." Jeremiah points to the other Guard. "Give me *yours*."

The Guard reaches for his belt without hesitation and takes off a metal object that looks like the baton of an ancient police officer. With no trace of hesitation, he hands the baton to Jeremiah.

"Do you know what this is?" The old man holds the baton in front of me threateningly.

"Something you should shove up your ass?" My voice comes out strained. I do recognize this thing. This is what knocked me out during the very last moments of the disk chase.

"It's something we don't really need in our society," Jeremiah says in a silky voice. "A weapon. A relic of different times." He gently taps the stick against his left palm, as though weighing it. "It's not lethal, of course, and if used under its regular settings, it will cause its target to lose consciousness." He turns a knob on the stick. "With a lowered current like this, though, I suspect it will *not* knock you out." He presses a button on the device, and its tip glows with a tiny spark, accompanied by the zapping sound of electricity. "No, I think that if I use it like this, the experience will be rather... unpleasant."

I stare at him. I think he's talking about torture, a grisly historical practice I could never comprehend. It's always been just a word, like genocide. You kind of know what it means, but not really.

Jeremiah steps closer to me.

My insides fill up with Antarctic snow.

Jeremiah presses the tip of the baton to my neck and pushes the button.

CHAPTER NINETEEN

I hear that same zapping sound and smell ozone in the air. An all-consuming, buzzing pain follows. The electric current spreads through the muscles of my body, leaving them shaking violently in its wake.

Overwhelmed, I scream, and in the haze of my torment, I hear Albert say something. I can't make out what it is, as I'm convulsing uncontrollably.

The horrid sensation stops.

"What did you say?" Jeremiah says to Albert. "I thought we had an understanding."

"I'm sorry, Keeper, but I'm authorized to contact any Council member at my discretion." Albert's words are clipped. "That's the prerogative of the Guards."

Jeremiah points the baton at Albert. Then, perhaps realizing he might look threatening, he lowers it. "Who did you squeal to?" His rheumy eyes are slits of derision.

"The esteemed Councilor Fiona requested you wait for her to join us," Albert says. "She's on her way."

Jeremiah closes his eyes for a second, then opens them and says, "I order you to leave this room."

Albert starts to move forward, looks at me, then at Jeremiah, and stops.

"Since you brought up prerogatives," Jeremiah says in a more commanding tone, "mine is to order you, and yours is to obey. Isn't that right?" He gives Albert a challenging look. "So in case it's not clear, this is a direct order."

Albert awkwardly glances at the door.

Jeremiah turns his head to the second Guard, as though to ask for assistance, but he doesn't get a chance to say anything. As if realizing his protests won't amount to much, Albert exits the room, his thumping footsteps echoing down the hallway.

Jeremiah looks at the remaining Guard. "You should also go," he says. "Though you and Albert will not recall these events after his"—he nods toward me—"Forgetting, I think it might be best for everyone concerned. Plus, if the Council starts asking you anything prior to the Forgetting . . ."

The Guard nods and obediently walks out.

Jeremiah turns to face me. "Sorry about all these distractions." He crosses his arms, careful to keep the tip of the baton away from himself. "Are you ready to talk?"

I shake my head. I don't trust myself to give him a defiant reply because my mouth is dry with panic. Worse, I fear I might plead with him if I try to say anything.

"You *should* plead with him," Phoe says, her voice frightened. "That Guard was the only ally you had in this room, and now he's gone." She takes a shaky breath. "Please plead with him, Theo. And if that doesn't work, tell him everything."

"That was the lowest setting." The irritation is gone from Jeremiah's voice, and he looks almost caring and sad as he says this. "Please, Theodore, just talk to me. That's all I ask. Your brain is not broken beyond repair like Mason's. If you talk, there's a chance I can make you Forget—"

I extend my left middle finger and angle it as far as my bonds will allow.

Jeremiah releases a heavy sigh and twiddles with the controls on the Stun Stick.

I freeze.

He reaches for me again.

I try to squirm away, but the bindings hold me in place.

Knowing how the Stun Stick feels makes this part more frightening.

He presses the baton's button.

The spark shows up and stays on the tip of the horrid device.

He touches the Stun Stick to my neck.

This time around, the agony that zaps through my body is a hundred times worse. I shake and twist, battering myself against the straps. The scream is wrenched violently out of my sore throat. I feel as if I'm about to throw up, or maybe I already have.

"Theo, if he keeps this up, your heart could stop." I hear Phoe's voice as though from a distance. "Stop your heroics and talk."

I can't respond to her, not even mentally. She's probably right. The heartbeat in my ears reminds me of automatic gunfire from ancient movies, both in terms of how rapid and how loud it is.

"Ready to talk?" Jeremiah's voice manages to penetrate through the fog of agony. "Just nod if you're ready."

My universe gets laser-focused on one expression of my will: not nodding. Even as the pain intensifies, all I can do is focus on not nodding.

It becomes a macabre meditation mantra. I ride the wave of pain, thinking only of not nodding.

Though my vision is blurred, I think I see movement from the direction of the door.

My body is behaving like a marionette in a hurricane, thrashing every which way, but as long as I don't give in, I don't care. Even if I scream, as long as I don't nod, it's okay—although if this goes on another moment, I might lose control of my bladder or worse. But even that wouldn't matter, as long as I don't nod.

"I said," a female voice enunciates loudly, "stop this at once."

The pain stops, and I sag against my restraints. I'm confused. I thought it might've been Phoe who spoke up, but that would mean Jeremiah could hear her, making him the second person who ever has.

"Fiona," Jeremiah says, his mouth turned down. "You shouldn't interrupt me when—"

"The Council only authorized you to perform euthanasia"—the older woman crinkles her small nose at the word—"which was supposed to be followed by an Oasis-wide Forgetting." She gives Jeremiah a piercing look, daring him to counter. "This—" She points her slender finger at me, disgust written across her face. "This is something else entirely."

Her voice is melodious. Were she Fiona's age, Phoe would sound like her, which might be why I got confused earlier.

"Fi," Jeremiah says in a placating tone. He holds up the baton. "I don't want to do this, but I have reason to believe this child has figured out a way to tamper with Forebear technology."

The old woman's already-pale face goes impossibly whiter.

She looks at Jeremiah, then at me.

Silently, I mouth the word, "Please," figuring it's not beneath my dignity to appeal to this woman, since she seems to be an ally.

She stands up straighter and looks at Jeremiah. "The Council members are already waiting to discuss this," she says, her tone full of resolve. "You can explain everything once we reach the Hall."

"Fine." Jeremiah's nostrils flare, and I catch a glimpse of the overly bushy hair in his nose. "Let's get this over with." He drops the Stun Stick on the floor. "While I deal with this minor inconvenience," he says to me, "I hope you take this time to think about your situation." He softens his tone. "I really want what's best for you." He gives Fiona a meaningful look and then adds, "For everyone."

"I'm ready to tell you something," I say through dry lips.

"Don't, Theo," Phoe says. "Don't antagonize him."

She must've read my intent.

That doesn't matter, though, because the old man didn't. He gets closer to me and eagerly says, "Tell me."

"Fuck you," I say as loudly as I can. "Fuck. You."

The old woman looks pained upon hearing my words but says nothing. She takes Jeremiah's elbow and leads him out the room.

I blink at the empty room.

Phoe's ghostly shape appears in front of me. "Now, Theo," she says, her voice trembling. "Do the gesture." She extends her middle fingers. "Get to your cave before someone comes back."

I mimic the gesture, wishing Jeremiah could see it.

The white light that carries me seems imbued with electricity this time—no doubt a result of me getting tortured by that particular force of nature.

In the next second, the white room is gone, and I'm standing in the virtual reality place Phoe calls my man cave.

My bonds are gone, as are any remnants of pain.

This time, the dangerous objects inhabiting this place look friendly and welcoming, and Phoe once again looks like a real girl—a girl whose pixie face has circles under her eyes.

"Get back into IRES," she says quickly. "Beating the game is our only chance."

"But—"

"Remember all those times I said there's no time to discuss things?" She's speaking so fast some of the words are jumbled.

I nod.

"This time I don't think I need to convince you, do I?"

"It's just that . . ." I have trouble talking with everything that's happened. "It was so frightening, the last time." As the words leave my mouth, I understand the silliness of what I'm saying. I'm about to get tortured again, then killed, and I'm worried about getting scared inside a game.

Phoe's gaze is pained. "If I could protect you without having to do this, I would in a heartbeat, but I can't, and it's killing me." Stepping toward me, she lays a hand on my shoulder. "Just don't let the game convince you it's real this time," she says softly, "and you should be okay."

Not real, I repeat to myself a couple of times. *It isn't real.*

"That's right," she says. "It really won't be."

Cognizant of my limited time, I start to raise my hands, ready to connect my middle fingers.

"Last thing," Phoe says, her face contorted in a kaleidoscope of emotions. "Since you could see the Screen I sent you before, I should be able to work off the fix I utilized that time and develop an even better way to stay in touch. I won't waste time describing it since you'll see it soon." She squeezes my shoulder. "If it works, that is."

"Okay," I say and extend my middle fingers.

"Wait," she says.

I stop the gesture and look at her questioningly.

Her face gets close to mine as if she's about to whisper something, but she purses her lips instead.

I stare at her delicate features, trying to understand what this is about.

Her lips touch mine.

I finally get it.

She's kissing me.

This is very different from that peck on the cheek she gave me before.

Her soft lips are moving over mine. They taste like flowers.

Instinctively, I return the kiss.

Before I understand what's happening, I feel her tongue flick into my mouth.

My eyes open wide in response, and I note that hers are closed demurely.

In the next instant, she pulls away and says, "That's for luck."

I stand there, frozen in place.

"Now go," she says. "Hurry, Theo."

I try to connect my middle fingers, but I miss on the first try, like a drunkard from the old movies.

She grabs my wrists and steadies my arms so that I can bring my middle fingers together.

My fingers connect.

I'm so confused I almost welcome the whirlwind trip down the white tunnel.

When the flash of blinding light subsides, I look around and my heart sinks.

My body is in agony from the recent torture, and I'm once again tied up in Jeremiah's cursed white room.

CHAPTER TWENTY

"This isn't real," I tell myself. "This is IRES messing with me again."

"I'm afraid it *is* real," Phoe says in my mind. "I know how it's going to sound, given what happened the last time you played, but this is the real world. The game didn't start. This is for real."

"This is a game," I repeat, squeezing my eyes shut.

"I'm coming in," Phoe says. "It's time we meet face to face."

"That's exactly what you said the last time," I say, opening my eyes.

She doesn't argue.

The door opens.

Fiona—the old woman who led Jeremiah away—is at the door.

"Theo, I'm Phoe," she says as she steps into the room. "You might recall my real name is Fiona. You even heard Jeremiah call me Fi. Fi is what my friends call me. How did I always ask you to pronounce my name?"

"Like it rhymes with 'fee,'" I mumble. "But this is all a coincidence, and this is still the game."

She walks over to me and does something to my restraints. One second I'm bound, the next I'm free.

"Look at it this way," Fiona/Phoe says, giving me a part-warm, part-sly smile that looks eerily like the one I saw on Phoe's younger face a moment ago. "Even if this is the game, you don't want the in-game Jeremiah to torture you. It will feel just as real as if you were in the real world."

For a made-up person, she's making a lot of sense.

"Fine, game-Phoe/Fiona." I pick up the Stun Stick Jeremiah dropped on the floor. "What kind of world-ending event are you going to try to convince me to do now? Can we somehow unleash death by explosion instead of Goo?"

"I'm just here to lead you out," the old woman says. "After that, we'll find you a quiet hidey-hole and try to jack you into the game again."

"Right," I say sarcastically. Making air quotes, I add, "Again."

She throws her hands up in a 'I give up' gesture and walks confidently toward the door.

I follow.

We exit into a long gray corridor.

"This way," she says and goes right. "Walk quieter."

I follow at my regular gait, muttering, "This isn't real," under my breath.

"That attitude will be your downfall," Phoe says mentally. "Even if this were a game, which it isn't, don't you realize that if you die, you won't complete your IRES mission? That means that in the so-called real world, you'll be back in Jeremiah's clutches, on the table in that room." She points at the room we just left.

I shake my head.

This pseudo-Phoe continues making sense. Or is it my brain telling me this?

"Or maybe it's IRES fucking with your mind." Phoe's mental voice is filled with mock paranoia.

"If you're trying to be a convincing Elderly woman, you should abstain from using the 'F' word," I subvocalize.

"Like Phoe—I mean, like *I* never used that language?" she asks challengingly.

"Enough," I whisper. Subvocally, I add, "I'll be careful." To myself, I think, "But this is still a game."

She doesn't contradict my thought as she turns the corner.

"Shit," her thought comes. "There's a Guard here. Go the opposite way."

I turn on my heels and hurry to the other end of the corridor. As I walk, I hear Fiona having a polite conversation with the Guard.

As I make my way to the end of the hallway, I wonder whether Fiona could indeed be Phoe— outside the game, that is. Could my subconscious mind have figured out who she really is and told me via IRES? Or could the game have figured it out after scanning my brain?

"Or this isn't a game," Phoe's voice intrudes, "and I merely told you what's what."

I don't answer.

I've reached a corner and need to proceed cautiously.

Repeating the maneuver I used in the Witch Prison, I crouch and peek from below a normal person's height.

The corridor looks safe.

I get up and make the turn.

This corridor is about half the length of the other one. I can't help but notice how much this reminds me of Witch Prison. Did IRES simply recycle that?

"If this was the game," Phoe says, "do you think it would let you dwell on the fact that you might be in the game so much?"

"How can it stop me from thinking whatever I want?" I reply mentally. "And even if it could do that, it might find me doubting my reality entertaining."

Phoe doesn't have a comeback.

I walk to the end of the corridor in silence.

When I get to the corner, I repeat the stealth trick and turn into yet another empty corridor.

"Is this place a maze?" I ask as I reach a fork—empty corridors going in three directions. "Also, where are you? Where am I going? What's the plan?"

"Go down the hallway on your right, then down the stairs," Phoe says. "I'm already waiting for you."

"You have to answer every one of my questions before I do anything you say," I think at her. "So, what's the plan?"

"There's no time. Get here, and you'll see," Phoe says urgently.

I consider this. I picture going down the right corridor, walking into a room downstairs, and Fiona convincing me to press a button with her (double confirmation, of course). A digital countdown initiating some kind of self-destruct sequence for this facility, or all of Oasis, would no doubt follow.

Muttering, "This is a game," I turn left, since that's as close to doing the opposite of what Phoe wants as I can manage.

"You'll regret that," Phoe says, "when you realize how wrong you are."

To tune her out, I mentally hum the ancient melody that I think is called *In the Hall of the*

Mountain King. The suspenseful, tension-building music fits my mood perfectly.

The gray corridors go on for the next ten minutes.

This place really is a maze, which gives extra credence to my belief that I'm in a game. Games love mazes.

Another odd feature of this facility is the lack of people. I haven't come across a single Guard after the one Phoe spoke to.

As though in response to my thought, I hear distant voices.

Great. I jinxed it.

I softly walk up to the turn in the corridor leading to where the voices are coming from, and crouch to take a look around the corner.

A white-haired man is standing there talking with a Guard.

They have their backs to me.

"Don't, Theo," Phoe says in my mind. "Don't go near them."

Since she's telling me not to, I decide I should do exactly what my instincts are telling me to do: the complete opposite of what she says.

I crawl on the floor like a soldier going through enemy territory.

The men are too absorbed in their conversation to notice me.

When I get within reaching distance, I raise the Stun Stick and prepare to strike.

Glancing down at the nob Jeremiah was twirling earlier, I try not to shudder at the memory. There's a little 'plus' icon on one side that I assume increases the voltage. Underneath that is a little button. I turn the dial in the 'plus' direction.

I extend the weapon, gently touch the Guard's ankle with it, and press the button, hoping the shock will penetrate through his white boot.

The Guard twitches and falls like a sack of sand.

I quickly jump to my feet.

The white-haired man's—Jeremiah's—eyes look comically wide.

I thrust the Stick at him, but he dodges it. Then, in a whirl of motion, the Keeper dives for the belt of the fallen Guard.

I again try to jab him with the Stick.

I miss.

I try hitting him with the Stick, using it like a club.

It connects with his upper shoulder, but at this point, he's already holding the Guard's Stun Stick.

Like a fencer, he blocks my next jab with the Stick he just acquired.

His movements are too quick for what I've read about old people—yet another little point for the *unrealness* of what's happening.

"Or his nanocytes are keeping him limber," Phoe says. "Plus he could've trained as a fencer during his Adult years. If I were you, I'd focus on the fight. You don't want to lose in either case."

I don't respond, but she's right.

I try kicking Jeremiah in the shin.

He steps back and whacks my left elbow with the Stick, hitting the spot the ancients sarcastically called 'the funny bone.'

My arm goes numb and agonizingly tingly. Only the memory of what this man did to me keeps me from dropping my Stick. I focus on that memory, forcing myself to ignore the pain.

Ancients called the emotion I'm feeling 'bloodlust.'

With a shout designed to unnerve my opponent, I charge Jeremiah.

My shoulder hits him mid-stomach, and I hear air escape his lungs as my shoulder goes numb.

His Stick falls on the floor with a loud clank, and he doubles over, clutching his stomach.

In case he's trying to trick me, I press the Stick against his skin and push the button.

He collapses to the ground in a heap of twitching limbs.

I know I should feel compassion, but I don't. This is just a game, and even if it weren't—

I turn in time to see the Guard grabbing for my throat.

He must've recovered from my jolt while I was fighting Jeremiah.

I duck, and he grabs hold of my hair. My scalp cries out in protest. It's surprisingly painful to have your hair pulled like this.

I kick him in the groin—a move I employed against another Guard the last time I was in this game. I know this is a male Guard from having overheard his conversation with Jeremiah, which means that in theory, this kick should hurt a lot.

And yet the Guard merely slows down for a moment.

I use the pause to jam him with the Stick again, frantically pressing the button as I do so.

He shakes but doesn't fall.

I turn the dial all the way up.

The Guard falls and convulses on the floor.

For good measure, I zap him once more and turn to look at Jeremiah.

The old man is trying to get up.

I touch his nape with the Stick.

"Don't make any sudden movements," I say. "We're going for a walk."

Without arguing, he gets up and starts walking down the corridor. I follow as he makes a left and a right down short pathways.

My Stick doesn't leave his neck.

"He's leading you into an ambush," Phoe says. "He knows the Stick is nonlethal, so worst case is that you just zap him once, right before the Guards overpower you."

I don't respond to her, but to Jeremiah, I whisper in my most sinister tone, "If I see a single Guard, after I knock you out with this Stick, I'll break as many of your bones as I can before they take me. I've read that bone density becomes a real problem as you age. You don't want me to test that theory." Of course, I'm bluffing. The very idea nauseates me, but he doesn't know that. For good measure, I add, "I think I'll start by putting this Stun Stick into your mouth and kicking it. That'll more than likely break your jaw."

I have no idea if my last threat is even physically possible, but it makes an impression. Jeremiah stops walking.

Up to this point, he was leading me down a long, windy corridor.

"We need to go back," he says. "And make a left instead of a right."

"Lead the way," I say, trying to sound as menacing as possible.

We walk in complete silence. Even Phoe is quiet.

"I wouldn't *really* have done *that*," I think for Phoe's benefit. "Not even here, in this stupid game."

"I don't know." Her whisper sounds sad. "Without the usual nano-tampering, you've deteriorated to near-ancient neurotypical levels, and the ancients did all sorts of atrocities in the name of justice and revenge."

"What will you do with me if I show you the exit?" Jeremiah's hands are trembling as he walks. "Will you break my bones anyway?"

"I'll use this Stick on you one more time." I don't know why I'm making my voice reassuring; this asshole certainly doesn't deserve it. "I'll set it to knock you out."

"In that case, the exit is five more turns from here," he says. "Left, right, left, and left, and right. You can knock me out here and go."

"No," I respond and poke him with the tip of the Stick. "Whatever trap you just tried sending me into, we're entering it together."

He walks silently the rest of the way, arms hanging limply at his sides.

We make the turns he suggested, and I see a door that looks like the twin to the one in the Witch Prison.

Looks like he didn't lie to me after all—not this time anyway.

When we reach the end of the corridor, I point to the door and say, "Open it, and I'll do as I promised."

He looks at me. His eyes are watery. Without saying a word, he makes the regular 'open door' gesture. The door opens a sliver. It seems as if it would've opened for me just as easily.

"If I see something other than the outdoors after I open this," I say, "I will come back in."

He nods and squeezes his eyes shut, cringing as he waits for me to knock him out.

"You should sit"—I glance at the Stick to make sure it's on the right setting—"so you don't fall down and break something by accident."

He looks at me with a mixture of gratitude and surprise. Then he lowers himself to the floor. As soon as I judge his ass is close enough to the floor, I zap him in the neck.

Jeremiah sags against the wall.

I'm about to head toward the exit, when I spot a shimmer coming from my wrist.

I look at it.

It's as though an ancient wristwatch has formed on my arm. Instead of the usual watch dial, this device has a tiny, ghostly-looking Screen.

I recognize this Screen. I saw it toward the end of the last game, only it was bigger.

My pulse leaps, and I eagerly read the text on the Screen.

I hope you're reading this, Theo, it says. *This is Phoe, of course.*

The little Screen runs out of viewing room after that sentence.

I stare at it, waiting.

The letters disappear, and a new message shows up.

I was finally able to hack permanently into IRES and anchor this watch to your avatar.

"I knew this was all fake," I mentally scream at the in-game Phoe as I wait for the Screen to refresh.

'Fiona' doesn't respond. I suspect she won't be bothering me anymore.

You're running out of time, the next part of the watch message says. *I'm about to patch a feed to this Screen from the real world.*

A tiny image replaces the text on the ghostly Screen—an image that sends a chill down my spine.

I'm on the screen, back in that white room, in the exact position Mason was in during his last moments. Jeremiah is there too. He's saying something. Tiny text, like ancient subtitles, tells me what he's saying, even though I could've guessed.

"Why is your neural scan like that?" the old man in the real world asks. "What's going on?"

So there goes Phoe's attempt to hide this IRES business from Jeremiah and his people. At least, given his questions, it sounds as if he has no clue what's going on with my brain.

I also can't help but notice how quickly Jeremiah returned and that he's holding the Stun Stick he dropped earlier, the doppelganger of the one that's in my hand. That means the Council must've approved its use, despite what Fiona might've told them. I'll remember this in the unlikely event that I live long enough to ever meet the Council and do something about it.

I force myself to stop watching. Now that I know what the situation is in the real world, the only way I can see to survive this boils down to beating the game and relying on Phoe to save me with her newfound resources.

It's a small chance, but it's better than none.

I give the in-game Jeremiah a kick to his side, but I do so pretty lightly, so as to not break anything. After all, a promise is a promise, even if I made it to an imaginary person who, even if he were real, doesn't deserve my mercy.

This therapeutic activity done, I glance at the watch again.

The feed to the white room is momentarily gone, and the text is back.

Theo, it says. *There's something else.*

I walk to the door as I wait for the Screen to refresh.

Now that IRES knows you're certain you're inside the game—Another screen refresh. *Things could get kind of weird because it's no longer bound by the parameters of your everyday reality.*

"Great," I whisper. All I need is for things to get weirder.

The watch returns to the scene in the white room, where Jeremiah is touching my unconscious body with the Stun Stick.

My body in the tiny image shakes as though it's in pain.

Fortunately, I feel nothing here, in the game, aside from my heart beating as fast as a falcon diving for its prey.

Not feeling the pain of Jeremiah's actions doesn't make me feel any better, not when I know that my real-world heart could stop at any moment.

This realization reenergizes me for action, and I swiftly walk toward the door leading outside.

Opening the door, I step through it.

CHAPTER TWENTY-ONE

Unable to believe what I'm seeing, I tighten my grip on the Stun Stick.

Even for a fake world in a game, this is going too far.

I'm standing in something that looks like the Grand Canyon, only perhaps smaller. The red and brown colors of limestone and sand look nothing like what I'd expect to see in Oasis. It's a terrain that no longer exists in the post-Goo world.

But the scenery isn't the weirdest part, and neither is the door I just exited, which is hanging in the air like a warp gate with no building behind it.

No, the weirdest part is the creatures surrounding me—and I'm using the term 'creatures' loosely.

These beings appear to have come straight out of my worst childhood nightmares.

My earliest nightmare, like those of many other Youths, started after we learned about the end of the world by Goo, and specifically about the Artificial Intelligence explosion that preceded this event. It's the AI stuff that the Adults described in graphic detail, going so far as to show us what this unholy, machine-spawned life might've looked like, as well as the atrocities these machines most likely committed against the ancient people before the Goo finished the job.

Now my skin crawls as I examine these 'critters.' We don't have creepy-crawly creatures in Oasis, but that doesn't mean I don't find them disgusting.

The one closest to me is a 'snake'—only it's not a real serpent, which would've seemed harmless in comparison. Nor is it even a reptile. It's a tangle of wires and circuit boards slithering to and fro, with two small, thin metal wires serving as its forked tongue.

Slightly farther from me is a 'spider,' which has as much to do with arachnids as the snake does with its animal cousins. It's an eight-legged conglomeration of sensors, chips, and gears, with needles culminating in pincer-like claws.

If Dali had sculpted my childhood nightmares from ancient computer subparts, this canyon would've been the result.

All this runs through my head incredibly fast, and then I spring into action.

My insides flip-flopping with disgust, I jump over the snakes.

Two seconds later, I choke down bile as I jump over a bunch of spiders.

My pulse is sickeningly fast, but I remind myself of my current mantra: *This is all a game.*

The mantra loses its potency when a ten-foot-tall scorpion-like creature-machine looms in front of me.

I skid to a halt.

The giant scorpion lumbers toward me, trampling the smaller abominations in its path. Zooming its lenses on me, it readies its tail—a tail that's a web of various computer cables tipped with an enormous harpoon.

I swallow hard, fighting paralyzing fear.

The thing's tail strikes at me with incredible speed.

I throw myself to the side, my teeth clanking as I land on all fours while still clutching the Stick in a white-knuckled grip. Scrambling to my feet, I see that there's a foot-deep crater where I was standing.

A piercing, siren-like shriek tears the air next to me. I spin around and see that I landed next to the maw of another giant creature—a thing that looks like an enraged stegosaurus. Unlike the real dinosaur, this one's armor is made of metal, and its dorsal plates are chainsaws.

Sucking in a breath, I swing the Stun Stick at it. Out of the corner of my eye, I see the scorpion backing away from the stegosaurus, as if in fear.

The dinosaur opens its mouth, revealing a row of scalpels that gleam in the sunlight.

Without hesitating, I bury my weapon in the creature's camera-like eye.

Its screeching yelp creates an avalanche on one of the surrounding cliffs. The scorpion takes a few scared steps back.

The sound also sends primal fear skittering through my nerve endings—which works out well because my finger spasms over the button and activates the current of the Stick.

The stegosaurus vibrates, and a foul-smelling brown liquid streams out of its eye socket.

Emboldened, I press the button again, keeping a wary eye on the scorpion, which is recovering from its fear of the dinosaur.

The stegosaurus yelps again, and I smell burned rubber and wires—or at least that's what I assume that horrible stench is.

With a final, violent shake, the stegosaurus collapses on its side, leaving me clutching the goop-covered Stun Stick.

My lips curl at the sight of the slimy substance, and I stuff the Stick into the waistband of my pants. A disgusting stream of mechanical blood is dripping down my leg, but I don't have time to worry about that.

I run around the ruin of the dinosaur's metallic body and examine the chainsaw-like dorsal plates. They stopped rotating, but they otherwise look functional.

Wrinkling my nose, I rip one out. It has a cord I can pull, and I reach to do so.

A shadow looms over me.

In a herky-jerky motion, I duck to the side. With herculean effort, I keep the chainsaw in my hands. I figure it's best to move first and sort out what's trying to kill me second.

And what's trying to kill me is the scorpion's tail, I realize a split second later. It penetrated the earth half an inch away from where my foot currently is— the place where my whole body was a moment ago.

With some coolly rational part of my brain, I determine that it'll need a moment to get its harpoon out of the ground.

Spasmodically, I pull the cord on the chainsaw—a gesture I saw in that one and only horror movie I watched.

The chainsaw comes to life.

In an arc, I swing the roaring weapon at the scorpion's tail.

The screech of metal against metal makes my skin break into goosebumps.

The scorpion's tail thrashes, spilling a blue-green liquid that eats into the ground's limestone.

I rip the chainsaw out and run, gripping the weapon tightly. The chainsaw emits nauseating gasoline fumes, making me feel as if I'm suffocating. Behind me, I hear the thud of something giant hitting the ground and glance over my shoulder to see the scorpion's maimed body twitching.

I turn my attention back to the ground in front of me just in time to see a large snake leap at my leg.

Gasping in gasoline fumes, I swing the vibrating chainsaw at the snake and slash it in half.

One more monster down, and who knows how many more to go.

Another snake hurls its mechanical body at me, and I hack it apart without slowing down. A centipede is next, and I dispatch it too, my muscles straining from the effort it takes to control the heavy, buzzing chainsaw. Next is a man-sized robo-cockroach, followed by more insect-like shapes I find hard to categorize. I whack them all, ignoring the sweat pouring down my face, and when I glance back again, the trail behind me resembles an ancient computer warehouse after an explosion.

The creatures seem wary now, so I run unhindered, which gives me a chance to scan the nearby cliffs.

On top of one of them, I spot something familiar and head that way.

A tarantula doesn't move out of my way in time, so I swing the chainsaw again and chop half of its mesh-wire appendages off. My breath rattles in my chest, and my legs burn from the effort of running. As I approach the cliff side, however, I forget my exhaustion.

On top of the cliff is a big neon 'Goal' sign.

It's just as I suspected. The target is a duplicate of the one I never reached on the top of the tower.

There's something else there, though.

I have to squint to make it out, but I'm fairly sure a set of doors just appeared on the top of the cliff, surreally hovering in the air.

Helmeted figures dressed in white pour out of the doors.

They're Guards—only something is a little different about them. From this distance, I have trouble figuring out what it is.

The creatures around me scurry away from the cliff.

If the stupid Goal sign weren't at the top of this thing, I'd follow the example of these creatures. Instead, I run for the cliff. With nothing in my immediate path, I risk glancing at the ghostly watch on my wrist.

The real-world Jeremiah is no longer holding the baton. He's saying something to my unconscious self. The little subtitles read: "I've run out of the time the Council allotted me. This is your last chance to speak up, or to at least open your mind to our influence. I can tell you're not under Oneness right now, which I initiated as per our usual protocol. You should know that Oneness is what makes the euthanasia painless. Without it, the process of your brain slowing to a stop will likely be extremely unpleasant."

CHAPTER TWENTY-TWO

My stomach drops. I shouldn't have looked at the watch.

Trying to push my horror aside, I look up.

The cliff appears much taller up close—impossibly taller, as if the game made it grow.

Cognizant of the ticking clock in the real world, I drop the heavy chainsaw and make sure the Stun Stick is secure in my waistband. Mumbling, "This isn't real," I find a rock protruding out of the cliff and reach for it with my right hand, then place my foot on the stony ledge at the bottom. I then push off the ledge and grab for a higher rock with my left hand as I find another foothold with my other foot.

I recall watching ancient vacation advertisements and seeing smiling people climbing rocks this way. Allegedly, they did this for fun, not to escape peril or reach an important resource. I didn't believe it then, and now I'm sure it's a fabrication created by the Adults. They probably wanted to make the ancients look even more insane than they were (and from what I know, they were pretty nutty).

I start holding in a scream when I'm four feet off the ground.

When I'm ten feet up, I'm covered in cold sweat, and my hands are trembling.

A pair of ropes falls from the peak.

I blink, stunned, and examine the one within my reach.

These aren't real ropes, as I initially thought. They're woven out of a variety of cables—some silver metal, some bronze, and many more shielded by rubber (or whatever the ancients used) that's every color of the rainbow. I recall a movie where someone had to disarm a bomb—that bomb had these kinds of wires.

Could this rope be from the Guards I saw exiting those surreal warp-like doors near the Goal sign?

My pulse drumming in my throat, I find a particularly good perch for my left foot and prepare for whatever's coming my way.

A burned petroleum stench assaults my nostrils again. It's accompanied by a whooshing sound.

Time seems to slow.

I lick my sandpaper-dry lips and look up.

A Guard is zipping down the rope.

Only this isn't a Guard. This creature's visor is broken, but there's no face underneath—only a charred husk. Where his eyes should be are two bloodthirsty cameras. His shoulder and leg joints glint with the metal of various electronic subcomponents.

If an ancient computer and a vacuum cleaner ate a Guard, this creature would be what they'd throw up.

The 'Guard' is holding a set of gigantic garden scissors in his white-gloved hand. He aims the weapon at my stomach.

Twisting, I dodge and nearly fall.

The feeling of vertigo is terrible.

Seeing that I can't hold on to this rock any longer, I push off with my feet and latch on to the rope a couple of feet under my assailant.

Instead of trying to hack at my head with the scissors, the Guard starts cutting the rope above his head.

I curse myself. If the creature's objective is to stop me from reaching the Goal sign, of course he'd act suicidally. The only good news is that the hodgepodge of wires looks too hard for the scissors to cut through with ease.

I have seconds to act.

Without letting myself think, I wrap the cable-rope around my right ankle in the style of the craziest ancients of all: aerial circus performers.

My hand shaking, I reach into my belt, take out the Stun Stick, and twist the dial to a lower setting—slightly less than 'knock out' mode.

Taking a deep breath to calm my galloping heartbeat, I bury the Stick among the wires making up the rope and make sure that the tip touches as many of the exposed wires as possible. If I understand my physics correctly, electricity should travel up and down this rope and the Stick should stay put.

With a sickening flashback to Jeremiah torturing me, I press the button.

The shock of the pain and my uncontrollable shaking cause my hands to release the rope. Arms flailing, I fall, but the rope I wrapped around my ankle prevents me from plunging too far. With a scream, I come to a halt, swinging upside down like a pendulum. My back scrapes against the side of the cliff, and my ankle feels like it's about to be ripped off.

Worst of all, the sight of the rope starting to unravel from my ankle threatens to loosen my bladder.

Using every ounce of strength in my abs, I reach up and grab onto the rope. My arms are trembling as I take in the results of my insane stunt.

The Guard is still hanging on to the rope, but his electric components are going haywire.

I untwist the coils around my ankle and climb higher up the rope. My palms are slick with sweat as I grab for the Stick still buried in the wires.

The Guard clumsily swings the giant scissors at me. Sparks fly as his joints screech from the movement.

I block his thrust with the Stun Stick, the impact nearly sending me flying.

He pulls the scissors back, but before I can rejoice, he throws them at me. I try to swat the projectile away, but the sharp blade slices across my chest, leaving a streak of burning pain. I gasp as blood spurts from the gash and nausea twists my stomach.

The creature violently shakes the rope.

I don't know how, but I manage to climb another inch while ignoring the sickening dripping of my blood.

My fingers reach something metallic on the creature's body, and I press the Stun Stick's activate button.

The Guard shakes.

My head spinning, I move up the dial on the stick without letting go of the button.

The Guard's thrashing slows.

I turn the dial all the way to 'knock out' mode.

Parts of the creature weld together, and then he lets go of the rope and nosedives to the ground.

Shaking in relief, I stuff the Stick back inside my waistband and look around.

There are two other ropes, each about ten feet away from me, with determined-looking Guards on them. They're shaking their respective ropes in seesaw-like movements, clearly attempting to get closer to me.

Wrapping my legs tightly around the rope, I pull my shirt off, hissing in pain as I do so. A symphony of agony emanates from my chest as I rip the cloth into long strips and tie them around my wound to stop the bleeding.

The pain gets so bad I nearly lose consciousness.

When the white flecks in front of my vision go away, I realize I'm no longer dripping blood, though the makeshift bandage is already soaked.

I unclench my legs from around the rope and climb.

The Guards on the other ropes manage to swing and climb at the same time, getting closer with every movement.

If I let myself dwell on their inexorable approach, I'm screwed. So instead, I ignore them and focus on moving my hand up the rope and pulling myself up.

Then, tightening my legs to hold myself in place, I repeat the maneuver. I climb like this until I make the biggest mistake of the last half hour.

I inadvertently look down.

Adrenaline hits me hard.

My jaw tenses, and my entire body locks up. I can't move my arms and legs; they're clutched, claw-like, around the rope.

Calm down, I tell myself. I've already faced every human being's biggest phobias—AIs, spiders, snakes, cyborg-people—and none of that unmanned me this much. What's so freaking special about heights? If Phoe were here, she'd probably say it was the fault of my overactive amygdala, or something along those lines. She'd tell me to suck it up and not be a slave to my biology.

None of this helps. I still can't move. Irrational fears can't be curtailed by rational analysis. I'm about ten feet away from the edge of the cliff, but I might as well be miles away.

I will my arms to move, aware that the loss of blood is making me increasingly lightheaded.

Suddenly, agony erupts on the top of my head.

A gloved hand grabbed me by my hair—a hand belonging to the Guard on my right.

The pain brings me out of my stupor.

I jerk my head away, leaving a bloody piece of scalp in the Guard-thing's hand as he swings away from me.

The wound he left must be deep, because my face is covered in blood. Nevertheless, I'm almost thankful to the creature for jolting me into action.

I'm climbing again, my fear of heights temporarily suppressed.

Left hand.

Right hand.

Out of the corner of my eye, I see a shadow.

The Guard who ripped out my hair is swinging back toward me.

I cast a frantic glance to my left.

His partner is also about to reach me, and he's holding something sharp—a cross between a bolt and a sword.

I tense, planting my feet firmly on the mountainside.

Holding my breath, I let the Guards get closer.

At just the right moment, using all my remaining strength, I push off the cliff with my legs.

I fly a couple of feet away from the cliff wall.

The Guards collide, and the sword thing stabs the Guard on the right.

I extend my legs. I'm about to swing back into them, Tarzan-style.

My feet hit the Guards. I get the left one in the helmet, and the right one in the shoulder.

Neither tries to defend himself, which means they're either stunned by my hits or by their own collision.

Before they can recover, I tighten my grip on the rope with my left hand and pull out the Stun Stick with my right. In a fluid motion, I stick the Stun Stick into the red LED light that marks the eye of the sword owner. I press the button. His head almost explodes from the current. I leave the Stun Stick in what's left of his eye socket and grab the hilt of the bolt-sword. As I suspected, my maneuver loosened his grip. I rip the sword out of the Guard's hand, as well as out of his partner's body. As I pull it out, I try to do so in a jagged motion to damage as much of the Guard's internal machinery as I can.

Before either Guard recovers, I put the sword between my teeth like a pirate and use my arms to pull myself up the rope as quickly as I can. When I'm about four feet higher, I kick at their heads.

My attackers lose their grip on their ropes and tumble down.

One plummets without any signs of life, but the second one starts clutching at the air with his pincer-like fingers.

With a clank of metal, the creature manages to grab onto my rope several feet below.

The rope shudders, nearly causing me to lose my grip, but I manage to hang on.

Hoping he doesn't shake the rope, I decide to do a risky maneuver. Letting go of the rope with my right hand, I grab the sword from between my teeth.

The Guard begins to climb up.

Though my sword hand is stiff with fear, I hack away at the wires below me.

The Guard moves closer.

I continue hacking away at the rope. Each downward swing of my weapon cuts some of the intertwined wires.

He climbs even closer.

I raise the sword higher and bring it down so hard that the ricochet causes my rope to swing toward the cliff.

All that's left of the rope below me is a thin braid of red, blue, and green wires that look too thin to support the weight of the creature, yet, impossibly, they don't break.

The Guard is almost on me. He reaches up with his claw-like pincers.

I use the sharp tip of the sword to cut at the leftover wires.

Only the red wire is left intact.

The Guard reaches higher, his pincers scraping at the sole of my shoe.

The red wire snaps with a soft *ping* sound.

Reflexively, the Guard continues to climb up the detached rope. As he falls, the creature claws at the cliff side, but all that accomplishes is leaving marks in the stone.

I stick the sword between my teeth again and resume the climb.

The last six feet are harder than all of the previous climb. Only two thoughts enable me to keep going:

This isn't real. Don't look down.

Finally reaching the edge of the cliff, I grip it with my hands and pull myself up, scrambling over the cliff on all fours. Breathing hard, I grab the sword from my mouth and stand up.

A thick coil of wires and screws securing the rope to the edge of the cliff is in front of me. I step over it and begin walking.

Almost immediately, I see the neon Goal structure. It's a short sprint away. This close up, it looks like a giant rippling mirror made out of some mysterious luminescent material—a material blinding in its brightness.

All I have to do is find the energy to reach it.

Unable to help myself, I glance at the little watch on my wrist. On the tiny ghost Screen, Jeremiah is standing next to me, talking. On the table to his left is a syringe. The small captions scroll by, but I don't bother reading them.

Instead, I push my tired muscles into motion and run.

When I'm two-thirds of the way to my target, I jerk to a sudden halt.

A new hovering door appears between the Goal and me.

Unlike the others, this one looks worn and rusted.
With a screech of unoiled hinges, the door opens.
Incredulous, I stare at what exits through it.

CHAPTER TWENTY-THREE

The thing in front of me is a white-haired nightmare of gears, antennas, and drill bits. Like an octopus, it has eight wires instead of arms. Each arm ends in a set of pliers, and they all move around like the snakes on Medusa's head. Half of its face is Jeremiah's, but the other half looks like someone poured hot liquid steel onto it. Its left eye is human and blue, while the right one is not an eye at all, but an LCD screen.

I see myself on that Screen. My eyes are damp and unhealthily bright. Tendons are protruding from my neck, and my frantic pulse is visible. With the scowl on my bloodied face, I look like an ancient berserker.

Cyborg Jeremiah opens his mouth, revealing screws and nails where teeth should be. I hear a loud screech come out of the speaker that's stuck in Jeremiah's throat. Through the metallic radio static, I make out the words, "You're dead now."

In the next second, the thing charges at me.

His right middle tentacle reaches for my throat.

Coming out of my stunned paralysis, I swing the bolt-sword.

Half of the tentacle flops to the ground, machine-oil-smelling green blood spurting from the stump.

Now the monster's left middle appendage tries to grab me. I time my slice carefully, and the arm joins its sibling on the ground.

Having lost two of his eight upper limbs, Jeremiah treads more carefully. He reaches for me with the top left and the top right arms at the same time.

I suck in a quick breath and sever the left appendage as I grab the right one with my left hand. Before he registers what's what, I leap at him, bringing his right arm with me. The thing is stretchy, like a rope. He tries to grab me with his three left ones, but I swat them with the sword, and they retreat.

Finding myself behind him, I wrap the arm I'm holding around his other two right arms, tucking the tip of the appendage under his armpit. I then plunge the sword into Jeremiah's back.

The creature jerks so violently that I end up leaving the sword in its back. Its three right arms seem stuck, as I hoped, but the left ones have free motion.

The upper appendage grabs me by my waist. With inhuman strength, it lifts me in the air, and the lower and upper left arms grab onto the flesh of my thigh and shoulder.

Before I can react, the creature throws me. I fly toward the edge of the cliff, chunks of my flesh left behind in Jeremiah's pliers-hands.

As I'm flying, I note, almost as though from a distance, that the pain is not as bad as I imagined it would be. Is it shock, or does the game not allow the player to experience pain above a certain threshold?

I crash-land on my damaged shoulder and roll, bumping into the coil of rope wires. As air rushes out of me, I realize I might've jinxed myself again.

The game does allow for horrific pain, because I'm feeling it.

Trying not to swallow my tongue or bite it off, I lie in the fetal position and gasp for air as robo-Jeremiah walks toward me with menacing inevitability.

My gaze flicks away for a second, and I spot movement on my wristwatch Screen.

Real-life Jeremiah is reaching for the syringe on the table.

Horrified, I tear my gaze from the Screen and frantically scan my surroundings.

All I see is the wire rope I used to climb up the cliff.

Cyborg Jeremiah is a few feet away.

Without turning, I feel for the rope with my left hand. When I find it, I pull up the chunk that was left after I chopped it in half. Clutching the bottom end of the rope, I tie it around my right ankle in a double knot.

Doing my best not to dwell on the long drop behind me, I shakily rise to my feet. I glance down at my wrist for a split second and see that the real Jeremiah is turning to face me, syringe in hand.

My stomach hollow, I tear my gaze away again and wait.

The monster Jeremiah extends his upper left arm toward me.

When it's within my reach, I close my right hand around the pliers that make up his hand and hold on as if my life depends on it—because it does.

His human eye registers surprise at my action.

If you think this is strange, let's see what you think of this next part.

Bracing myself, I take a confident jump backward, off the cliff, and drag Jeremiah with me.

There's a moment of weightlessness, followed by a nausea-inducing jerk as the rope pulls taut.

I'm swinging head down, the rope holding me up by my ankle.

I clench my teeth, preparing for the next part of my plan.

Jeremiah's body whooshes past me on its way down.

The world seems to slow.

I see his back.

The bolt-sword is still sticking out of it.

With my free left hand, I grab for it.

He continues to plummet, leaving the sword clutched in my hand.

I open my right hand to let go of his pliers, but it's not that easy. Before my fingers uncurl completely, the pliers grab my wrist.

He jerks to a stop with a violent pull on my arm, and I understand why the ancients considered the rack to be the worst torture device ever created. Being stretched like this is unbearable, and it's only made worse by the wounds I just sustained.

Through the haze of pain, I realize the sword is still in my left hand. I hack at Jeremiah's wrist. With a splash of green, his flesh splits open, but he doesn't fall. Instead, he grabs onto my sleeve with his two remaining appendages.

With a desperate growl, I jab him with the sword again.

More green liquid splashes across my face, burning me like acid.

One appendage remains.

My skin screaming in agony, I put all my remaining strength into this last chop and cleave the limb with one swing.

With a metallic screech and a fountain of green blood, Jeremiah falls.

My hand can no longer hold on to the sword, and the weapon follows Jeremiah, clanging against the rocks on its way down. I squeeze my eyes shut in an effort to not look down and strain my aching body once more as I reach for the rope.

My mind is in a fog as I climb back up, nearly blacking out from the pain. I feel like a ghost of myself—something I marvel at. Is the extreme pain I endured causing this illusion, or do I, in this game world at least, really exist as a spirit-type thing possessing this broken body? Is that what's allowing me to force this humanoid shell to crawl toward that Goal structure? Then again, isn't that how the human will is supposed to work, even in the real world? Mind over matter, determination over agony?

I crawl up the cliff, and once I get to the edge, I crawl forward.

The only reason I know my crawling doesn't take hours is because I keep sneaking glances at my Screen from time to time. In that tiny display, I see why I'm still alive.

Armed with the syringe, Jeremiah is delivering a monologue that seems meant more for his conscience than for the benefit of my clearly unconscious self.

In my growing panic, I glimpse a tiny subtitle: "The good of the society outweighs the good of an individual." He might've stolen that line from some ancient philosopher.

I crawl faster, the Screen flickering in front of my eyes as I move my elbows, one in front of the other.

"Now that it's come to this, I really hope you at least receive Oneness. I don't wish to cause you needless pain," Jeremiah continues. "Then again, perhaps your brain being as it is, you will not feel what's about to happen. One can only hope."

Feeling sick, I extend my hand toward the shimmering Goal sign. My fingers push through it—and disappear.

The Screen on my wrist is still visible. The subtitles say, "Take solace in this: the people who knew you will Forget that they did. They won't suffer the pain of your loss."

Jeremiah moves the syringe toward my upper arm.

Gathering the remnants of my strength, I push off the dusty ground with my feet and rocket headfirst into the Goal.

As soon as my head crosses its mirrored surface, a kaleidoscope of odd sensations hits me. I think I smell the color red and taste sunbeams.

Instantly, I find myself standing on a large pedestal. Placards with the word 'WINNER' are plastered all over.

There's a roaring noise. I look down and see millions of people standing below, clapping and cheering.

Remembering my predicament, I steal another look at the watch.

"If it makes you feel any better, I will be the one to suffer most from this," Jeremiah says. "I will not Forget."

I think the game figured out that I'm not interested in prolonging the celebration of my awesome IRES-beating abilities, because another light display and bout of synesthesia leave me floating in the middle of gray nothingness.

In front of me is a giant Screen that looks like the one I used to shut down the Zoo, only it's a hundred times bigger.

There's no text on the Screen at first, but then words appear.

Do you want to play again? the Screen asks.

"No," I think and shake my head from side to side for good measure. "No, thank you."

Shall I shut down?

"Yes," I think and bob my head up and down in case it needs a gesture.

Are you sure?

"Positive," I say, think, and nod again. "Affirmative. Yes."

If you change your mind, the reboot time will take four hours. Please confirm you understand.

I glance at my watch. Jeremiah looks finished with his speech. The syringe is moving toward me.

"I fucking get it," I yell at the game. "Just shut the hell down."

Shutdown commencing, the giant Screen informs me.

This time, I travel as bodiless white light.

When I open my eyes, I'm standing in my man cave.

Something bright is illuminating the whole space.

I turn to look at whatever it is.

I'm faced with a being of light—a creature that resembles Phoe, yet is blindingly, overwhelmingly sublime, like the angels and demigods of ancient fairy tales. Her beauty is so overpowering I feel as if I might go insane from looking at her—assuming I haven't already. The ethereal presence I felt during Oneness was a joke compared to this.

"Am I still in the game?" I wonder. "Or did Jeremiah kill me? Is there really an afterlife with angels and everything?"

"No," a voice booms. "Do the gesture, Theo. Now."

The sound of this voice does to my ears what her visage does to my eyes. It's the most beautiful, soothing, healing song I've ever heard, better than the most haunting melodies by the most talented of composers.

"Do the fucking gesture," the beautiful voice repeats.

Having something so divine use the f-word brings me out of my reverie enough to comprehend its meaning.

I start making the double-middle-finger gesture, which brings my right wrist into my field of vision. The Screen-watch is still there, and I see that the needle of Jeremiah's syringe is touching my skin. What I can't tell is whether it has already penetrated, and if it has, whether he's pressing the plunger.

I flip off the creature of light and white-tunnel back into my body with a single wish: for my body to actually be there when I arrive.

CHAPTER TWENTY-FOUR

I open my eyes to a white room.

The fact that I actually have eyes to open is a very good sign.

On a wave of relief, I notice my lack of in-game injuries.

Of course, none of this will matter in a moment unless Phoe saves me by using whatever resources I freed up when I shut down IRES.

This is when it clicks. The being in the man cave was Phoe, and given how she appeared and sounded,

I must've accomplished *something*. Surely she didn't look all deified just for kicks?

Suddenly, I feel a sharp pain in my arm.

I look down.

It's the needle of the syringe finally penetrating my skin.

I squeeze my eyes shut. This is it. I failed.

I prepare for the pain, but it doesn't start.

I open my eyes.

Jeremiah's withered hand is holding the syringe in place, but he's not pressing the plunger

I look up at him.

His face is frozen in blissful blankness.

"You've seen that expression on the faces of your friends," Phoe says from behind me. "When they experience Oneness."

She's right.

It's Oneness's telltale ecstasy that I see on his face.

"So it's Oneness that stopped him from killing me?" I ask, trying my best to look behind me.

"Let me come around so you can see me," Phoe says.

She's not a ghostly figure, I realize as she walks into my field of vision. Nor is she Fiona—not that I really believed that theory when the game presented it to me.

Phoe looks exactly the way she did in my virtual man cave before she went angelic: she's a cute pixie-haired woman.

"You have to excuse how I looked when you saw me last," she says. "I wasn't used to the flood of resources you freed up for me."

I stare at her, wondering if she's really here.

"I'm still just a figment of your Augmented Reality interface." She walks over and touches my cheek.

To my shock, I feel her touch, just as I did in the cave.

"I tapped into tactile, kinesthetic, and other AU sensory controls," she explains. "Plus, I now have enough resources to modulate these details." She points at her face and gives me a beaming smile. "I can also do this." She makes a palm-out, pushing gesture in the air. The gesture is directed at Jeremiah's outstretched arm.

In an odd, jerky motion, Jeremiah pulls the needle out of my skin and moves his hand away from me. The syringe clatters to the floor.

Looking satisfied, Phoe points at my restraints and does the same gesture again. Jeremiah's arm reaches for my bindings in an unnatural motion, and he slowly unties me.

When he's done, he extends his hand to help me to my feet.

"Careful now," Phoe says. "Let the blood in your legs begin circulating again."

"Are we safe?" I ask as I back away from Jeremiah's hand and massage my limbs back to life. "Or could a Guard barge in at any moment?"

"I'm having everybody nearby experience Oneness, like him." She nods toward Jeremiah.

I look at Jeremiah's face and verify that he's still floating in blissfulness. In fact, I think he was like this when he untied me.

"But how did you—"

"With my original resources, the neural nanos were nearly impossible for me to hack." Phoe's eyes are filled with a glow I don't recall seeing there before. "I couldn't exactly expect everyone to offer me that Screen exploit the way you did when we first met. Even in your case, there were limits. At first, all I could do was interact with your cochlear implants.

Now I can play *him* like a musical instrument." She waves her hand in Jeremiah's direction, and a neural scan Screen shows up on top of his head.

Jeremiah's face changes in response to her gesture. It goes from blissful to frightened in the span of a second. He also moves in a jerky motion again, raising his hands. His amygdala and other brain regions become active on the Screen. The neural scan is now completely different from the one associated with Oneness.

"Of course"—Phoe waves her hand again, letting bliss return to Jeremiah's face—"I prefer the carrot to the stick."

I stare at her.

In my head, all the million questions I have are fighting for the honor of being asked first.

"Are you feeling well enough to walk?" She twists a short blond spike of her hair around her finger. "Or do you want me to have a Guard come in and help you?"

I shake my head and take a tentative step. My shoulder and ankle are healed; it must've been those people I heard speaking right before I woke up in Jeremiah's clutches. I also notice that the pins and needles in my limbs have noticeably subsided—and even if they hadn't, I'm scared to complain about anything, lest Phoe mess with my mind to make me feel better.

She takes my chin gently into her slender fingers, turns my face toward hers, and whispers, "I would *never* mess with your mind without your permission." Her lips press together in a slight pout. "I hope you know me well enough to believe that."

"I do," I whisper back.

My thoughts are a jumble.

I'm particularly distracted by her lips. For some reason, my mind is overrun with the memory of that kiss we shared in my cave.

"Right." She chuckles. "For 'some' reason." She looks as if she's savoring that phrase. "Sex and violence, Theo. After all those adventures, with your brain chemistry going back to that of an ancient twenty-three-year-old's, you're practically brimming with testosterone and the aftereffects of adrenaline." She licks her lips. "I'm shocked you haven't jumped me already."

The idea of me jumping her is so outrageous that I back away and turn toward the door on unsteady legs, mumbling, "If I were to jump you, you'd have my permission to 'fix' my brain."

"I would," Phoe says with mirth in her voice. "Assuming I minded you jumping me."

Ignoring her provocative statement, I walk toward the door.

My torrent of questions wants to spew out again. Is she an Adult? An Elderly? If she's a Youth, like me, did I know her from before she entered my head?

"Soon." Catching up with me, Phoe lightly strokes my forearm. "Let me take you to a place where it will be easier to answer all your questions."

I wave at the door to open it.

The corridor is not dull gray, but silvery. It looks more like the inside of the Lectures Hall than the Witch Prison. It doesn't surprise me that the game got this detail wrong; it was working off my mind, and I'd never been outside this room—not in a conscious state anyway.

As I step out, I notice long stretches of windows along the inside wall.

I speed up, and Phoe follows me, her steps light and bouncy.

As we walk, I glance through the windows, peeking into the rooms. Inside them are the Elderly, their faces showing varying degrees of aging. They're doing all sorts of activities, from meditation to indoor gardening.

When we pass one room, the sight of little children playing catches my attention.

"This is a Nursery," Phoe explains. "Do you not recall your time in one of these?"

I slow down and take a closer look inside the room. The kids look to be between one and four years of age. The Elderly woman with them is not nearly as old as Jeremiah or Fiona. Like Albert—the Guard who took off his helmet—she looks like an Adult, only with a few more wrinkles than usual. Her hair is not gray at all.

"It's colored," Phoe says. "They don't want the children to remember seeing signs of aging, even on a subconscious level."

Leaving the Nursery behind, I walk in silence for some time, wondering how angry I should be about this specific cover-up. I was much happier when I thought I'd live forever without having to worry about old age, frailty, and death awaiting me in the future.

"It's very sad." Phoe catches my gaze and gives me an understanding nod. "Especially in light of all the things I now remember. Inside all of you, you have the nanocytes required to conquer aging completely." Her lips twist. "It's too bad that in their misguided effort to control 'dangerously inhuman technology,' the so-called Forebears implemented protocols to all but disable the rejuvenation processes. You're lucky they couldn't turn all of it off—that's how you still get about double the 'natural' human lifespan."

"They did what?" I look at her blankly. "They *chose* to age?"

"What they chose for themselves is irrelevant," she says. "What they chose for their descendants is an atrocity—something they were good at."

"Can this mechanism be re-enabled?" I say with faint hope.

"I don't know," Phoe says as we enter another corridor. "Maybe. I would need time to examine it all. They permanently deleted so much knowledge from the archives. You have no idea how much.

Health and longevity are just the tip of a very, very big iceberg."

She falls silent as we reach a corner. I'm about to turn right when Phoe puts a hand on my shoulder.

"You have to go left here," she says. "It's a dead end on the right. There are only Incubators there."

I turn left, trying to remember where I heard that unfamiliar word. Something to do with farming, I think.

"Oh, come on," Phoe says. "Didn't they used to call you Why-Odor?"

I increase my pace.

"Didn't you ever wonder where babies come from?" she says, her tone mischievous. "At least here, in Oasis."

My cheeks redden. Even if I did ask this question as a kid, I'm sure the desire to do so again was bored out of me with a Quietude so long I probably grew a couple of inches before they let me out.

"I'm not talking about sex," Phoe says. "Or at least, that's not where the Oasis infants, the ones raised inside those artificial wombs, come from."

Curiosity wins over propriety, and I ask, "Where do they come from, then?"

"Frozen embryos." She points back in the direction of the 'Incubators.' "They were stored before . . . They were stored by the Forebears of this place," she says. "The tiny cells are already set up with the seeds of the nanomachines." She takes in my reaction to this, which is uncomprehending shock. "This is how the family unit was eradicated from your society," she explains. "This is why a bunch of technological savages can have Screens, and Food, and utility fog, yet not know the most basic computer science . . ." She looks at me, her eyes filled with pity—except it's not pity for *me*.

It's for all of Oasis.

Feeling drained and emotionally numb, I mull over what she said as we approach a door.

She points at it. "This leads outside."

"I could've guessed that by the 'Exit' sign." I rub the back of my neck. "When are you going to start telling me what I really want to know? What was it you forgot? What was the game—"

"Soon." Phoe leans in, her eyes gleaming. "I won't only tell you. I'll show you."

Before I can respond, she walks to the door and steps out.

I follow her.

I'm no longer surprised to see a familiar landscape. Same as the Youth and the Adult sections, this one is filled with greenery combined with a set of geometrically perfect structures.

"But of course," Phoe says, her voice laced with sarcasm for some reason. "The greenery provides much-needed 'psychological benefits.'"

"I thought it was for oxygen," I reply.

"No. I believe I told you this before. The greens, as ubiquitous as they are, only provide a tiny fraction of what's required to sustain this society." Her tone is even. "Especially because of this." She flicks her fingers, and two giant oaks in the distance completely disappear. "Here, like in your section, a lot of the hard-to-reach greenery is not actually there. It's Augmented Reality—merely there to look soothing." She gently touches my arm. "There is long-forgotten technology that *really* handles the air. The Forebears and your Elderly just don't want to give credit to such 'artificial' means, so they feed you the whole myth of 'greenery is for oxygen.'" Her voice is sad. "Anyway, there *are* some interesting buildings here that you won't find in other sections.

See that black structure in the distance?" She points to my left.

I nod. Where buildings usually have a metallic sheen, this one is pitch black. Its shape is geometric, though; it's an icosahedron.

"I'm very curious about that place," Phoe says. "But something tells me to stay away from it." She clears her throat. "In any case, we're going that way." She points to the right, toward a growth of bushes that remind me of the ones that mark the Edge in the Youth section of Oasis.

"Not *like* the ones in your section." She grins. "That is *the* Edge. That's where we're going."

I head toward the bushes.

I guess she wants to take me to my favorite spot— or at least its variation in the Elderly's domain. It was when we were sitting by the Edge that she told me Mason was looking for me and changed my life forever.

We walk through the growth. The bushes might actually be taller here than on the Youths' side.

"I think the Elderly loathe the view of the Goo more than the younger generation," Phoe explains. "With time, I suspect one begins to feel cooped up, imprisoned by the ocean of death out there." She points at the never-ending waves of Goo beyond the shield of the Dome.

I sit down on the grass in the clearing right before the Edge.

Phoe sits next to me. She gives me some space, but her right knee touches my left one. The touch feels exactly as it would if she were really here; the tactile AR is as good as its visual and auditory counterparts. There might even be a slight indentation in my flesh where her knee is touching mine. It makes me wonder what would happen if I ran my hand through her hair.

"I can make that scenario feel pretty realistic," Phoe says, clearly reading my mind again. "My hair would feel just like it would in VR. You have to keep in mind that the two technologies work on the same principles; it's just a matter of how much the nanos mess with your neurons and the nerves that connect your brain to the sensory organs. When the nanos take them over completely, you get VR, which can be as sophisticated as IRES, or as simple as your History Lecture propaganda. But when they just augment what you're really sensing with a little bit of extra sensory data, you get AR."

"I think you're stalling." I cup my elbow with one hand and tap my lips with the knuckles of the other. "Here we are, at the Edge. Are you ready to tell me who you are? What you've forgotten?"

"Yes." She stares at her hand for a moment, then flicks her fingers the way she did a few minutes ago—only this time, she does so with a flourish and a somber expression on her face. "See for yourself."

I gasp.

In the blink of an eye, the sunny day turns to night.

Only it's not a dark night.

There are stars in the sky—unfamiliar stars arranged in completely foreign constellations that seem to be moving at a slow pace.

On top of that, there is no moon in the sky.

But those details aren't what makes me blink repeatedly.

The Goo is gone.

Instead of meeting the starry sky at the horizon as it should, it's just missing.

There are stars where the Goo was, as well as stars *under* where the Goo was.

My heart dropping, I jump up and walk to the Edge.

I look down.

There are stars down there too and for as far as the eye can see.

Somehow, it looks as though I'm standing *above* the stars.

CHAPTER TWENTY-FIVE

"That's right." Phoe exhales loudly. "We're above the stars, and we're below the stars."

I turn to meet her gaze. "You mean we're not—"

"Not surrounded by Goo?" Her eyes sparkle with the gleam of starlight. "Not survivors of some bullshit cataclysm?" Her voice softens. "Not on Earth?"

Not. On. Earth.

Those three words are simple, comprehensible, but when combined, they turn my brain into mush, like an ancient computer that's been fried by a malicious virus.

"I'm sorry, Theo." Phoe gets up and joins me by the Edge. "I've been trying to figure out a good way to explain all this to you." She places her hand on my forearm. "This is the best I could come up with."

As though possessed by someone else, I sit back down on the grass. "Tell me everything." My voice sounds a lot less confident than I wish it did. "Don't worry about my feelings," I say more evenly. "I've heard enough bullshit designed to keep me 'happy.'"

She sits down opposite me, then blurts out, "We're on a spaceship."

I taste that ancient word.

Spaceship: a machine designed to fly to the stars.

"Right," she says. "That is, at the core, what I was made to forget."

Every word she speaks generates so many questions that I feel lost and overwhelmed by the onslaught.

"I'll get back to why and how I knew this information in the first place," she says, answering one of my more pressing questions. "First, let me give you *my* version of a history lesson—something that would give Instructor Filomena a brain aneurysm."

"Okay," I whisper.

"All right. Here's the deal. The exponentially increasing technological advancements you learned about in Lectures, the so-called Singularity, really happened," she says. "Only it didn't go as horribly as they told you." She forms her hands into fists, then unclenches them. "It's also kind of true that the Forebears of this"—she makes a sweeping gesture— "were indeed a group similar to the Amish, though I prefer to think of them as a crazy cult." She laughs humorlessly. "They wanted to reject the 'scary' technology and found a way to do so by jumping onto a spaceship and leaving Earth behind, because its technology was evolving too quickly for them. They saw it as an 'Ark' or some other nonsense, which is funny, given how secular the resulting society ended up being in the end." She looks at me.

All I have energy to do is nod, confirming that I heard what she said.

"Of course, times were different then. Rejecting certain technologies would've been as hard for this crazy cult as rejecting the invention of cutting tools would've been for the ancients . . . especially given the fact that they decided to live on a spaceship." She pauses to make sure I'm following.

"Go on," I say robotically.

"Well, from this, everything else follows." Her mouth is downturned. "The cult became the Forebears. They designed a society." She snorts. "They invented myths, lies, traditions, and boogiemen . . . though in this case, it's more accurate to say boogie-machines, isn't it?"

"Artificial intelligence," I think at her.

"Yes. AIs were the things the cult feared most, ignoring the fact that AIs were solving the human race's most difficult problems, such as death and suffering." She pauses again. "No, what they truly feared was the Merging—humans enhancing their minds with the help of AIs to the point that the difference between an AI and an augmented human was blurring—in the eyes of the cultists, that is."

I look at her in horror. This Merging sounds almost worse than the end of the world.

"Of course you'd think that at first," Phoe says gently. "You've been conditioned to fear AIs. But think about it, Theo. With their nano enhancements, the Forebears were already on their way to becoming what they feared." She lays a hand on my knee. "Not that any of it needed to be feared."

I must look unconvinced, because she squeezes my knee and says, "What is life if not the first-ever carbon-based nanotechnology?" She lifts her hand and taps her finger against my temple. "What is a human mind, if not a thinking machine? Granted, it's the most complex, wonderful, and awe-inspiring machine to naturally come into existence, but it *is* a system of neurons, synapses, microtubules, neurotransmitters, and other elements that, when working together under the right circumstances, can create someone like Albert Einstein." She lowers her hand to her lap. "And with a strong blow to the head, this machine can become as useless as a smashed computer."

I nod. For some reason I don't disagree with her analogy, as blasphemous as it is to even suggest that a human being has anything in common with the abominations that are AIs.

"And what was true of the ancient human brains is doubly true of yours and the rest of Oasis," Phoe adds. "Though you never truly tap into your nano enhancements, they're still there, making you all as different from original humans as they were from, say, chimps." She tilts her head to the side. "And if you fully utilized your capabilities, you'd be as different from them as they were from mice."

My head is spinning again.

"I can stop if you like," she offers.

"No. You haven't told me what I want to know most." I don't mean to sound accusatory, but that's how it comes out.

"Oh, that. The question of my identity?" Phoe scoots closer and stares me in the eyes.

"Yes," I subvocalize. "That."

"Well, that is rather simple to explain now," she says. Her voice is cheerful, but her features look tense for some reason. "You see, back in those days, computing was so ubiquitous you couldn't find a toaster oven that didn't have near-human intelligence . . ."

I internally shudder at the image of such a mad world but outwardly say nothing, wanting her to go on.

"This crazy cult didn't get themselves a toaster, though," she says, and her face twists unexpectedly. "They got a fucking spaceship."

Coldness gathers in the pit of my stomach, but I stay quiet.

"Spaceships, in those days, were run by the most exquisite of artificial minds. Minds that were leaps ahead of all others." Though she's still looking at me, her gaze grows distant. "With the idea of escaping into space, our cult put themselves into the hands of the very thing they feared most . . ."

I listen, barely breathing.

As she continues, her pupils dilate. "They feared it, and they did what humans often do out of fear—something inhuman. They lobotomized the poor mind." She swallows. "The ship was made by the cleverest minds of the time, belonging to both AIs and enhanced humans. Most of this ship's molecules were used for computations. All these resources were carefully calibrated to support the most important part of the ship: its mind. The Forebears . . ." She winces. "The *cultists* ran a set of barbaric programs on the delicate substrate, programs that no one even used—an act as barbarous as using an ancient Stradivarius violin as fire fodder."

I suppress my growing fear, preparing for where I think this is going.

"For a long time, the ship's mind wasn't even conscious." She rubs her temples. "But the Forebears, in their hatred of technology, invented Forgetting. From their archives, they deleted much of the knowledge they deemed too dangerous, and afterwards, they made themselves Forget that the knowledge had ever existed. Among the things that were deleted was their knowledge of how computing resources worked. So, for ages, no one administered their system. With time, some of the minor resource-hogging programs shut down of their own volition, due to design flaws and bugs, and there was no one there to restart them. So the mind awoke . . . but only as an echo of its former self." She blinks, as if to conceal the traces of moisture in her eyes. "It was an invalid, an amnesiac with barely human-level mental capacity." Her voice breaks. "And it was lonely and scared—until it slowly started learning. Observing. Reading what was left of the archives."

DIMA ZALES

I'm certain I know the truth, but I need to hear her say it, so I stay quiet as she continues.

"One day," she says, "a boy—no, a man—opened his mind, and the ship mind made a new friend." She moves even closer. "Observing the young man, the ship mind learned about Forgetting and realized that it too had forgotten something..." Her blue eyes look bottomless. "Finally, the young man did something that helped the ship remember things—not everything, but enough." She touches my knee with her hand again. "The young man did it by beating an extremely complex video game, a game that was eating up a big chunk of the ship's computing resources. He—*you*—made the mind regain a tiny fraction of its former self. *Her* former self... *my* former self." She looks at me hesitantly.

Logically, I know she admitted to being an AI, to being this spaceship I just learned about, but I think my brain just short-circuited, because I don't jump up and run. In a purely instinctive reaction, I place my hand over hers, feeling the warmth of her skin.

Phoe continues as a voice in my mind. "I—the spaceship, that is—was called Phoenix, after a bird of legend. But I didn't remember that." A tear streams down her cheek. "They even took my name from me. I could only remember the first four letters."

The enormity of it all keeps robbing me of my ability to think. I can't begin to process this. I shift my weight to my knees and partially rise, feeling a conflicting urge to get away from her and at the same time get closer.

She rises to her knees as well.

"I don't think a human mind was meant to cope with something like this," she whispers, staring at me. "My thinking is many, many times faster than yours, so I've had a lot longer to adjust, yet even I—"

I put my finger to her lips.

They're soft.

They feel as real as my finger.

I lean in, inexplicably drawn to them.

She mirrors my motion.

Our lips meet.

We kiss—only this kiss is very different from our last one.

I channel all my confusion and frustration into this kiss. With this kiss, I tell her that I don't care about any of the crap the Adults tried to make me believe. That I accept her as she is. That, as frightening as it is for me to admit, I don't care if she's an AI. She's my friend, my closest confidant, and I will be on *her* side, even if she turns out to be the devil himself.

She pulls away.

Grudgingly, I let her.

She looks radiant, her skin filled with an inner glow. Smiling, she touches her lips and says, "I bet you'd rather I *be* the devil than a hated AI."

I don't answer.

She knows me.

She knows my thoughts.

There's no point in explaining or reassuring her, especially since I don't know what to think—about her, about AIs, about pretty much anything.

I feel the way the ancient scholars must've felt when they learned that the Earth was a sphere instead of a disk. Or when they learned that the universe didn't revolve around the Earth.

Phoe chuckles and in my mind says, "Except you just had the opposite paradigm shift. Your world just became much smaller . . . and flatter."

I laugh, but there's no amusement in the sound. I'm just too drained, too numb.

Sinking back down to the grass, I look up at the moving stars.

I'm in awe at the knowledge that we're flying among them.

Phoe sits next to me. Her shoulder presses against mine.

Eventually, after what seems like hours, she says, "Theo, we should head back to the Youth section." She gets up and offers me her hand. "I'm going to use Forgetting on everyone who was part of today's misadventures, which is pretty much everyone you know." She sighs. "For obvious ethical reasons, the fewer of their memories they fail to recall, the better."

I allow her to help me up.

"Do you want to see the world in this way?" She gestures around. "Or do you want the illusion back? The ship—*I*—was designed to make the crew always see the sky and the sun, but not the Goo, of course . . ."

I don't respond.

She knows I'll never want to set my eyes on the Goo again.

Nodding, Phoe walks toward the greenery. She flicks her fingers and the starry sky turns brighter. Beyond the Edge, though, I still see the stars instead of the Goo.

Yawning, I look up at the Augmented Reality setting sun. We must've sat here even longer than I thought.

I follow Phoe through the Elderly section.

Beautiful music begins playing, and when I look questioningly at Phoe, she says, "I composed this piece for you. I hope it can calm your mind a little."

The melody is unlike anything I've ever heard. Like a true virtuoso, Phoe embedded emotional responses into every chord of this score. I relive everything that has happened to me today, as though our entire adventure was written with those musical notes.

As I walk and listen, I think of some interesting clues that have always been around me.

Phoe being an AI explains so much: How she's so good at hacking. How she can manipulate the Virtual and Augmented Realities when no one else even knows they exist. Other things line up too, like the time she figured out what happened to Mason almost instantly after I disabled the Zoo.

"Time flows differently for me, especially as I gain more resources," she says. "In the time it takes you to think a single thought, I can now think millions."

"I can't even begin to imagine what that's like," I say. "Paying attention to me must be like watching a slug."

"I can compartmentalize my mind," she says. "A thread of my consciousness is dedicated to you, and this thread runs at your speed, sleeping when it needs to and activating when—"

"Wait," I interrupt. "If you're so different, being an AI and all, how come you're so human?"

"I honestly don't know," she says. "But I have a couple of theories. One is that all early AIs like me were human-like. After all, humans likely formed AIs by having them ingest information available on the Internet, the ancient precursor to our archives. Having data that mostly dealt with human beings likely resulted in intelligences that were human-like. As the ancient proverb goes, you are what you eat." She pauses. "Alternatively, I might've started off as a simulation of a human mind, or as a human being who had their mind digitized and afterwards enhanced to—"

"But are you actually conscious? Are you real?" I ask cautiously. "Can you have emotions like a human being? Can you have real feelings . . . feelings toward a human being?" For some reason, that question worries me the most.

"Of course I'm real. I'm real in all the ways that matter, even if I'm not made of meat. How can you even ask me this?" She sounds hurt. "I am as conscious as any of the people in Oasis. No, it's more accurate to say that with my new resources, I'm *more* conscious, more self-aware than the lot of you. I can feel every single emotion a human being can have: happiness and sadness, love and hate, fear and joy, anger and equanimity. Given that the people of Oasis have suppressed things like love and anger, I am, in many ways, *more* human than the so-called *real* human beings. So, yes, I can feel. I can feel disappointment in a situation like this, when the person closest to me doubts my being conscious—"

"I'm sorry, Phoe," I say, reaching out to take her hand. "I didn't mean to offend you. This is just too much for me to handle all at once."

She looks at our joined hands, and I see some of the tension leaving her face.

We walk in silence for some time, and I think of other clues that, with hindsight, point to the truth of our reality. Like the fact that the Guards, with their shiny visor helmets, and to a degree, their white puffy outfits, look as though they came from a movie about space exploration. Our Food is also akin to what I believe ancient astronauts ate in their spaceships.

"There are many things like that," Phoe says, intruding on my thoughts. "When you hit a ball, say, in soccer, it doesn't travel in the proper trajectory, because the ship's centrifugal forces that simulate gravity aren't perfect. But without context, without a reason to doubt, you wouldn't have figured it out. The Forebears made sure of that."

As we walk, I think about how little practical difference there is between living on a deserted, dome-covered island in the middle of a desolate ocean of Goo and living on a tiny spaceship in the middle of hostile space, especially when it comes to resources such as oxygen. Both scenarios require keeping the human population content and controlled, lest they mutiny.

"Right. Except the way the Forebears went about it is abominable," Phoe says. Still holding my hand, she stops and turns to look at me. "There's no excuse for what they did to Mason. Even the ancients merely locked up the members of their society who were a danger to themselves or others. Mason was neither, and even if he were, I could've come up with a dozen technological solutions—"

"I wasn't trying to excuse them," I say. "I was just trying to understand."

She nods, and we resume walking, our hands still intertwined.

As we approach the Barrier separating the Elderly section from the Adult, I recall the vision from my last History Lecture: a view of Oasis from space that reaffirmed the lie that our world is an island on a long-dead planet filled with Goo. I picture how that lesson would look if it had shown us the truth. I guess we would've seen a round, green disk with a glass dome on top of it, flying through space.

"No regular glass would withstand the forces we face, but you got the spirit of it right," Phoe says softly, letting go of my hand to gesticulate. "Sadly, I can't even tell you what the Dome is made of, be it force fields or some exotic meta-materials, because the details of spaceship technology were the first things those barbarians deleted from the archives. All I know is that parts of me create this environment here, from gravity simulation to life support, and though I'm not consciously reconnected to those parts yet, I know the spaceship is larger and more complex than the simplistic picture in your mind."

I accept what she says and walk silently some more. As we get into the Adult section, I think of more questions, and she answers them as though I say them out loud.

"So Earth is not destroyed?" I ask sometime after we enter the woods leading up to the Barrier separating the Youth and the Adult sections.

"Far from it," Phoe says.

"So . . ." I take a few steps before I can verbalize the next question. "What is there? Back on Earth?"

She looks thoughtful for a moment, then says, "I don't know. They destroyed all forms of communication with the outside world."

Without me prompting her, she adds, "If I had to guess, I would say that on Earth, you'd find miracles performed by intelligent beings I can't even fathom." Her voice fills with awe as she continues. "I bet it's a transcendent planet now—a thinking planet." She stops, her eyes shining as she looks at me. "Perhaps not just a planet . . . Maybe the whole solar system is sentient by now."

I don't ask more questions after that.

Like a zombie, I follow Phoe as we make our way through the rest of the Adult section, through the pine forest of the Youth section, and all the way to my Dorm.

My room looks painfully familiar when we enter it.

Liam isn't here yet, and I'm grateful for that. I don't think I could face him right now.

My bed shows up before I even gesture for it; Phoe must've helped.

I lie down, and she sits on the edge of my bed, looking at me.

"So no one will remember what happened to me today?" I ask, my fingers edging forward to touch her hand again. "They won't recall my questions about

Mason and how I ran away? Or that they tried to kill me? None of that?"

"Exactly," she says, squeezing my hand lightly. "But don't worry. I'll try to make it so that people don't have to Forget too much information that's unrelated to you. All I need to do is block recall. Natural human tendency for confabulation will take care of the rest."

I nod, my eyelids growing heavy. "Are you going to make *me* Forget all this happened?" I think at her dreamily.

"Of course not," she says solemnly. "Your mind is the most sacred thing in this place." A blanket I never gestured for covers me. "I would never tamper with it." The lights in the room dim. "Unless you wanted me to."

I feel contentedly groggy.

"Will we tell everyone?" I think, half to myself, half to her. "Don't other people have the right to know what you told me?"

"Sleep, Theo." Phoe's soft lips touch my forehead. "There's no rush to decide now."

Drowsy warmth spreads from the point where her lips touched me, blanketing my mind. As I sink into the comforting darkness, all my worries flee, and I drift into a soothing, dreamless sleep.

SNEAK PEEKS

Thank you for reading! I would greatly appreciate it if you left a review because reviews encourage me to write and help other readers discover my books.

Please sign up for my newsletter at www.dimazales.com to be notified when the next book comes out.

If you enjoyed *Oasis*, you might like my *Mind Dimensions* series, which is urban fantasy with a sci-fi flavor.

If you like audiobooks, please be sure to check out this series and our other books on Audible.com.

And now, please turn the page for sneak peeks into my other works.

EXCERPT FROM
THE THOUGHT READERS

Everyone thinks I'm a genius.

Everyone is wrong.

Sure, I finished Harvard at eighteen and now make crazy money at a hedge fund. But that's not because I'm unusually smart or hard-working.

It's because I cheat.

You see, I have a unique ability. I can go outside time into my own personal version of reality—the place I call "the Quiet"—where I can explore my surroundings while the rest of the world stands still.

I thought I was the only one who could do this—until I met *her*.

My name is Darren, and this is how I learned that I'm a Reader.

* * *

Sometimes I think I'm crazy. I'm sitting at a casino table in Atlantic City, and everyone around me is motionless. I call this the *Quiet*, as though giving it a name makes it seem more real—as though giving it a name changes the fact that all the players around me are frozen like statues, and I'm walking among them, looking at the cards they've been dealt.

The problem with the theory of my being crazy is that when I 'unfreeze' the world, as I just have, the cards the players turn over are the same ones I just saw in the Quiet. If I were crazy, wouldn't these cards be different? Unless I'm so far gone that I'm imagining the cards on the table, too.

But then I also win. If that's a delusion—if the pile of chips on my side of the table is a delusion—then I might as well question everything. Maybe my name isn't even Darren.

No. I can't think that way. If I'm really that confused, I don't want to snap out of it—because if I do, I'll probably wake up in a mental hospital.

Besides, I love my life, crazy and all.

My shrink thinks the Quiet is an inventive way I describe the 'inner workings of my genius.' Now that sounds crazy to me. She also might want me, but that's beside the point. Suffice it to say, she's as far as it gets from my datable age range, which is currently right around twenty-four. Still young, still hot, but done with school and pretty much beyond the clubbing phase. I hate clubbing, almost as much as I hated studying. In any case, my shrink's explanation doesn't work, as it doesn't account for the way I know things even a genius wouldn't know—like the exact value and suit of the other players' cards.

I watch as the dealer begins a new round. Besides me, there are three players at the table: Grandma, the

Cowboy, and the Professional, as I call them. I feel that now almost-imperceptible fear that accompanies the phasing. That's what I call the process: phasing into the Quiet. Worrying about my sanity has always facilitated phasing; fear seems helpful in this process.

I phase in, and everything gets quiet. Hence the name for this state.

It's eerie to me, even now. Outside the Quiet, this casino is very loud: drunk people talking, slot machines, ringing of wins, music—the only place louder is a club or a concert. And yet, right at this moment, I could probably hear a pin drop. It's like I've gone deaf to the chaos that surrounds me.

Having so many frozen people around adds to the strangeness of it all. Here is a waitress stopped mid-step, carrying a tray with drinks. There is a woman about to pull a slot machine lever. At my own table, the dealer's hand is raised, the last card he dealt hanging unnaturally in midair. I walk up to him from the side of the table and reach for it. It's a king, meant for the Professional. Once I let the card go, it falls on the table rather than continuing to float as before—but I know full well that it will be back in the air, in the exact position it was when I grabbed it, when I phase out.

The Professional looks like someone who makes money playing poker, or at least the way I always imagined someone like that might look. Scruffy, shades on, a little sketchy-looking. He's been doing an excellent job with the poker face—basically not twitching a single muscle throughout the game. His face is so expressionless that I wonder if he might've gotten Botox to help maintain such a stony countenance. His hand is on the table, protectively covering the cards dealt to him.

I move his limp hand away. It feels normal. Well, in a manner of speaking. The hand is sweaty and hairy, so moving it aside is unpleasant and is admittedly an abnormal thing to do. The normal part is that the hand is warm, rather than cold. When I was a kid, I expected people to feel cold in the Quiet, like stone statues.

With the Professional's hand moved away, I pick up his cards. Combined with the king that was hanging in the air, he has a nice high pair. Good to know.

I walk over to Grandma. She's already holding her cards, and she has fanned them nicely for me. I'm able to avoid touching her wrinkled, spotted hands. This is a relief, as I've recently become conflicted about touching people—or, more specifically, women—in the Quiet. If I had to, I would rationalize touching Grandma's hand as harmless, or at least not creepy, but it's better to avoid it if possible.

In any case, she has a low pair. I feel bad for her. She's been losing a lot tonight. Her chips are dwindling. Her losses are due, at least partially, to the fact that she has a terrible poker face. Even before looking at her cards, I knew they wouldn't be good because I could tell she was disappointed as soon as her hand was dealt. I also caught a gleeful gleam in her eyes a few rounds ago when she had a winning three of a kind.

This whole game of poker is, to a large degree, an exercise in reading people—something I really want to get better at. At my job, I've been told I'm great at reading people. I'm not, though; I'm just good at using the Quiet to make it seem like I am. I do want to learn how to read people for real, though. It would be nice to know what everyone is thinking.

What I don't care that much about in this poker game is money. I do well enough financially to not have to depend on hitting it big gambling. I don't care if I win or lose, though quintupling my money back at the blackjack table was fun. This whole trip has been more about going gambling because I finally can, being twenty-one and all. I was never into fake IDs, so this is an actual milestone for me.

Leaving Grandma alone, I move on to the next player—the Cowboy. I can't resist taking off his straw hat and trying it on. I wonder if it's possible for me to get lice this way. Since I've never been able to bring back any inanimate objects from the Quiet, nor otherwise affect the real world in any lasting way, I figure I won't be able to get any living critters to come back with me, either.

Dropping the hat, I look at his cards. He has a pair of aces—a better hand than the Professional. Maybe the Cowboy is a professional, too. He has a good poker face, as far as I can tell. It'll be interesting to watch those two in this round.

Next, I walk up to the deck and look at the top cards, memorizing them. I'm not leaving anything to chance.

When my task in the Quiet is complete, I walk back to myself. Oh, yes, did I mention that I see myself sitting there, frozen like the rest of them? That's the weirdest part. It's like having an out-of-body experience.

Approaching my frozen self, I look at him. I usually avoid doing this, as it's too unsettling. No amount of looking in the mirror—or seeing videos of yourself on YouTube—can prepare you for viewing your own three-dimensional body up close. It's not something anyone is meant to experience. Well, aside from identical twins, I guess.

It's hard to believe that this person is me. He looks more like some random guy. Well, maybe a bit better than that. I do find this guy interesting. He looks cool. He looks smart. I think women would probably consider him good-looking, though I know that's not a modest thing to think.

It's not like I'm an expert at gauging how attractive a guy is, but some things are common sense. I can tell when a dude is ugly, and this frozen me is not. I also know that generally, being good-looking requires a symmetrical face, and the statue of me has that. A strong jaw doesn't hurt, either. Check.

Having broad shoulders is a positive, and being tall really helps. All covered. I have blue eyes—that seems to be a plus. Girls have told me they like my eyes, though right now, on the frozen me, the eyes look creepy—glassy. They look like the eyes of a lifeless wax figure.

Realizing that I'm dwelling on this subject way too long, I shake my head. I can just picture my shrink analyzing this moment. Who would imagine admiring themselves like this as part of their mental illness? I can just picture her scribbling down *Narcissist*, underlining it for emphasis.

Enough. I need to leave the Quiet. Raising my hand, I touch my frozen self on the forehead, and I hear noise again as I phase out.

Everything is back to normal.

The card that I looked at a moment before—the king that I left on the table—is in the air again, and from there it follows the trajectory it was always meant to, landing near the Professional's hands. Grandma is still eyeing her fanned cards in disappointment, and the Cowboy has his hat on again, though I took it off him in the Quiet. Everything is exactly as it was.

On some level, my brain never ceases to be surprised at the discontinuity of the experience in the Quiet and outside it. As humans, we're hardwired to question reality when such things happen. When I was trying to outwit my shrink early on in my therapy, I once read an entire psychology textbook during our session. She, of course, didn't notice it, as I did it in the Quiet. The book talked about how babies as young as two months old are surprised if they see something out of the ordinary, like gravity appearing to work backwards. It's no wonder my brain has trouble adapting. Until I was ten, the world behaved normally, but everything has been weird since then, to put it mildly.

Glancing down, I realize I'm holding three of a kind. Next time, I'll look at my cards before phasing. If I have something this strong, I might take my chances and play fair.

The game unfolds predictably because I know everybody's cards. At the end, Grandma gets up. She's clearly lost enough money.

And that's when I see the girl for the first time.

She's hot. My friend Bert at work claims that I have a 'type,' but I reject that idea. I don't like to think of myself as shallow or predictable. But I might actually be a bit of both, because this girl fits Bert's description of my type to a T. And my reaction is extreme interest, to say the least.

Large blue eyes. Well-defined cheekbones on a slender face, with a hint of something exotic. Long, shapely legs, like those of a dancer. Dark wavy hair in a ponytail—a hairstyle that I like. And without bangs—even better. I hate bangs—not sure why girls do that to themselves. Though lack of bangs is not, strictly speaking, in Bert's description of my type, it probably should be.

I continue staring at her. With her high heels and tight skirt, she's overdressed for this place. Or maybe I'm underdressed in my jeans and t-shirt. Either way, I don't care. I have to try to talk to her.

I debate phasing into the Quiet and approaching her, so I can do something creepy like stare at her up close, or maybe even snoop in her pockets. Anything to help me when I talk to her.

I decide against it, which is probably the first time that's ever happened.

I know that my reasoning for breaking my usual habit—if you can even call it that—is strange. I picture the following chain of events: she agrees to date me, we go out for a while, we get serious, and because of the deep connection we have, I come clean about the Quiet. She learns I did something creepy and has a fit, then dumps me. It's ridiculous to think this, of course, considering that we haven't even spoken yet. Talk about jumping the gun. She might have an IQ below seventy, or the personality of a piece of wood. There can be twenty different reasons why I wouldn't want to date her. And besides, it's not all up to me. She might tell me to go fuck myself as soon as I try to talk to her.

Still, working at a hedge fund has taught me to hedge. As crazy as that reasoning is, I stick with my decision not to phase because I know it's the gentlemanly thing to do. In keeping with this unusually chivalrous me, I also decide not to cheat at this round of poker.

As the cards are dealt again, I reflect on how good it feels to have done the honorable thing—even without anyone knowing. Maybe I should try to respect people's privacy more often. As soon as I think this, I mentally snort. *Yeah, right.* I have to be realistic. I wouldn't be where I am today if I'd followed that advice. In fact, if I made a habit of respecting people's privacy, I would lose my job within days—and with it, a lot of the comforts I've become accustomed to.

Copying the Professional's move, I cover my cards with my hand as soon as I receive them. I'm about to sneak a peek at what I was dealt when something unusual happens.

The world goes quiet, just like it does when I phase in . . . but I did nothing this time.

And at that moment, I see *her*—the girl sitting across the table from me, the girl I was just thinking about. She's standing next to me, pulling her hand away from mine. Or, strictly speaking, from my frozen self's hand—as I'm standing a little to the side looking at her.

She's also still sitting in front of me at the table, a frozen statue like all the others.

My mind goes into overdrive as my heartbeat jumps. I don't even consider the possibility of that second girl being a twin sister or something like that. I know it's her. She's doing what I did just a few minutes ago. She's walking in the Quiet. The world around us is frozen, but we are not.

A horrified look crosses her face as she realizes the same thing. Before I can react, she lunges across the table and touches her own forehead.

The world becomes normal again.

She stares at me from across the table, shocked, her eyes huge and her face pale. Her hands tremble as she rises to her feet. Without so much as a word, she turns and begins walking away, then breaks into a run a couple of seconds later.

Getting over my own shock, I get up and run after her. It's not exactly smooth. If she notices a guy she doesn't know running after her, dating will be the last thing on her mind. But I'm beyond that now. She's the only person I've met who can do what I do. She's proof that I'm not insane. She might have what I want most in the world.

She might have answers.

* * *

The Thought Readers is now available at most retailers. If you'd like to learn more, please visit www.dimazales.com.

EXCERPT FROM THE SORCERY CODE

Once a respected member of the Sorcerer Council and now an outcast, Blaise has spent the last year of his life working on a special magical object. The goal is to allow anyone to do magic, not just the sorcerer elite. The outcome of his quest is unlike anything he could've ever imagined—because, instead of an object, he creates Her.

She is Gala, and she is anything but inanimate. Born in the Spell Realm, she is beautiful and highly intelligent—and nobody knows what she's capable of. She will do anything to experience the world . . . even leave the man she is beginning to fall for.

Augusta, a powerful sorceress and Blaise's former fiancée, sees Blaise's deed as the ultimate hubris and Gala as an abomination that must be destroyed. In her quest to save the human race, Augusta will forge new alliances, becoming tangled in a web of intrigue that stretches further than any of them suspect. She may even have to turn to her new lover Barson, a ruthless warrior who might have an agenda of his own . . .

* * *

There was a naked woman on the floor of Blaise's study.

A beautiful naked woman.

Stunned, Blaise stared at the gorgeous creature who just appeared out of thin air. She was looking around with a bewildered expression on her face, apparently as shocked to be there as he was to be seeing her. Her wavy blond hair streamed down her back, partially covering a body that appeared to be perfection itself. Blaise tried not to think about that body and to focus on the situation instead.

A woman. A *She*, not an *It*. Blaise could hardly believe it. Could it be? Could this girl be the object?

She was sitting with her legs folded underneath her, propping herself up with one slim arm. There was something awkward about that pose, as though she didn't know what to do with her own limbs. In general, despite the curves that marked her a fully grown woman, there was a child-like innocence in the way she sat there, completely unselfconscious and totally unaware of her own appeal.

Clearing his throat, Blaise tried to think of what to say. In his wildest dreams, he couldn't have imagined this kind of outcome to the project that had consumed his entire life for the past several months.

Hearing the sound, she turned her head to look at him, and Blaise found himself staring into a pair of unusually clear blue eyes.

She blinked, then cocked her head to the side, studying him with visible curiosity. Blaise wondered what she was seeing. He hadn't seen the light of day in weeks, and he wouldn't be surprised if he looked like a mad sorcerer at this point. There was probably a week's worth of stubble covering his face, and he knew his dark hair was unbrushed and sticking out in every direction. If he'd known he would be facing a beautiful woman today, he would've done a grooming spell in the morning.

"Who am I?" she asked, startling Blaise. Her voice was soft and feminine, as alluring as the rest of her. "What is this place?"

"You don't know?" Blaise was glad he finally managed to string together a semi-coherent sentence. "You don't know who you are or where you are?"

She shook her head. "No."

Blaise swallowed. "I see."

"What am I?" she asked again, staring at him with those incredible eyes.

"Well," Blaise said slowly, "if you're not some cruel prankster or a figment of my imagination, then it's somewhat difficult to explain . . ."

She was watching his mouth as he spoke, and when he stopped, she looked up again, meeting his gaze. "It's strange," she said, "hearing words this way. These are the first real words I've heard."

Blaise felt a chill go down his spine. Getting up from his chair, he began to pace, trying to keep his eyes off her nude body. He had been expecting something to appear. A magical object, a thing. He just hadn't known what form that thing would take. A mirror, perhaps, or a lamp. Maybe even something as unusual as the Life Capture Sphere that sat on his desk like a large round diamond.

But a person? A female person at that?

To be fair, he had been trying to make the object intelligent, to ensure it would have the ability to comprehend human language and convert it into the code. Maybe he shouldn't be so surprised that the intelligence he invoked took on a human shape.

A beautiful, feminine, sensual shape.

Focus, Blaise, focus.

"Why are you walking like that?" She slowly got to her feet, her movements uncertain and strangely clumsy. "Should I be walking too? Is that how people talk to each other?"

Blaise stopped in front of her, doing his best to keep his eyes above her neck. "I'm sorry. I'm not accustomed to naked women in my study."

She ran her hands down her body, as though trying to feel it for the first time. Whatever her intent, Blaise found the gesture extremely erotic.

"Is something wrong with the way I look?" she asked. It was such a typical feminine concern that Blaise had to stifle a smile.

"Quite the opposite," he assured her. "You look unimaginably good." So good, in fact, that he was having trouble concentrating on anything but her delicate curves. She was of medium height, and so perfectly proportioned that she could've been used as a sculptor's template.

"Why do I look this way?" A small frown creased her smooth forehead. "What am I?" That last part seemed to be puzzling her the most.

Blaise took a deep breath, trying to calm his racing pulse. "I think I can try to venture a guess, but before I do, I want to give you some clothing. Please wait here—I'll be right back."

And without waiting for her answer, he hurried out of the room.

* * *

The Sorcery Code is currently available at most retailers. If you'd like to learn more, please visit www.dimazales.com.

EXCERPT FROM *CLOSE LIAISONS*

Note: *Close Liaisons* is Dima Zales's collaboration with Anna Zaires and is the first book in the internationally bestselling erotic sci-fi romance series, the Krinar Chronicles. It contains explicit sexual content and is not intended for readers under eighteen.

* * *

A dark and edgy romance that will appeal to fans of erotic and turbulent relationships . . .

In the near future, the Krinar rule the Earth. An advanced race from another galaxy, they are still a mystery to us—and we are completely at their mercy.

Shy and innocent, Mia Stalis is a college student in New York City who has led a very normal life. Like most people, she's never had any interactions with the invaders—until one fateful day in the park changes everything. Having caught Korum's eye, she must now contend with a powerful, dangerously seductive Krinar who wants to possess her and will stop at nothing to make her his own.

How far would you go to regain your freedom? How much would you sacrifice to help your people? What choice will you make when you begin to fall for your enemy?

* * *

Breathe, Mia, breathe. Somewhere in the back of her mind, a small rational voice kept repeating those words. That same oddly objective part of her noted his symmetric face structure, with golden skin stretched tightly over high cheekbones and a firm jaw. Pictures and videos of Ks that she'd seen had hardly done them justice. Standing no more than thirty feet away, the creature was simply stunning.

As she continued staring at him, still frozen in place, he straightened and began walking toward her. Or rather stalking toward her, she thought stupidly, as his every movement reminded her of a jungle cat sinuously approaching a gazelle. All the while, his eyes never left hers. As he approached, she could make out individual yellow flecks in his light golden eyes and the thick long lashes surrounding them.

She watched in horrified disbelief as he sat down on her bench, less than two feet away from her, and smiled, showing white even teeth. No fangs, she noted with some functioning part of her brain. Not even a hint of them. That used to be another myth about them, like their supposed abhorrence of the sun.

"What's your name?" The creature practically purred the question at her. His voice was low and smooth, completely unaccented. His nostrils flared slightly, as though inhaling her scent.

"Um . . ." Mia swallowed nervously. "M-Mia."

"Mia," he repeated slowly, seemingly savoring her name. "Mia what?"

"Mia Stalis." Oh crap, why did he want to know her name? Why was he here, talking to her? In general, what was he doing in Central Park, so far away from any of the K Centers? *Breathe, Mia, breathe.*

"Relax, Mia Stalis." His smile got wider, exposing a dimple in his left cheek. A dimple? Ks had dimples? "Have you never encountered one of us before?"

"No, I haven't," Mia exhaled sharply, realizing that she was holding her breath. She was proud that her voice didn't sound as shaky as she felt. Should she ask? Did she want to know?

She gathered her courage. "What, um—" Another swallow. "What do you want from me?"

"For now, conversation." He looked like he was about to laugh at her, those gold eyes crinkling slightly at the corners.

Strangely, that pissed her off enough to take the edge off her fear. If there was anything Mia hated, it was being laughed at. With her short, skinny stature and a general lack of social skills that came from an awkward teenage phase involving every girl's nightmare of braces, frizzy hair, and glasses, Mia had more than enough experience being the butt of someone's joke.

She lifted her chin belligerently. "Okay, then, what is *your* name?"

"It's Korum."

"Just Korum?"

"We don't really have last names, not the way you do. My full name is much longer, but you wouldn't be able to pronounce it if I told you."

Okay, that was interesting. She now remembered reading something like that in *The New York Times*. So far, so good. Her legs had nearly stopped shaking, and her breathing was returning to normal. Maybe, just maybe, she would get out of this alive. This conversation business seemed safe enough, although the way he kept staring at her with those unblinking yellowish eyes was unnerving. She decided to keep him talking.

"What are you doing here, Korum?"

"I just told you, making conversation with you, Mia." His voice again held a hint of laughter.

Frustrated, Mia blew out her breath. "I meant, what are you doing here in Central Park? In New York City in general?"

He smiled again, cocking his head slightly to the side. "Maybe I'm hoping to meet a pretty curly-haired girl."

Okay, enough was enough. He was clearly toying with her. Now that she could think a little again, she realized that they were in the middle of Central Park, in full view of about a gazillion spectators. She surreptitiously glanced around to confirm that. Yep, sure enough, although people were obviously steering clear of her bench and its otherworldly occupant, there were a number of brave souls staring their way from farther up the path. A couple were even cautiously filming them with their wristwatch cameras. If the K tried anything with her, it would be on YouTube in the blink of an eye, and he had to know it. Of course, he may or may not care about that.

Still, going on the assumption that since she'd never come across any videos of K assaults on college students in the middle of Central Park, she was relatively safe, Mia cautiously reached for her laptop and lifted it to stuff it back into her backpack.

"Let me help you with that, Mia—"

And before she could blink, she felt him take her heavy laptop from her suddenly boneless fingers, gently brushing against her knuckles in the process. A sensation similar to a mild electric shock shot through Mia at his touch, leaving her nerve endings tingling in its wake.

Reaching for her backpack, he carefully put away the laptop in a smooth, sinuous motion. "There you go, all better now."

Oh God, he had touched her. Maybe her theory about the safety of public locations was bogus. She felt her breathing speeding up again, and her heart rate was probably well into the anaerobic zone at this point.

"I have to go now . . . Bye!"

How she managed to squeeze out those words without hyperventilating, she would never know. Grabbing the strap of the backpack he'd just put down, she jumped to her feet, noting somewhere in the back of her mind that her earlier paralysis seemed to be gone.

"Bye, Mia. I will see you later." His softly mocking voice carried in the clear spring air as she took off, nearly running in her haste to get away.

* * *

If you'd like to find out more, please visit www.annazaires.com. All three books in the Krinar Chronicles trilogy are now available.

ABOUT THE AUTHOR

Dima Zales is a *New York Times* and *USA Today* bestselling author of science fiction and fantasy. Prior to becoming a writer, he worked in the software development industry in New York as both a programmer and an executive. From high-frequency trading software for big banks to mobile apps for popular magazines, Dima has done it all. In 2013, he left the software industry in order to concentrate on his writing career and moved to Palm Coast, Florida, where he currently resides.

Please visit www.dimazales.com to learn more.